D0292028

DEAD DINOSAURS

By the same author

Blood Sacrifice

DEAD DINOSAURS

A Luis Balam Mystery of the Yucatán

GARY ALEXANDER

DOUBLEDAY
New York London Toronto Sydney Auckland

PUBLISHED BY DOUBLEDAY
a division of Bantam Doubleday Dell Publishing
Group, Inc.
1540 Broadway, New York, New York 10036

DOUBLEDAY and the portrayal of an anchor with a dolphin are trademarks of Doubleday, a division of Bantam Doubleday Dell Publishing Group, Inc.

All of the characters in this book are fictitious, and any resemblance to actual persons, living or dead, is purely coincidental.

Book Design by Dorothy K. Urlich

Library of Congress Cataloging-in-Publication Data

Alexander, Gary, 1941–
Dead dinosaurs : a Luis Balam mystery of the Yucatán / Gary Alexander. — 1st ed.
p. cm.
1. Private investigators—Mexico—Yucatán (State)—Fiction.
2. Yucatán (Mexico : State)—Fiction. I. Title.
PS3551.L3554D42 1994
813′.54—dc20 94-6496
CIP

ISBN 0-385-46896-2

Printed in the United States of America
October 1994
First Edition
10 9 8 7 6 5 4 3 2 1

por Shari, *mi esposa*

for Gonzalo Guerrero

The Spaniards suffer from a disease of the heart, for which gold is the specific remedy.

—Hernán Cortés

Poor Mexico. So far from God and so close to the United States.

—Porfirio Díaz

DEAD DINOSAURS

1

The tourist's teeth were brilliantly white and absolutely straight. They were so perfect that Luis Balam thought of them as a facial deformity he could repair with a fist.

"What I'm saying, what I'm trying to get across, is that black coral is an endangered species," the tourist said to Luis's younger daughter. "You people continue diving and chipping coral off the reef, pretty soon it's history. It's your heritage you're squandering, not mine."

Rosa Balam smiled sweetly, held thumb and index finger an eighth of an inch apart, and said, "Sorry. Me speak tiny little bit English."

Luis also smiled, but not sweetly. This tourist and his woman, along with another pair of women, were Black Coral's only customers. Luis would let Rosa and Esther, his other daughter, take care of business. They often told him that he was around so seldom he didn't know what was going on, anyway.

The tourist grimaced and spoke, a serious face accompanied by sweeping hand gestures. Serious communication, serious pidgin, serious negotiation was about to commence, Luis knew. "Down in sea. Water. *Agua.* Black coral. Yes?"

"Yes," Rosa said, nodding vigorously.

"Soon no more," he said, shaking his head. "Soon all gone. Too *mucho* many necklaces, too *mucho* many bracelets. Soon black coral all gone. Poof! Gone."

The tourist's woman was handling a bracelet of black coral, lapis lazuli, and silver. Both were young. They had blue eyes, yellow hair, and bronzed skin.

Luis had seen their type at Cancún. In their expensive underwear, with their stereo headsets, they ran along the boulevard or on the beach every morning of their stay, running to nowhere. Luis had thought running would be one activity in their daily routine that North Americans sought to escape on their costly vacations.

But no. Running was fun and fitness. Luis was skeptical about the fun. Slogging along in the heat and humidity, their expressions were funless, as if a blowtorch was being held to their genitals. Luis Balam did not run unless somebody was chasing him.

"I like this, Denny," the woman said.

"I know you do, Joyce," Denny said, winking. "You make them feel guilty, put them on the defensive. Then you turn the screws. That's how you Jew these people down."

Joyce looked up at Denny, half in admiration, half in disgust. "There are times when you can be such a shit."

Then to Rosa, he said, "Little tiny bit money is all me pay. Maybe police no let us take out of Meh-he-co. Endangered species, *comprehendo?*"

"God, Denny," Joyce said, giggling.

"One hundred dollar," Rosa said.

"One hundred dollars! No can do. Negative. *Nada.* Bad to sell black coral, bad to buy, bad for environment. Trouble is, I no buy, someone else buy. What'm I gonna do? Joyce, my señorita lady, she like semi-*mucho. El cheapo* necklace. Thirty dollar. Thirty Yankee dollar, I can do."

"You right, señor," Rosa said. "Me sort of *comprendo.* Black coral too much brought up from reef, will be gone soon. You very smart señor. Ninety-five dollar. Cheap. Almost free."

"How soon?" Joyce said, folding a hand around the necklace.

Rosa touched a finger to her lips. "Who can say? Very. Black coral can anytime be quitted. Everybody will want."

"Forty dollars," Denny said. "My best offer. Going, going, gone."

"Wait a second," Joyce said to Rosa. "Do you know something we don't?"

Luis drifted toward Esther. Rosa had things under control. He hoped she hadn't laid on her feigned ignorance of English too heavily. He forbade his girls to lie outright to the customers, but he had no problem with encouragement of misconceptions, the nurturing of greed.

The Mexican government would sooner or later clamp down on the black coral trade, though not in the next ten minutes, as Joyce and Denny were beginning to believe. When that time came Luis would have to replace the handmade BLACK CORAL sign on the front of his tent with—what? FINE JEWELRY AND MOSTLY JUNK? LAST CHANCE TRINKET SHOP UNTIL YOU COME TO THE NEXT ONE?

Esther's prospects were more pleasant. They were stout middle-aged ladies with baggy shorts and Texas twangs. Perhaps schoolteachers on a long weekend. If you had the money, why not? Dallas and Cancún were only two airline hours apart.

The ladies and Esther were laughing. They were calling

her "dear," making her blush. No sale, Luis supposed. They had the look of browsers, entertaining themselves on the way back to Cancún from the ruins at Tulum or Cobá.

Esther wouldn't care if she made the sale. Meeting nice people was for her its own reward. Rosa, on the other hand, would be edgy from the outset with these women, correctly reading them as congenial tightwads, resentful that her time was being wasted.

Luis went outside, again amazed how unlike his babies were. They had different mothers, yes, but his girls might as well be from different planets.

He walked across the dusty, pocked lot to the highway. Highway 307 was the north-south thoroughfare that paralleled the Mexican Caribbean and ran from Cancún to the Belize border. Two lanes of blacktop, it slashed through the scrub jungle and flat-as-a-tortilla limestone shelf that was the Yucatán Peninsula.

Three-oh-seven was the aorta of the tourism boom, pumping visitors and their hard currencies to Cancún, Cozumel Island, and the other resort spots that were fast filling the seaside.

Luis frequently observed the highway. He was analyzing the economy. Traffic was his economic indicator. He wasn't counting cars, he was feeling the flow, sensing money racing from here to there. The size of the trucks and their loads. The number of people crammed into rental cars and taxis and buses. Tour buses, especially.

Tour buses drove the economy of the highway. The drivers disgorged tourists at shops such as his, citing his crudely hand-lettered BLACK CORAL sign as an indicator of low overhead. A bargain trove, it was. Relatively undiscovered.

Off the beaten gringo path. Luis wished more of them would pull into Black Coral.

There were plenty of them out there, buses and shops. It was March, late in the high season. Winter in Yucatán was warm and dry. It had been described as the ideal California summer.

Chic, affluent North Americans fled ice and snow and swarmed southward. They spent money crazily, until it was gone. What didn't go for hotel suites and fine cuisine and disco tequila was taken at the posh Cancún malls and boutiques. What money remained was grabbed by highway handicraft markets who bribed drivers to disgorge tourists at *their* relatively undiscovered bargain troves of blankets and bracelets.

Thus Luis's problem. He was an hour from Cancún. He could not afford to bribe the drivers to stop at Black Coral in high season when they were out in quantity with capacity North American loads. He could only afford to bribe them in the sweltering, steamy summer months when passengers were reluctant to leave their air-conditioned coaches.

His second vocation was not going well either. As a pure-blooded Maya fluent in English and Spanish, he had been in demand as a part-time tour guide at Tulum and Cobá. Now they were going to full-timers with regular schedules and spiffy uniforms.

Luis was given a choice: all or almost nothing. No thanks on the "all," Luis told them. He had a business to operate too. What he didn't tell them was that he could not endure questions about the sacrifice of virgins five days a week. Luis had then been placed on call, as an illness fill-in. He did not have a telephone. Nor did they.

A tour bus howled past. The slipstream rocked Luis on his heels. He held his breath to avoid the diesel stench. The window seats were occupied. Some people gave him a glance —another Indian idling by the side of the road.

Luis was a thirty-seven-year-old Yucatec Maya of average height: five foot two. The bus passengers had seen and by now forgotten a round face, prominent cheekbones, an aquiline nose, and almond eyes brought across the Bering land bridge millennia ago. Should the riders have retained any image of the lazy roadside Indian, it may have been of stockiness without fat, a deceptive musculature.

Luis headed back to Black Coral. There were moments when he wondered what he was going to do, what was going to become of his girls. This was such a moment.

A Jeep braked hard and turned into the lot, jouncing through potholes, boiling up the dust. It was candy-apple red with chrome wheels, shiny as new. The top was up, sealing in the air-conditioning. The glass was blacked out and Luis couldn't see inside. As a former traffic policeman, Luis despised privacy glass. You pulled a vehicle over, you never knew what sort of creature was inside waiting for you.

The Jeep parked at the entrance. The twangy Texans were exiting Black Coral, chattering and waving back to Esther. Luis discerned no shiny baubles on their plump bodies.

He went inside as a happy Joyce admired her necklace and matching earrings with a pocket mirror. Denny was tearing off and signing traveler's checks, a twenty and two fifties. His perfect white teeth were hidden behind clenched lips.

One hundred and twenty U.S. dollars, Luis thought. Probably eighty for the necklace and forty for the earrings, the last of their endangered kind. Luis's floor on the necklace had been sixty dollars, on the earrings twenty-five. Environmentally responsible Denny had singlehandedly made the day a financial success.

When they had gone, Luis considered proper words of praise for Rosa, carefully editing in his head. He did not want to make such a production of the sale that Esther's feelings would be hurt. He opened his mouth as his daughters opened theirs, squealing in unison, "Mr. Martínez, Father."

He turned and saw Ricardo Martínez Rodríguez emerge from the Jeep. Ricky Martínez was the leading client of his third vocation, the most pitiful of the three—private detective.

The driver stepped out too. He was dressed in khaki pants and shirt. The shirt had epaulets and any number of pockets. He had binoculars around his neck and sunglasses parked on a billed cap. He had the look of an anthropology professor who had watched too many old adventure movies.

Luis tagged him the Desert Fox.

2

Esther, age eighteen, was quiet and serious. She wore the traditional Maya *huipil,* a gaily embroidered white dress. Rosa, age sixteen, favored blue jeans and neon tops. She was addicted to cola drinks and North American rock music.

They were identical in one respect. They both had crushes on Ricardo Martínez Rodríguez, a handsome and dapper Cancún City attorney in his thirties.

Once, Luis had chanced upon a television program in a cafe. It was an old North American comedy serial entitled *I Love Lucy.* Shave the waxed pencil mustache and Ricardo Martínez Rodríguez could be the twin of Ricky Ricardo, the Cuban bandleader. Like it or not, Ricardo had been Ricky to Luis ever since.

"Father, who is that strange man with Mr. Martínez?" Rosa asked. "His Jeep is gorgeous. Why is he wearing a uniform?"

Luis shrugged. "You can be certain that Ricky will eventually explain."

"When Mr. Martínez comes to see you, Father, he takes the bus," said a puzzled Esther.

Ricky Martínez could not afford a car. He had a marginal law practice in Cancún City. His fees were invariably squandered on oversexed women and pie-in-the-sky business deals. Whenever Luis submitted a private investigation bill to Ricky that was paid, he felt giddy, recipient of a miracle.

"He is moving up in the world," Luis said. "He has a chauffeur and an obedient one at that. Look. He holds up his hand and the Desert Fox halts."

"The what?" Rosa asked.

Ricky Martínez came into the tent, shook Luis's hand, and said, "Luis, hello to you and your lovely daughters."

Ricky kissed their hands. They retired to the rear of the tent, tittering, cheeks crimson.

"Ricky, where did you find the Desert Fox? Tobruk? El Alamein?"

"What, Luis?"

"My first impression was professor, but with that uniform, my second impression is soldier. Erwin Rommel, the legendary German general, the Desert Fox whose Nazi armored divisions nearly pounded on the gates of Alexandria before Montgomery pushed him back into the Sahara."

"Luis, there are times when you annoy the holy hell out of me showing off this obscure knowledge of yours."

In the 1970s, when Luis had worked as a construction laborer at Cancún, he had been befriended by North Americans who helped him master the English language. The 1974 World Almanac and Book of Facts was his primary text. Read it, said the best of his Anglo buddies; you'll learn English and damn near everything else.

Read it he did, until the binding disintegrated and humidity and handling reconverted the loose pages into pulp. Luis had acquired through repetition and his spongelike brain a mental warehouse of trivial facts and statistics. Rolling some of them out the door occasionally was a character fault he had no intention of correcting.

"Look at him, Ricky. Did you see the movie? Except that he has expensive sunglasses on his cap instead of tank goggles, your friend is the Desert Fox."

Ricky sighed and said, "Vance Dugdale is in field attire, Luis. He is not a tourist and would not appreciate being regarded by you as a frivolous person. He is a professional and an entrepreneur."

Ricky's unfrivolous Vance was fanning himself with his campaign cap. Luis guessed him to be in his forties. Sun exposure had migrated on his face and crown in the form of large freckles. Limp strands of graying brown hair hung from the rim of his head to his shoulders. He had a raptor's nose and darting eyes. Luis revised first and second impressions. No halls of ivy for this character, no drill fields. He was a hustler, a predator.

"He is dressed to conquer North Africa for my sake? Invite him in out of the heat."

"I came in first to lay the groundwork. Do not be offended, Luis, but you can be rude and suspicious to strangers."

"Me?"

"Vance therefore suggested I speak to you first."

"To lay the groundwork?"

"Yes."

"Have you?"

"No, Luis, I have not."

"Lay your groundwork later. Invite him in before he faints, Ricky. Don't be so rude and suspicious. Who precisely is your friend?"

Ricky waved at Vance. "Vance Dugdale is a close business associate. He is an international entrepreneur and a gentleman of substance. While he is a recent client of mine, I know his credentials to be impeccable."

Recent, Luis thought. Ricky met him in a bar last night. "A legal client?"

"I have both a legal role and a business advisory role," Ricky said thoughtfully, stroking his handsome jaw. "A complex holistic situation. Luis, the potential is absolutely staggering!"

Ricky was drunk when he met Dugdale in the bar, Luis thought further. His last North American client with absolutely staggering potential had been a college boy on holiday who had attempted to climb a beachside coconut tree as he had seen it done on *Hawaii Five-O.* He was trying to impress a group of college girls, but his choice of tree was bad. It was weak and topless, a victim of either a virus or Hurricane Gilbert. The trunk snapped and the boy came down hard.

Ricky went to the resort manager and demanded negligence damages, citing his client's pain, which was not unlike chronic whiplash. The manager said to come back later. The owner was flying in from Mexico City that afternoon. The resort owner did not negotiate with Ricky; he referred him to his administrative assistant, a gentleman with a thick neck who wore sunglasses indoors and out.

The administrative assistant walked Ricky to the beach at dusk and asked how long he could hold his breath underwater. Ricky asked why he asked. The administrative assistant said that he was just wondering if Ricky would have time to pray to the Virgin of Guadalupe, to beg forgiveness for his greed. End of case.

"What potential is staggering us today, Ricky?"

"Check this out, Luis," Ricky said, pointing at the Desert Fox and his vehicle. "The ice chest Vance is bringing out of the Jeep is not an ice chest. It is a portable refrigeration unit you plug into the cigarette lighter. Vance is paying an arm and a leg to the rental agency for this deluxe vehicle and its equipment. The man is a class act if I ever saw one."

Vance Dugdale, the impeccable international entrepreneur, brought in a briefcase and the portable refrigeration unit. He set them on a table beside a tray of middling-quality silver and onyx pieces.

"Whew," he said, wiping his glistening pate. "Hotter than a popcorn fart. Hi, I'm Vance Dugdale."

He gave Luis a moist, vigorous handshake, and continued. "Nice establishment, guys, but can we scoot into a privacy mode? Canvas walls have ears."

Luis looked at Ricky, who said, joining thumb and forefinger into an O, "This is a ground-floor opportunity, Luis. Vance is in possession of priceless information."

Luis led them through the flap that separated Black Coral's shop from the private area. He spread his hands apologetically to Esther and Rosa, who went up front to await customers. Luis invited his guests to sit on the packing crates that served as chairs. On a rickety table, beside the hot plate and griddle upon which they cooked luncheon tortillas, Vance Dugdale placed his portable refrigeration unit.

He removed from it three bottles of Leon Negra beer and gave Luis and Ricky theirs.

"Cold Leons, Luis. *Cold,*" Ricky said. "Nice touch?"

"Yes, a nice touch," Luis had to admit, opening his.

Leon Negra, rich and dark and brewed in the Yucatán state capital of Mérida, was his favorite beverage. Vance Dugdale had gone to considerable trouble to please him. Why?

Dugdale raised his bottle, clinked the others, and said, "To a long and prosperous partnership. *¡Salud!* Rick, lemme toss the ball in your court. Whip a general overview on Lu if you would."

"Luis, Vance is known north of the border as the king of the cultural theme parks."

"Shucks, Rick, you make me out to be a P. T. Barnum. I don't own the facilities. Wish I did. No, I'm strictly a consultant. Call me an arbitrageur of good taste and cultural advancement and you won't hear a peep of complaint outta this kid, no sir."

Lu? Rick? "Disneyland?"

"Uh uh. No way. No ducks and mice. None of that roller coaster shit either. We operate on a higher level, a whole separate tier of quality. My philosophy is that the physical setting and the visual aid, the diorama and/or a tasteful skit, they're primary. No schlock, but you'd be a fool not to kick in some entertainment value too. Then you stand back and watch the knowledge soak in and the smiles light up. It's awesome, it's spiritual. A kid who's gone to a park with the Dugdale signature on his summer vacation has a blast and he hits the floor running in history class that September."

Luis did not respond. He was imagining tasteful skits with the Dugdale signature, Yucatán version. Costumed Maya sacrificing voluptuous virgins. Maya in warrior regalia battling the Spaniards. Prone, gasping women followed by a Three Musketeers extravaganza.

"Vance has consulted in numerous American Civil War–oriented parks and he is involved in fossils unearthed—where, Vance?"

"Peripherally involved, though I love the kind words, Rick. In Montana. Nothing may come of it. You have a population density shortfall up there that turns off the bean counters, but when you're a sucker for antiquity, hey, who can say what challenge will rear its head next."

"Have I missed the point?" Luis asked. "A point? Any point?"

Vance Dugdale grinned and raised a fist. "Lu, if I had a doubt about you before, bite my tongue. You passed the ol' acid test. You're my guy. No way on God's green earth would I take on an executive liaison who wasn't a card-carrying cynic."

Executive liaison? Luis stared at him.

"Vance, show Luis the newspaper clippings, the photographs, and the NASA report," Ricky said.

Dugdale took from his briefcase an eight-by-ten photograph of a colorful illustration. In the foreground, prehistoric birds were flying above the clouds. In the background, a huge celestial object hurtled through the overcast, shock waves accompanying it like parasites.

"Those are pterodactyls, Luis. Aren't they, Vance?"

"Sure are," Dugdale said, chuckling. "I'd hate to have those suckers build a nest in my yard. Lu, you're a knowledgeable guy. You've heard the theories regarding the demise of the dinosaurs."

Luis did not reply. Dugdale removed stapled papers. On the cover page was the letterhead of NASA, the National Aeronautics and Space Administration.

"Well, you've been gazing at a talented artist's accurate

rendition of the fateful moment. Now, it's cut and dried in the scientific community that sixty-five million years ago, a comet or an asteroid smacked into the planet. The impact pushed so much dirt and crud into the atmosphere that sunlight was screened out. Plants couldn't grow and the Earth got colder than a witch's tit. Dinosaurs couldn't chow down, so they went extinct. The mystery was where the thing hit, what part of the world got creamed. Lu, that mystery has finally been solved."

"Luis, I have examined the documents microscopically," Ricky said. "The fact pattern is indisputable."

Luis paged through the clippings. CRATER TIED TO END OF DINOSAURS. NASA HELPS IN HUNT FOR SECRETS OF THE DINOSAURS. HOW DINOSAURS DIED FROM A HEAD-ON COLLISION.

Dugdale put away the NASA papers too quickly to suit Luis and handed him another eight-by-ten, a black-and-white aerial photograph. "You take it from here, *amigo*. Show and tell. What's wrong with this picture?"

Luis studied it. He presumed from its absence of detail that it had been taken from a high altitude. He recognized squarish patches of agriculture in a texture of whites and grays. Narrow straight lines—roads—were short and few, dead-ending at the agricultural squares. An array of white dots formed a shallow arc from side to side. Luis could not identify them.

"What's wrong with this picture?" Luis said.

Vance Dugdale clapped his hands in glee. "Lu, I thought you'd never ask. *Nothing* is wrong with this picture! This is a satellite snapshot taken from four hundred and thirty-eight miles, a very relevant sample of the nine-mile-by-nine-mile shots taken all the way across the Yucatán Peninsula. Click, click, click from up there in outer space.

Except for some NASA sharpie noticing what he noticed on the pictures, us guys, we'd never be schmoozing at this point in time. What he was looking for was water sources used by your ancestors, Lu, before they went off to the Happy Hunting Ground.

"Okay, whoa, back to school for a sec. Lu, what's this fantastic Yucatán Peninsula of yours made of? Geologically speaking. Rick, no fair prompting. Lu's as sharp as a tack anyhow."

"Limestone," Luis said.

"Give that man a gold star. Lu, c'mon, guy, expand on the subject."

Luis said nothing. This was the Desert Fox's game, not his.

"All right. What the Yucatán is is a limestone shelf flatter than my second ex-wife. In terms of bodies of water, the Yucatán isn't exactly Minnesota."

"Land of ten thousand lakes," Luis said, thinking: 1974 World Almanac, page 718.

"There you are. Except for the rare lake, the Yucatán's principal body of water is the cenote. Which is? C'mon, Lu."

Luis sighed and said, "Sinkhole wells in the limestone. The limestone collapses and fills with water from the water table."

"And guess what those white dots on the picture are, Lu. I'll answer. The question's too easy. Cenotes. Yeah. The white dots are cenotes, surface water that's been enhanced by high-tech NASA voodoo. Lay these outer space snapshots next to each other and you have—"

Dugdale withdrew from his briefcase a line map of northern Yucatán. On it was drawn a circle. The upper half was in the Gulf of Mexico, the lower 180 degrees on the mainland.

"This sucker was one hundred ten to one hundred twenty-five miles in diameter. Can you visualize the hell raised when it struck? The eggheads say the bang was bigger than all the nukes us and the Russkies ever made. Combined! The cenotes correspond perfectly with the semicircle perimeter of that comet. These sinkholes weren't random chance situations, Lu. The impact fractured the crust and the water's been oozing up from then on. And if that's not enough, these heavenly bodies are loaded with iridium, a rare rare rare earth metal worth *mucho dinero.* The Yucatán is filthy with iridium traces. That's what the scientists say."

Luis looked at Ricky, whose eyes had the wild glaze of someone remembered fondly in a will. "Trust Vance on this, Luis. He is the impresario of cultural amusement parks."

Before Luis could ask what Vance, as a non-Disneyland impresario, had to do with homicidal comets, Vance said, "Lu, guess whose village touches the cenote ring?"

And before Luis could say "Whose?", Ricky clasped his shoulders and cried, "Luis, we are going to be rich!"

3

"Bottom line, Luis, that sexy North American term. Bottom line is that there are hundreds and hundreds of cenotes on the deadly ring, and we must be the first to establish a cultural center in this region," Ricky said.

"The key word, Lu, is jobs," Dugdale said. "What's the name of your village again?"

"Ho-Keh."

"Yeah, Ho-Keh. We get this thing in the air, it's a Ho-Keh operation for Ho-Kehers. I draw a piddling consulting fee, capital investment payback, and an eensy-teensy percentage of the gross. The gravy is yours."

"You are so generous because you are strictly a consultant?" Luis said.

"You got it, Lu. Ouch. Got to do something about this road right off the git-go. They bob and pitch on the cruise ships, but that won't prepare them for this."

"Road improvement for the buses, Luis," Ricky explained.

Luis asked a question that was not answered. "Cruise ships?"

Four kilometers south of Black Coral, they had turned off the highway onto a narrow, rutted road. Low, dense brush scraped the Jeep's candy-apple side panels.

"*¡Ay caramba!* Fingernails on a blackboard. And what am I gonna tell the car rental folk? Lu, you Mayan folks have vehicles, don't you?"

"The Maya travel by bicycle. Some have cars," Luis said.

"Luis has the only car in Ho-Keh," Ricky said. "A Volkswagen Beetle."

Dugdale said something else, but Luis wasn't listening. He was in the back of the Jeep, thinking and watching the Desert Fox jerk behind the wheel like a rag doll at every pothole. What was Ricky Martínez dragging him into? He worked for the attorney as a detective. Vance Dugdale's oily patronization, his offer of the executive liaison post, it appeared, was recruitment for some manner of pimp duty.

They emerged after two kilometers in the village clearing. Ho-Keh consisted of fifteen homes of traditional Maya construction—elongated huts with thin sapling or stucco walls and steep thatched roofs. Only the electrical lines drooping from meters to poles denoted the century. Rural electrification was a modernization priority of Mexico City. The Indians could wait for sanitation and schools.

Ho-Keh was a small village, an extended family. One home was occupied by Luis and his daughters, another by his mother and father, others by uncles and aunts, first and second cousins.

"Picturesque. I love it," Vance Dugdale said. "What's Ho-Keh stand for?"

"Ho-Keh is Yucatec Maya for five deer," Luis said. "So

the story goes, an unknown ancestor at an unknown point in time walked into the clearing and saw five deer. These days you are lucky to see five in a year."

"Makes sense to me," Dugdale said. "How do we get to the cenote?"

Luis considered telling him to park and they would walk the one hundred meters. But no. There were people outside. Women were hanging laundry on lines. Men were watering potted herbs and seedlings, on raised platforms, away from scavenging pets, chickens, and turkeys, with which the children were playing.

They paused to stare at the strangely gaudy Jeep with the smoked windows. Luis was grateful for the privacy. He would not admit shame to himself, but he did not want to be seen by his people with Ricky and the Desert Fox in the throes of executive liaison.

"Left past the last house. You can go in fifty meters until the road narrows to a path, then we'll walk."

"Groovy," said Vance Dugdale.

At the cenote, he said, "Small."

"You've been to Chichén Itzá?" Luis said.

"Yeah. Their Sacred Cenote, it's one hurkin', humongous well. Round, vertical walls, the area of a football field, a long, long drop to the surface, and some deep, deep water. I'd of hated to've been a virgin with an attitude.

"They draw tourists by the gross. We'll never match their volume. They've dredged bones and jewelry out of there, you know, from the babes that were tossed in."

"Men, women, and children were sacrificed," Luis corrected.

"Whatever," Dugdale said, lighting a cigarette, gazing

at a greenish body of water surrounded by rocks, spindly trees, and scrub jungle. "This is a little bigger than your basic backyard swimming pool, but not by a whole hell of a lot. It's frankly not what I pictured."

"Irrelevant, Vance, in terms of historical significance," Ricky said quickly.

"Sure, *no problema.* Rick, what's the ownership situation?"

"Well, this is communal property," Ricky said, looking uneasily to Luis for verification.

Ricardo Martínez Rodríguez's legal knowledge was not extensive. Complexities and ethics learned in law school had been all but lost in a subsistence practice devoted to whiplash and other petty torts. A typical detective assignment for Luis entailed using his hotel contacts to investigate the credit card limits of North American tourists unfortunate enough to have tapped the rear bumper of one of Ricky's clients with their rental cars.

Mexican police could impound the negligent driver's car until damages to the other party were paid, and insurance coverage through the rental agency was rarely adequate. But this was just the beginning of the tourist's problems. Ricky would then solemnly bring to the person's attention the lengthy bureaucratic procedures likely to befall any foreigner who injured a Mexican national, not to mention the unspeakable conditions in Mexican jails. Negotiation and settlement were usually quick. Ricky accepted traveler's checks and the currency of most nations.

"This is communal land," Luis said. "According to Article Twenty-seven of the Constitution of the United Mexican States, it belongs to us."

"That was my assessment, Vance," Ricky said, nodding confidently.

"Which means all we're lacking is the green light from the Ho-Kehites," Vance said, looking at Luis.

"A job for an executive liaison," Luis said.

Dugdale winked at Ricky and said, "Hey, you told me, stud. Lu's as sharp as a tack."

"What are your plans?" Luis asked.

"Right off the top, Lu, nothing too elaborate. We'll kind of phase into it. Palapas for protection from the elements. Benches and chairs. Refreshments. Some makeshift dioramas until we can have professional stuff made up. Fiberglass dinosaurs, twelve feet tall. This outfit in São Paulo does them *el cheapo* for carnivals. We're shipping them in from Brazil in pieces and will assemble them on site, preferably here. They're on order and should arrive any minute.

"I'll provide the staffing at the start, but we'll train and transition your people into the thing. We'll have to hack down some brush and move some rocks, but environmental impact won't amount to diddly. This ain't gonna be any Chichén Itzá. I don't reckon we'll have a daily turnstile count of over fifty to a hundred, max."

"Vance and I plan to establish a chain of Dead Dinosaurs Parks along the ring," Ricky said.

"Dead Dinosaurs is a name Rick and me brainstormed last night. It's open to review, naturally, but you have to admit it's got some serious topspin."

"This will be the only location near the coast highway, however," Ricky said. "You'll have the Cancún and Cozumel tourists to draw from, Luis. Hotels, condos, cruise ships. We're developing connections. It's a gold mine."

"Fifty to one hundred people? Every day?" Luis said. "Dead Dinosaurs Parks? To not see dinosaurs that died sixty-five million years ago?"

"Your people, Lu, we'll definitely want them in uniforms," Dugdale continued, unhearing. "They'll be done in good taste. No folk dancing and skits, either. I hate that shit. The position of chief supervising guide, Lu, by the way, is yours for the asking. You have the talent to wear two hats. I know you do. We'll eventually set up a gift shop, leaning heavily into books and the educational. No schlock that glows in the dark, although we'll begin park operations at night."

"Why at night?" Luis asked.

"Good question, Lu. Our propwork won't look so cheesy at night, especially before the dinosaurs arrive. You got a romantic ambience and I have ideas for a sound and light show. We'll bring in a generator, rig speakers, blow off fireworks, and give the customers your basic vicarious feel for what it must of been like when that baby clobbered the planet sixty-five million years ago.

"So, Lu, basically the ball's in your court. We have to move fast. This comet thing's been getting a lot of press lately."

"As executive liaison," Luis said. "And chief supervising guide."

"There you go. Whatever your consensus process is, you know, to get the green light. Rick says you pack *mucho* clout around here."

Luis said nothing.

"Luis and Francisco—what is his last name and what is he to you, Luis?"

"Francisco Ek. Second cousin," Luis said.

"Luis and Francisco, Vance, if they agree the rest will follow and it's a done deal."

"You and this Ick dude, Lu, are you *mucho simpático* pals?"

"Yes," Luis lied.

"Super. So you'll set up a powwow or whatever you Mayans call them, and get us our go-ahead?"

"Yes." Luis was not lying. Despite their differences, despite a mutual contrariness that placed Luis and Francisco on opposite sides of most issues, there was no chance Francisco would reject Luis's recommendation to send Dugdale and his dinosaurs down the road. He was a sensible man who had a sick wife for whom to care. "I'll arrange a meeting. Maybe as soon as tomorrow."

"Dynamite," Dugdale said, flicking his cigarette into the cenote. "Oops. Sorry 'bout that. It's dry as tinder and only you can prevent forest fires, but, hey, that was tacky of me. I'll fish it out if you like."

Luis shook his head.

"I mean, is your cenote sacred too?"

"In a way it is sacred," Luis said.

"Past sacrifices and curses and religion, that it?"

"No. Because it is our only source of water."

4

The black Dodge Dart sedan bristled with antennae that fed signals to nonexistent radios. Spotlights were mounted on each front door. Other equipment included dual exhausts, mismatched alloy wheels, and, of course, blackened windows.

Vance Dugdale stopped at the edge of the Black Coral lot to let Luis out, giving the Dodge darting glances and plenty of room. Although he couldn't take his eyes off it, he asked no questions. Ricky could have provided answers, but he only volunteered a sigh. Luis could have answered more questions, but he just smiled and got out.

He walked by the Dart, wondering how many confiscated guns, how much confiscated ammunition Héctor had inside the trunk today. You carried a firearm in Héctor's jurisdiction, you'd better have a reason that suited him, or your gun was his gun.

The Dart's tail end was drooping, but whether that was weight or worn-out shock absorbers, Luis couldn't say. In any case, the Dart terrorized pulled-over motorists. North Americans invariably drew comparisons to the Mel Gibson *Road Warrior* films. Héctor never received an argument when he said that the speed limit had been exceeded. Tell them that they had been clocked at Mach three, they would apologize and pay the fine.

Luis went past his tables of silver and black coral and lapus lazuli and hematite, and through the tent flap to the rear of Black Coral. Rosa was shaping tortillas with practiced hand slaps and Esther was frying them. Black beans simmered in a pot.

Inspector Héctor Salgado Reyes of the Quintana Roo State Judicial Police sat on a crate and ate the tortillas as fast as Rosa could shape and Esther could fry them. He was washing them down with beans and Leon Negra from Dugdale's refrigerator.

"Luis," Héctor said. "Late lunch, early dinner, whichever, the timing is always perfect for a meal. And this wonderful gadget, it plugs into a car lighter?"

Luis sat across from him. "Yes."

"The beer is still cool. Your lovely daughters say it was a gift from a strange client of your lawyer associate."

"That is an interesting story."

"I know you will enlighten me as soon as you have refreshed yourself," Héctor said, giving him the last Leon.

Luis accepted a tortilla from Esther and ate, watching Héctor, mentor and former superior when they were together at the Tránsito, the traffic police. Héctor was more than a little curious, but he was a patient and instinctive interrogator. Whether you were Luis, his best friend, or a murder suspect, whether it was a harmless tale or a felonious pack of lies, Héctor wanted first to listen to the speaker's own words.

Forty-five years old, round as he was tall, and half bald, Héctor Salgado Reyes was dressed like Luis in slacks, white shirt, and sandals. He rejected the military-style uniform favored by many of his colleagues, as he did the departmental squad car. Khaki trousers and a brown shirt with epaulets would have made him a caricature, a comic figure in an operetta. Héctor could be rude and his speech was laced with profanities, but he was a kind and fair man.

A relatively honest cop with a wife and seven children, he could not afford to be pristine. His salary was the equivalent of five hundred U.S. dollars per month. Out of that came expenses such as car repair, gasoline, and typing of official reports. Héctor stole without joy. He stole to feed his family.

Luis waved Esther off after the fifth tortilla. "Shall we go out front now, Father?" she asked.

"Not yet," he said. Unlike some Mexican males, Luis Balam did not treat his female offspring as an inferior species. He felt guilty for chasing them out earlier. What Héctor could hear, his babies could hear. Within reason.

"Interesting is an understatement," Héctor said when Luis was done. He laughed. "Ricky Martínez, that slick pretty boy. Ricky chasing another of his rainbows."

Héctor quivered when he laughed and Luis was afraid the packing crate would collapse under his bulk. In this laughter was a sharp trace of resentment. Héctor had been a poor peasant boy from Oaxaca State on the south Pacific coast. He had completed the six compulsory years of grammar school and drifted from various jobs to police work.

Any further education was impossibly beyond his means, but Héctor was relentlessly self-taught. He understood the law better than any attorney Luis knew, certainly far far better than Ricky. He had won countless barroom bets by reciting verbatim Articles of the Constitution of the

United Mexican States. His vocabulary was also exceptional, if profane and overused. Héctor was one-half Zapotec Indian, like Luis a member of an underclass who had made his own way. Thus a natural affinity between the two men.

"Ricky is all right, Héctor. He isn't bad."

"Please, Luis, do not tell me next that he means well."

"I would never do that," Luis said. "Ricky can't make a decent living slowly, so he wants to get rich quick. Ricky is Ricky."

"If I am to comprehend properly, North American space scientists, according to their orbiting spy satellites, possibly bored because they are not required to peek at the Kremlin any longer, have determined that a comet or a meteor landed in Yucatán and the resulting dust and crud blocked the sun's rays and altered the world's climate to the extent that dinosaurs froze and starved to death."

"Dugdale didn't allow me to study the documents in detail, but what I saw was convincing."

"Regardless. Nevertheless," Héctor said, looking from Rosa to Esther to Luis, "we must contemplate a flawed fallacy in this Dead Dinosaurs Park tourist proposition."

Rosa took her sister by the arm and said, "Come on. Inspector Salgado is going to use dirty language."

Esther went along, saying, "Hurry. Otherwise we might learn a new word."

"Horrors!" Rosa said, tittering through the tent flap.

Héctor grinned and shook his head. "Your daughters are too bright for your own good, Luis. Would you care to venture a guess in conjunction to my flawed fallacy tourist assertion?"

"Why would tourists come to Ho-Keh?" Luis said. "Would they care?"

"Precisely," Héctor said, hoisting a thumb. "No affront intended to your charming little village, Luis, but why indeed?"

"Charming and picturesque," Luis said, nodding. "But not charming and picturesque enough."

"Not remotely enough. The North Americans travel to Cancún to avoid for a few precious days their vicious Arctic winters. They come to Cancún for sun and fun. They come to bake beneath our sun. They come to party, to shop, to disco. They come to eat and drink and party and sun and swim and shop and disco and fuck. They come to fuck the companion they have come with, or if they are incredibly lucky, to fuck a complete and total stranger.

"The gringo sun worshipers are not attracted by plastic dinosaurs and apocalyptic lectures on history they would not give a shit about in any circumstance. Dugdale's anthropological tamale stands along a cenote ring created by a rock from outer space, they do not strike me as moneymakers. Some of these tourists, a tiny percentage, they visit Maya villages in arranged tours, but then you are expected to perform. Plant corn or speak your old language or string a hammock or whatnot."

"Sacrifice a virgin," Luis said.

"That might be effective. You would draw gigantic crowds, but keeping reliable virgin employees would be difficult. The tourists would come in throngs to steep themselves in ancient Maya culture. Dead dinosaurs, on the other hand, don't have a fucking thing to do with anything. That comet, it was a problem between them and it."

"Agreed," Luis said.

"The tourists desire to steep themselves in ancient Maya culture with less effort than going out to some isolated village. They climb on an air-conditioned bus, go over to Chichén Itzá or on down to Tulum. They walk around and listen to guides such as yourself describe what went on hundreds of years ago when there were actual people living there. Ninety out of a hundred North Americans, Luis, this is how they culturally steep themselves. They get it accomplished in an afternoon, and return to Cancún to sun and swim and eat and drink and shop and party and disco and fuck. The dead dinosaurs are bullshit."

"True," Luis said.

"So what is Dugdale's angle?"

"Money."

"Thank you so much for your insight, Luis. How does he bring the money rolling in with this stupid little cultural park that nobody will want to come to? That is the vital question."

Luis shrugged.

"What is Dugdale's background? How long has he been in Yucatán? What do you know of him aside from your lawyer friend's information?"

Luis shrugged again. "It doesn't matter. Francisco and the others will never approve the scheme."

"Ricky Martínez met Vance Dugdale in a bar, unquestionably. I will check on this promoter and see what we can find out for you," Héctor said.

He leaned forward and took out his wallet. "I always love coming to your establishment, Luis, but this is not exclusively a social call. On the subject of money, filthy lucre, I have not just an interesting, but an astoundingly amazing tale for you."

Héctor paused and, widening his eyes for effect, took from the wallet a one-hundred-dollar bill, flexed it so it snapped, and gave it to Luis. "Crisp and crackly new, Luis. Lovely, is it not?"

Luis had often seen one-hundred-dollar traveler's checks, but seldom the denomination in pure dollar form. Benjamin Franklin, the North American patriot, gazed benignly at him. Luis held the bill to his face and inhaled. Nothing smelled quite like a United States of America banknote.

He tried to return it to Héctor, who threw up his hands as if to surrender. "No, no, Luis. The money is yours. *Can* be yours should you accept an assignment. Permit me to tell you my spectacular tale."

Luis pocketed the hundred in his shirt. "Take as much time as you need, Héctor."

"You are naturally familiar with the Cancún InterPresidential Hotel, Luis?"

This obviously did not require a reply. Almost new, the InterPresidential was a glass and concrete pyramid that would have staggered the imaginations of his ancestors. In scale and in vulgarity, Luis thought.

"During your interim working construction in Cancún, Luis, you were involved in massive projects, but nothing of this ostentatious grandiosity. Government ministers, international rock stars, and professional athletes attended its opening last year. In excess of a thousand rooms. A dozen restaurants and bars. Activities and boutiques for everybody. And a swimming pool half a kilometer long!

"Two hundred Yanqui dollars per night in high season, minimum. For that lofty sum you do not even get a suite. You get a nice room with satellite television and a lanai. In such a room is your prospective client, Mr. Bob Chance."

"Why is this Mr. Bob Chance hiring me?"

"Mr. Bob Chance is a demented gringo millionaire," Héctor said. "He is, as we speak, holed up in his wonderful room, existing like a paranoid recluse."

"Like Howard Hughes?" Luis asked.

Héctor fluttered a palm. "Less money. Not yet as deranged, but nevertheless on the road to the status of a major psycho mental case. Unless, that is, you step in, Luis, and become his confidant and his salvation."

Luis smiled and took out the hundred.

"No, no, no, you misunderstand," Héctor said. "He is not requesting somebody to read him the Bible or lick his dick. Nothing remotely that odd and perverted."

"What is Mr. Bob Chance requesting, Héctor?"

"I must backtrack. The hotel night manager is a friend of mine. He telephoned me and asked if I might come by and consult regarding a confidential and sensitive problem."

"Consult," Luis said, smiling. "How much?"

"Not much," Héctor said. "Shut up, please, and permit me to continue. The InterPresidential night manager was alarmingly concerned. Mr. Bob Chance, a bizarre individual by any standard, had not been seen or heard from outside of his room in two days. The man spent the bulk of his time in that room anyway and subsisted on North American-style room service gourmet food. Pizza, fried chicken, tacos made with American cheese. Also copious quantities of beer and videocassettes.

"But he was no longer even having supplies delivered. The Do Not Disturb sign was permanently on the doorknob. The manager requested that I investigate. Should Mr. Chance have expired, the situation would be unseemly. Not to mention malodorous. Hardly an image the hotel wishes to project."

"The manager didn't check out Chance with his passkey?"

"He did. Chance would not respond and his door was jammed, as if a piece of furniture had been wedged against it."

"Then you were consulted?"

"I was. I yelled an introduction and pounded on the door. Eventually our Mr. Chance moved the dresser and granted me entry. He was not near death, although he was disheveled and absolutely terrified."

"Of what?"

"Virtually everything, it appeared at the outset. We spoke and narrowed his terror to specifics, specifically a fellow North American by the name of Mikey Smith, who was described as a virtual beast. Mr. Smith has been in pursuit of Mr. Chance for a while and seems to have caught up with him. Mr. Smith apparently desires to commit extreme bodily harm upon Mr. Chance. Strangling him with his own intestines, if you can believe Mr. Chance, who may or may not be exaggerating."

"How long has this Mikey Smith been in pursuit?"

"Chance is not sure. Chance departed his home city of Seattle, state of Washington, three months ago, on or about Christmas Day. He has been traveling throughout Mexico. Not the real Mexico, but Mexican enclaves for the affluent gringo tourist. La Zona Rosa in Mexico City. The chic hotel districts of Monterrey and Guadalajara." Then ticking them off on his fingers, "Los Cabos, Mazatlán, Puerto Vallarta, Ixtapa, and not to be forgotten, Acapulco."

"Expensive," Luis said.

"Extremely. Acapulco was his undoing. Mr. Smith apparently took up the hunt late, but closed in rapidly. Fortunately Mr. Chance spotted Mr. Smith before Mr. Smith spotted Mr. Chance, and hopped an airplane for Cancún. Mr. Chance perceives Mexico in a travel guidebook context. The Mexico beyond the pool bar and the margarita is a separate land altogether. Cancún was logical. Cancún is his final significant destination resort, the ultimate."

"Mikey Smith and Bob Chance think alike."

"They do, Luis. Smith picked up the trail and, according to Chance, is in Cancún. Several days ago, Smith and Chance spotted each other simultaneously, an unfortunate passing at a market. Chance managed to escape to his room."

"Does Smith know where Chance is, Héctor? Has he been to the InterPresidential?"

"Not to anyone's knowledge, but he will find him, if not today or tomorrow, the day after or the day after the day after. There are one hundred and fifty hotels and counting in Cancún. Mr. Smith is dogged. It is a matter of time.

"Chance has stupidly cornered himself. Think about it, Luis. Cancún, for all its luscious charms, is isolated. You have Highway 307 southward to Chetumal and the Belize border. You have Highway 180 going west to Valladolid, Chichén Itzá, and Merída. You have Cancún International Airport, at the end of a single access road. What remains? A refreshing swim to the western tip of Cuba, a mere two hundred kilometers? I don't think so. Bob Chance is built as spherically as yours truly and is somewhat softer. Mikey Smith can hire a little help and easily cover Chance's exit routes. Mr. Chance is trapped."

"What is Smith's problem with Chance?"

"Smith's problem is the funds with which Chance financed his extended fleeing to and vacationing in our fair land. The North Americans have lotteries as we do. Bob Chance won an enormous sum of money. Smith claims he was an equal partner with Chance on the winning ticket, so Chance stated, but Chance fled to Mexico before Smith could express that view to Chance, which is what he is attempting to do presently. Chance swore to me that Smith's claim is invalid and that Smith is a murderous opportunist."

"Do you believe him?"

Héctor laughed. "Luis, a shameful question. We were policemen together. I never believe just one side. It is one half of a story. Is Chance lying? Is Smith a figment of a tormented paranoid imagination? I don't know."

Luis touched the hundred but didn't withdraw it from his shirt.

"A meaningful gesture, Luis. You have accepted the assignment." Héctor took another crisp hundred from his wallet and kissed it. "An identical twin to yours. We are partners, you and I. Mr. Chance, for his faith and his generosity, deserves the benefit of the doubt, yes? His word against the virtual beast's?"

"What am I to do for him?"

"He is vague. These North Americans, their deviousness and indirection are maddening. He tells me he is stir crazy, claustrophobic, and wishes a bodyguard and companion to accompany him out of the room occasionally until he decides his next move.

"He evidently believes the stereotypes regarding Mexican police officers and therefore insists that his bodyguard be a civilian. I recommended you on the basis of your tenacity, your integrity, your toughness, and our friendship, which will insure continued partnership in this venture, a piece of whatever service fee you can negotiate with him."

"Twenty-five percent?" Luis said.

"One third," Héctor said. "That is not an unreasonable commission."

"All right, one third. Bob Chance wants to go sightseeing with me to protect him from Mikey Smith?"

"Yes. He mentioned a bullfight. He has never attended a bullfight."

"Did he discuss this next move of his?"

"No, but I have a hunch he might to you."

"I'm not doing anything that will land me in your jail, Héctor."

"Perish that thought, Luis. Anything you do illegally, I insist that you conceal it from me."

"When is he expecting me?"

"Soon," Héctor said, standing. "Answer me this question. Bob Chance is an incredibly rich and an incredibly sad man. How can a man so rich be so sad?"

"I don't know."

"Me neither. I wonder, is there a correlation between wealth and sadness?"

"I don't think so," Luis said.

"I don't either, but who knows. Maybe *I* should be poorer. Maybe I should pray to God that I knock up my wife again. With triplets."

5

Luis Balam had bought his VW Beetle from a Cancún car rental agency when renters would no longer tolerate the shimmy, the sputtering, the tattered upholstery. Its suspension had been bruised by bad roads, its engine malnourished on 81 octane gasoline. Cracks in the windshield were milky. Its body shell was dented and corroded. The front bumper was loose and fluttery. Oxidized blue paint closely matched the color of the exhaust smoke. Luis kept his car patched with bicycle tools and luck, and was thankful that rust-through had not reached its structural panels.

Luis knew the rental agency manager, who instructed him how the game was to be played. Luis received a ten percent discount on a low purchase price and returned five percent to the manager as an "administrative rebate." The manager split his "rebate" with the agency accountant, who rendered the process invisible.

Luis drove northward on 307, thinking of that cash legerdemain and thinking of Dugdale and Chance, two shifty foreigners who were going to make him rich. He thought too of the continual wheeling and dealing demanded at Black Coral. He wondered if anything would ever work out the way it was designed. He wondered if there would ever be room in his life for a straightforward deal.

Highway 307 was two lanes and shoulderless. Thick scrub jungle crowded the inland side. Now and then, the Caribbean peeked through on the other. Every day, it seemed that more dump trucks lumbered along the highway. They were excavating half the coast to build on the other half.

Luis drove hard, his foot to the floor, going around slower traffic, ignoring the blinking headlights of oncoming vehicles, squeezing back into his lane. He was in no hurry, but it was not his nature to coddle a machine.

Especially not the Beetle, which was manufactured only in Mexico now. Mexico City cabbies were known to get a decade of use from one of them on the world's most anarchistic streets and to routinely shoehorn in a family of six plus luggage. A masochistic breed of car, Luis thought. It loved the sting of his spurs.

The Cancún hotel zone was a desolate sandbar, skinny and brushy, 7-shaped and a dozen miles long. A quarter mile wide, and separated from the mainland at both ends by narrow channels, it was an island by the strictest definition.

Until the late 1960s Cancún had been a remote fishing village. Then it became the creature of a Mexico City computer and its masters, who decided that since Acapulco was booming, why not create another from scratch? Today, their creation boasted thousands and thousands of hotel rooms, malls and boutiques, tennis courts and discotheques, marinas and condos, cafes and restaurants, and the obligatory golf course.

Local cynics tagged Cancún *gringolandia*, but they did so with good cheer. Visitors came at a rate of a million per year, spending dollars and francs and marks and pesos and plastic. The parable of the golden goose was lost on no one, least of all Luis.

He turned onto the island at the south bridge. Cancún was developing from the north, so scraggly patches of untouched land remained at this end. Headed northward on the only thoroughfare, Kukulcán Boulevard, he could still see the lagoon to his left, the sea to his right.

But this view was doomed, Luis knew. A covey of construction cranes (designated the official bird of Cancún by the same cheerful cynics) stood perched at hotel and condominium projects still in the skeletal stages. Given time, and not a lot of it, the Caribbean side would be a solid column of Nouveau Maya heroic architecture, the lagoon side a clutter of marinas and jet ski rental shops.

Luis wondered again how he felt about the place. Yes, resort construction work had been his ticket out of the cornfields. It also had led to a disgraced police career and a dependence on cash money. One night he had gone drinking with an anthropologist acquaintance. Luis liked the man and disliked the man's profession. He was informed late in the evening by his overeducated and inebriated companion that Cancún had for Luis Balam "permitted socioeconomic elevation from the agrarian to the mercantile level without loss of ethnocentric core values."

Despite himself, the man made sense. Cancún had also, in Luis's honest estimation, reconciled his conscience and suppressed his ego, permitting him to haggle over the price of beads alongside his babies.

Good or bad? he debated for the umpteenth time. To the same nebulous conclusion.

Luis parked across Kukulcán from the Cancún Inter-

Presidential. He would have been conspicuous in the hotel's circular drive, a blemish on the immaculate pavement and the rainbowlike landscaping.

As he neared the hotel, the word that came to mind was *loom.* As massive as the pyramidal stone temples at Chichén Itzá and Cobá, he thought; perhaps even the towering monster at Tikal.

Luis had never been inside the InterPresidential. The lobby was startling—an atrium surrounded by layers of balconies. Skylights beamed the sun to palm trees. Lighted fountains cascaded as if made of lava. Glacial air-conditioning tingled his arms. Floors were, of course, polished marble. Cancún hotel designers lavished marble on floors, counters, even walls. The mineral was not native to Yucatán, and Luis often wondered where they got it all and whether a single slab of marble still existed anywhere else.

Luis stepped into a glass-enclosed elevator before he began gawking. He wore dark blue slacks and a light blue shirt, his Traffic Police uniform sans insignia. His shirt pocket was stuffed with pens and he carried a clipboard. He was an illusion, a valet or a supervisor of domestics or a maintenance man. Any Indian who did not pass for an employee would quickly attract attention.

He rapped on Bob Chance's door, waited, rapped again, waited, and rapped again, longer and louder.

"Read the thingie hanging off the doorknob, señorita. *Comprehendo?*" yelled a voice from within. "*No disturbo.* No do maid service today, okay?"

There were guests in the hall, so Luis did not yell a response. He wrote his name and Héctor's on the Do Not Disturb tag and slipped it under the door.

"You're that cop's guy?"

"I am."

"How do I know that?"

"You don't," Luis said.

"Can't live forever, I guess."

The latch clicked. Luis entered a darkened room. The suspicious voice came from an overweight silhouette outlined by the throbbing glow of a color television. The silhouette was sitting rigidly on the edge of the bed, clutching a short, dark object. Luis squinted, trying to focus. A gun? A truncheon?

"Remote control," Bob Chance said, hoisting it like a torch. "I shut off the sound."

Now shut off the odor, Luis thought. He smelled stale food, beer, and sweat. This room, which cost more per night than he earned in some months, reeked like a cheap bar, a cantina where you could get food poisoning and gonorrhea at no extra charge. He advanced to see the TV and stepped on an empty beer can. On the set was a VCR, on the screen a North American football game.

"Super Bowl highlight flicks," Chance said. "They're available down here, would you believe. This is one of the Miami Dolphin wins."

"Miami 14, Washington 7. The 1973 game," Luis said, browsing in his 1974 World Almanac storehouse. "Los Angeles Coliseum. Csonka, one hundred twelve yards rushing. What is 'rushing'?"

"Yards gained from scrimmage running the ball," Bob Chance said. "Jesus, who the hell are you?"

"Turn on a light and turn off the television."

Chance complied but in the opposite order. In the dark, he stumbled on another beer can, cursed, and pawed a wall for a switch. Luis blinked at the visage of a Caucasian his own age or slightly older. Bob Chance had a blotchy complexion and multiple chins. He was bulging out of plaid shorts and a Hard Rock Cafe T-shirt. His hair was graying and shaggy. Not hippie shaggy, Luis thought. He was simply overdue for a haircut.

Chance wore a kindly, hapless, larcenous expression, with playful-sad eyes and the trace of a smirk. Luis had seen the type. Bob Chance looked like a time-share condominium salesman not quite clever or immoral enough to make his quota.

Chance plopped back on his bed. "The cop didn't say you were an Indian."

Luis replied with a stare.

"Indian. You know, noble red man. I'm no racist. Savvy da lingo?"

"Don't call me an Indian," Luis said. "That's no different than me calling you a gringo. I am Maya."

"Jesus, sorry. I've seen you carved in stone. I'm a fan. You guys and ten points against Cortés instead of those Aztecs he clobbered way back when, I'd of taken you and the points."

"Four million Maya live in Mexico and Central America, not just on ancient stone. Speak properly to me. I speak English."

"Okay, fine. My Spanish consists of *cerveza* and *turista.* The cop, whatshisname, he said you were a hardass, but I guess that's what I'm paying for."

"The cop is Inspector Salgado to you," Luis said, taking in his surroundings. Food-encrusted plates, countless empty beer cans, and dirty laundry were scattered throughout the luxurious room, in plush chairs, on hardwood dressers and the marble floor. A man who would not pick up after himself if he were smothering in rubble, Luis observed; a forty-year-old not long weaned from his mother.

"Like you probably heard from Inspector Salgado, I've been a little paranoid lately," Chance said in a shrugging apology. "I didn't want anybody in this room. Chambermaids, nobody. I order up and they leave the stuff in the hallway."

"Tell me about yourself," Luis said.

"Well, Christmas Eve I hit the Lotto for—"

"No, I mean about your life, your background."

"Okay. First, you want a beer? I've got Bud or Miller."

"No Mexican beer?"

"Nope." Chance shambled to a refrigerator by the television and removed a Budweiser. "Mexican beer is made from Mexican water. Nothing personal, but I'm in plenty of trouble without compounding the situation with a queasy stomach."

"Not taken personally."

"In Mazatlán, I ate this beefsteak, thought I was gonna puke my guts out. I was laid up for—"

"Before your Christmas fortune, who were you?"

"I worked for the Boeing Company in Seattle. They make the big jets."

"The airplanes that fly the tourists to Cancún?" Luis said.

"Yep. Would of had seventeen years this June. Started there a week after I graduated from college. Talk about being in a rut."

"What did you do at the Boeing?"

"I was a planner." Chance sat heavily on the bed, popped the Budweiser tab, and laughed. "What I didn't do is give two weeks' notice. I cashed that winning ticket, beelined it to Sea-Tac Airport, and said fly me somewhere hot and dry. Know what Seattle's like in winter?"

"No."

"Well, it's not the North Pole or anything like that, but that day was your basic, typical gray, wet, and cold. Everybody and their brother's at Sea-Tac on the holidays, going and coming, and the lines were a mile long, like they were selling playoff tickets, but this one ticket guy, he had a cancellation to Cabo, except it was first-class, and I go, man, money is literally no object."

"What did you plan at the Boeing?"

"Production scheduling. In a little cubicle in a huge office building. I gave the last five years to engine nacelles. Boring."

Chance hesitated and sighed. Thanks to his soft bulk, the exhalation rippled flesh. "Goddamn, boring sounds really great right now."

Luis looked at an opaque curtain. On the other side was a lanai and a glorious view of the sea. For North Americans who came to Cancún this time of the year, the sea was high on their list of reasons. The Caribbean was the color of emeralds and blue topaz, as warm as bathwater. People came to this sea from their Chicagos and Buffalos, where if you wanted to see the water you had to saw a hole in the ice.

Luis pointed at the curtain. "Do you like the view?"

"No way. If I can see out, he can see in from the beach."

Luis had won a wager with himself. He said, "Married? Children?"

"Just finalizing my divorce. Judy filed and was handling the whole thing. A do-it-yourself manual. No lawyers. We hadn't talked for a while, but I assume it was finalized around late November, early December. We didn't have much community property worth fighting over, so I'd asked her to put it off till January. I made lots more money than her and I needed her as an exemption for the tax writeoff.

"Then a few days after she said she would, we had us a big beef, so I'm assuming she said to hell with me and went ahead and finalized as soon as she could. A terrific little gal. She'll never win any beauty contests, never be a Dallas Cowgirl, but she's too good for me in a lot of respects, though she's a real ditz."

"Ditz?"

Chance swirled an index finger by an ear. "You know, flaky, goofy, spacey. Judy's younger than me and into things I'm not. Birdwatching and gardening. Running. Things like that. No interest whatsoever in football, but like I said, a terrific gal. We didn't have any kids, thank goodness."

"Judy Chance doesn't share in your lottery fortune?"

Chance shrugged. "I'm afraid she's out of luck. We're divorced. She put me on waivers. She put the moccasins outside the teepee—oops, again, no offense—before I snatched the brass ring. We ever cross paths, I'll do the right thing, I'll do something for her."

"You won how much?"

"Three million bucks. It's weird. I never in my life won so much as a stuffed animal at a carnival, and then I go and beat seven-million-to-one odds, which is what the Washington State Lotto is."

"Nine billion old pesos or nine million new ones. Our Lotería Nacional has a nice top prize, but not in that range."

"It's not actually as swell as it seems. They dole it out to you over twenty years after the IRS whacks twenty-eight percent off the top. That's one hundred and eight grand per annum net."

"The same as over three hundred million old pesos or three hundred and some thousand new pesos," Luis said. "You came south with that much money?"

Bob Chance laughed without a discernible smile. "It's not the fortune it sounds like, man, not when you go as hog-wild as I did."

"You spent it all?"

He rapped on his forehead with his knuckles. "Knock on wood. Lucky I had the smarts to hang on to some, to sock some away in a kitty."

"Explain your problem with this Mikey Smith. Inspector Salgado said that Smith, a maniac, believes you cheated him out of his share of the ticket. He followed you to Cancún and is preparing to kill you."

"Yeah. That's it in a nutshell."

"Did you cheat him?"

"Well, that's kind of a complicated question open to interpretation. If it were a football play, you'd review it on instant replay."

Luis walked to the cooler for a North American light beer, and sat in a chair. "I have time."

"Okay," Chance began after a long pull on his beer and another tremor of a sigh. "Mikey Smith owns Mikey's Sports Bar, that's located in Seattle a long rolling punt from the Kingdome. The Kingdome, in case you didn't know, is a domed stadium where you play professional football and hold other events.

"Mikey's Sports Bar attracts a clientele that's into sports. Obviously. You don't have to shell out thirty smackeroos a seat for a Seahawks game. You can watch it on the big screen at Mikey's. Mikey Smith played some ball himself. Community college all-conference at linebacker and junior college all-American honorable mention. He was too short in height and grade-point average to go on to a four-year school.

"Get this. Above his backbar, mounted on a wood plaque like antlers, is this helmet split right down the middle. Mikey put a fullback in the hospital with that hit. Ruptured diaphragm and busted ribs. Boom! Talk about playing with intensity. They took Mikey in for observation too, you know, for a concussion. The brain scan was inconclusive. You can take that two ways."

A grisly story told with adoration. Luis said nothing.

"Luis, you're frowning like you're not reading me. Are you with me? A lot of this stuff is a situation where you'd have to be there. You'd have to be born and raised in America."

"Mikey Smith is powerful and dangerous," Luis said. "I understand that."

"Great. Fantastic. So you know what we're dealing with."

"*We* are not dealing with anything yet. What about you and Smith and the ticket?"

"Okay. You're a hard sell. That's fine. I'd been a regular at Mikey's for a while. We were friends, me and him. We had kind of a ritual where every Wednesday and Saturday, before the Lotto drawing, we'd each invest five bucks in tickets."

"You were partners?" Luis said.

Chance fluttered a hand. "Except this last time, which

is kind of a gray area. Mikey was gone for a couple of days. I bought the tickets. I *always* picked up the tickets, *always* did the legwork, and Mikey reimbursed me.

"Well, I had the winner and Mikey wasn't there. Technically he wasn't involved. I'm not what you'd call a spontaneous kind of guy, but there I was, sitting at the bar, when they drew the numbers on TV. I sat there dazed, with this ticket burning a hole in my pocket, and on comes this airline commercial for Mexico where they're showing beaches and palm trees and cupcakes in bikinis.

"Next morning, Christmas Eve, I cashed in. By noon I was packed and at Sea-Tac."

"You bought the usual ten dollars' worth, for you and Mikey?"

"I did, but like I said, he was drinking hot toddies with relatives or someone. You know how the holidays are. The fact remains, I saw him in Acapulco and then again right here. In both situations, we made eye contact."

"You're certain it was Mikey Smith?"

"Trust me, you make eye contact with Mikey Smith when his nose is out of joint, you know it."

"Why not talk to him? Offer next year's money and every other year from then on."

"That's an option I've considered. Trouble is, I'm registered as the winner and he's not gonna take my word."

"You could have an agreement drawn up by a lawyer. A good friend of mine is a lawyer. He could do it."

"I'll sleep on it, but you don't know Mikey. He doesn't think like normal people. We're at the point, probably, where if he could screw my head on backward and rip me a new pooper, it'd be better for him than all the tea in China."

"You cheated him out of a fortune," Luis said. "I would be angry too."

"Well, like I said, that's open for interpretation. Besides, what's the greater sin, a little bit of grand larceny or a torture-murder? Just give me a small portion of your time and I'll pay you anything reasonable."

"We can arrange a fee if I decide to. The one-hundred-dollar bill is fine for now."

"Okay. Tell me something about the guy who's gonna protect me. Fair's fair. You know about me, but all I know is what your cop buddy said, about you being tough and sticking up for your principles, which got you fired when you were on the force together. No details given."

"I went away from the village to work construction in Cancún. I hated being away from my family, but I liked the money and the new experiences," Luis said. "I would be restless if I returned to the village and grew corn. The Traffic Police was the answer, I thought. I could live at Ho-Keh and be a policeman. I liked police work. It's hard for a Maya to find a job with any authority, but Héctor had befriended me and got me on. He was and is my mentor."

"But he couldn't save you from the trouble," Chance said. "He had this sad look in his eyes when he said he couldn't."

"I was on duty one night when a rich man, speeding and drunk, struck and killed a Maya family. The rich man was driving a Mercedes-Benz. The family was on the side of the highway on a bicycle. We Maya can fit more people on a bicycle than anybody.

"The man and his wife were killed instantly. The bicycle was a pretzel. We didn't find the little boy and little girl until daylight. They had been riding on the handlebars. The girl catapulted twenty meters from the road and was wedged in a tree. The boy was smashed against another tree.

"I investigated. I had reliable witnesses. They gave a good report and a good description of the car. There were no skid marks. The driver hadn't touched his brakes. I traced the Mercedes to a garage. They had fixed the car, but I recovered the bumper and fender. I spent my own money on film and photographed everything.

"Much bigger money changed hands. My report was altered. A phantom driver was the official conclusion. I wouldn't quit. I complained. I was too noisy. Infractions were manufactured against me. I was fired for inefficiency. Héctor tried to help. He jeopardized his own career trying. He was helpless in the system too. Héctor moved on to an improved position at the State Judicial Police, but he is aware that nothing changes."

"I'm impressed. You're my guy if you're game. Let's go to a bullfight."

"They're on Wednesdays, the day after tomorrow. Why a bullfight?"

"I've never seen one, and surprise of surprises, I'm a sports fan. Even with the Super Bowl tapes, I'm going nuts cooped up in this room. The walls are closing in. I need to unwind, have a little fun."

"Bullfights are public. Smith may find you. Why not hire me to escort you to the airport?"

"And bug out to where? Mikey traced me to Acapulco and on to Cancún. How he did, I don't know, but he did. Mikey's got the momentum going for him."

"Don't you want to go home?"

"I don't know, I really don't. I burned my bridges. I'm not going to be welcome. I fire off a postcard once in a while. That's about it. I really don't know. For the time being, I'd just like to get out of this room, breathe some fresh air, and sort out my thoughts, you know."

"You won't be welcome by whom, your airplane company employers?"

"Nah. They don't care. My mother. I stood her up for Christmas dinner and I haven't talked to her since. I know Mom. She was brutally pissed and she's still steaming."

"What killed the dinosaurs?"

"Huh?"

"What killed the dinosaurs? Do you know?"

"If that's a sports trivia question," Bob Chance said, "you're asking the wrong guy. You must be thinking of a soccer team. There's no NFL club named the Dinosaurs."

6

Luis asked Chance for his spare room key. Chance asked why and Luis said, so I don't have to yell from the hallway if I have to visit you again before the bullfight. Chance said, hey, what about my privacy, can't you just knock? If you're passed out drunk, what good would it do to knock? Luis didn't say. If you have another visitor, Mr. Smith, for example, and he is twisting your head around, what good would it do to knock? Luis did say. You have a point, but, Chance said, holding on to the key, how would Mikey get in? I'm barricading the door when you leave. Smith tracked you thousands of miles, Luis said, and he has the momentum. Good point, Chance said, tossing him the key.

Luis drove from Cancún Island to Cancún City, adjacent on the mainland. As the hotel zone sprouted, the city grew too, but its growth was stunted, low to the ground and homely. Construction workers such as Luis who built on the island built the city as a home while they built on the island. Some were gone, replaced by younger laborers, and by taxi drivers, bartenders, and janitors. Cancún City was Cancún Island's bedroom and marketplace. It was boisterous and proletarian. Downtown Cancún was old Mexico, circa 1977.

The city's main thoroughfare was a hectic four-lane named Avenida Tulum. Other noisy avenues of commerce also honored Yucatán's ancient cities: Uxmal, Bonampak, Yaxchilán, Cobá, Chichén Itzá, Palenque, Kabah.

Ricardo Martínez Rodríguez's law office was in Cancún City, in a nondescript cement-block building, on the second and top floor above a bar. If the street had a name at all, it contained no reference to glorious history. The cheap overhead was a blessing, Ricky frequently remarked, as was the proximity of doctors willing to supply gloomy prognoses for his injured clients.

Luis went into the alley that separated Ricky's from another dreary building, and up the stairs. The door to the bar's kitchen was open. Luis smelled cigarette smoke and hot grease. It was close to nightfall. Luis was uncertain whether Ricky would be at his office, but he was.

The lawyer unlocked the door, let him in, and said, "Luis, the very person I want to see. My good luck holds. Come in and sit."

Luis sat on one of three folding chairs in the single room that Ricky described to women he met as a "corporate legal suite complex." The remaining furnishings consisted of a wooden table that served as Ricky's desk, a rust-pocked filing cabinet, and, hanging on a wall, the lonely portrait of Lázaro Cárdenas, a revered statesman and President of the United Mexican States in the 1930s. The corporate legal suite complex was directly above the bar. Luis could hear laughter and the horns and strings and yipping of jukebox mariachi.

Ricky said, "You missed Vance by moments. I'm sorry you didn't connect. We were doing a meeting and I have to say, I'm excited."

Luis could not bring himself to say that he was also sorry he had missed Dugdale, so he said nothing.

"The project is gathering no moss, Luis. We see no advantage in delaying expansion to other villages readily accessible to highways and tourist buses."

"No advantage," Luis repeated, unable to think of how else to respond.

"Vance feels that the key is the executive liaisons. A senior executive liaison, as it were, Luis. You."

"An executive executive liaison," Luis said.

"Luis, please don't make fun of me. I hate it when you do, especially because I am never sure when you do."

"Me?"

"Luis, would you be interested in the position? You would in essence be an advance man. Your job would be to recruit the Maya executive liaison in each prospective village."

"I'll consider the offer," Luis lied. "Will the company supplying the plastic dinosaurs be able to meet the demand?"

"Not a problem. Vance's vendor in Havana has an adequate inventory and is shipping the material as we speak. Vance says the vendor can produce to meet any demand. Expansion is a medium to long-term situation, so take your time considering. Vance is seeking further capitalization."

"Havana? Dugdale told us São Paulo. And what does 'further capitalization' mean? Doesn't Dugdale have any money?"

Ricky spread his arms. "Cuba, Brazil, whichever. Perhaps I am confused. What is the distinction, actually? And as far as Vance's finances go, he is extremely solid on Ho-Keh and subsequent projects on the short term."

"Cuba doesn't know where its next meal is coming from, Ricky. How can they turn out Dugdale's dinosaurs like they're Volkswagen Beetles?"

"Luis, Luis. Luis. You are missing the point by concentrating on minute details. The bottom line is, we are going to be rich!"

Ricky's voice was giddy, his eyes glazed. Luis pictured that face on the Spaniards who had crashed through the Valley of Mexico in gold lust, on the scent of Aztec riches. He was eager to interrogate Ricky on Dugdale. Who is he, where is he from? Fruitless, he realized. To Ricky, Dugdale, fact or fantasy, there was no difference.

He instead related his conversation with Bob Chance, without displaying the one-hundred-dollar bill. Mr. Benjamin Franklin and his greenback would top off a life-threatening accumulation of stimulation. Even a young, robust man like Ricky might overdose on greed and suffer a seizure.

"Oh, Luis, three million Yanqui bucks. That is what in pesos?"

"Nine million pesos today. Tomorrow, who knows? Ten million. He receives only one hundred and eight thousand dollars per year."

Ricky's eyes bulged. "Only?"

"And that is what he started with on Christmas Eve. Three months of traveling, eating and drinking expensively, and paying InterPresidential room rates, I wonder how much money is left."

"Plenty, Luis. Plenty. Mexico is cheap for gringos and Chance has a king's ransom. This Mikey Smeeth, this cretin, how dangerous do you anticipate him to be?"

"Smith," Luis said. "S-m-i-t-h. Smith."

"Luis, please do not correct me. I am a college graduate. As I said, S-m-i-t-h, Smeeth. How dangerous?"

"Smith."

Ricky sighed. "You are stubborn beyond comprehension, Luis. Very well. Smith. How perilous to Chance and to you? Is Chance misrepresenting or is Smith Smith Smith likely to kill him should the opportunity arise?"

"Chance cheated him out of his share."

"Situational ethics enter the equation," Ricky said, furrowing his brow, stroking his long, handsome jaw. "This is a gray area. Smith was away from his cantina on holiday on the day of the fateful lottery drawing. Their verbal contract could be interpreted as altered, not as binding as normally. Mr. Bob Chance is a substantial citizen. We should not be hasty to condemn."

"Chance cheated Smith, Ricky. I agreed to escort him to a bullfight, anyway. The ideal would be a settlement. Chance's life is saved and Smith is given his rightful money. Chance's former wife, I think, is entitled to money too."

"I am ignorant of North American law, Luis. I could execute a contract between the men, but how binding by their law it would be, I would not hazard a guess. Their criminal law system is backward from ours; you are innocent until proved guilty. They have a rigid definition of corruption and those caught in the process of election fraud are treated like mass murderers. Those people up in the north are Puritans. They are emotionally and jurisprudentially constipated."

"They would be making promises on paper," Luis said. "The psychological is more important than the legal. If they sign and shake hands, maybe there won't be bloodshed."

"A sensible approach. I can draft the document," Ricky

said, nodding. "When your Mr. Chance decides to do the smart thing, notify me. We will do a meeting, you and me and Chance and Smith-Smeeth."

String and vocal music wafted through the floorboards. Substandard flooring vibrated underneath Luis's sandals. "La Bamba." A neighborhood mariachi trio was in the bar, serenading a table of tourists. Five dollars bought you a tune, your request. They always requested "La Bamba," Luis thought. Always.

Ricky Martínez grimaced and jabbed a thumb downward. "Luis, have I told you lately how much I despise 'La Bamba'?"

"Yes, you have, Ricky."

"Whenever I hear 'La Bamba,' I ask myself if my ship will ever come in. My dream is—was—to buy the thickest carpet in Yucatán, to drown out the tune. But alas, my ship continually sinks prior to reaching port. Thanks to Vance Dugdale, Luis, that ship of mine is steaming in."

"I hope so, Ricky. I hope you get your thick carpet."

Ricky grinned. "The carpet is an old dream, Luis, an obsolete dream. To hell with this dump. I'm moving to the hotel zone and establishing my office in the nicest mall with the nicest fountain and the nicest view of the sea and the nicest offices and boutiques that employ the prettiest girls."

7

At the Tulum ruins there were diesel and sunscreen fumes in the air, but no work for Luis Balam. The tour buses from Cancún arrived early to beat the heat, disgorged their passengers, and howled at fast idle to power their air conditioners. It was not yet ten o'clock and Luis counted eighteen buses.

Tulum was a cliffside ruin erected a thousand years ago and still inhabited at the time of the Spanish conquest as a trading center. It had been built after the decline of the Maya city-states by the Toltecs, ruffians from up north. The buildings were squat and ornate, a compact compound inside stone walls.

Though it lacked the towering classic-Maya majesty of a Tikal or Cobá, Tulum was said to be the busiest ruin in Mexico. Its walls and seaside outlook were unique in an ancient Yucatán world of inland cities. It was by far the largest fortified site on the Quintana Roo coast and was easily accessible.

Regardless, permanent guides were in sufficient quantity today to accommodate visitors. Luis would not be permitted to organize groups to walk through and narrate the sights, and to collect a dollar apiece for his efforts. Maybe the next day or the next. Maybe not.

He had dropped Esther and Rosa at Black Coral, eight kilometers to the north, with the hope of picking up fifteen or twenty dollars for half a day's work. He drove the Beetle out of the hot, congested Tulum parking lot and turned right on 307, bound for Black Coral.

Luis pondered why he was scrounging work that seldom existed, why he was wasting time and gasoline. In his pocket was the crisp one-hundred-dollar bill, in his memory Ricky Martínez's assurance of imminent Dead Dinosaurs riches. Additionally, he had a bullfight escort assignment tomorrow with Mr. Bob Chance, the North American lottery tycoon.

Skepticism to the verge of cynicism, that was the answer. An unfailing distrust of his fellow man. An abnormally dubious attitude blackened further by insecurity. But a healthily abnormal attitude, he decided.

Business at Black Coral was slower than slow. One blue-eyed family came in. Father, mother, and five children descending in a two- or three-year pattern from Rosa's age to preschool. They were looking for something in silver, plain bracelets or rings, but good stuff, not the crapola those beach peddlers shoved in your face. They wanted quality souvenirs, lasting mementos of the vacation of a lifetime made possible by Dad's frequent flier miles and Mom's coupon-clipping thrift. Luis presented his best price. It was thrice what the blue-eyes said they could pay.

Despite the bargainlike image of its tent, Black Coral sold only genuine silver, .925 pure as decreed by law. The beach vendors with their valises of rings and the bracelets stacked on their forearms as if they were Cambodian princesses, Luis explained patiently and truthfully, couldn't claim a gram of silver total in their inventory. What the junk was made of, he didn't know. Scrap metal from cars, maybe. And where it came from? Taiwan? You pay next to nothing for garbage or you pay a little tiny bit more—cheap, almost free—for quality. Your choice, sir. Your choice, ma'am.

The father of the blue-eyed baby factory said sadly that they were on a budget. Luis said he sympathized, but you got what you paid for. They parted friends, although it was unlikely they would ever do business. A giggling Rosa said that since Father could not close an easy sale, would he please do them a favor. Go home for a couple of things we forgot this morning; please, Esther piped in. My Madonna cassette and headphones, Rosa said. And hair barrettes for me, said Esther; the red plastic butterfly clips.

Luis scowled and asked if he looked like an errand boy. But he drove back to Ho-Keh smiling. This was the first useful thing he had done all day.

At Ho-Keh, at the foot of the cenote path, were two strangers. They stood by their motorbike, a shiny Suzuki with crudely painted orange flames on the gas tank. They were smoking cigarettes, looking around, yawning, scratching their heads. One man had a notebook, the other a measuring tape. Both wore machetes in scabbards.

Whoever they were, whatever they were up to, the men did not impress Luis as dynamos. He walked toward them, wondering where everybody was. Francisco Ek and some of the men would be in the fields, yes, but not every man. The women should be doing laundry and preparing tortilla dough for lunch. The children should be playing. Ho-Keh wasn't deserted; Luis saw a woman hanging up clothes. Two kids chased a dog out of Francisco's house and ran back in. There was neither alarm nor curiosity about the strangers. Evidently everyone else was inside their homes or Francisco's. Considering María Ek's illness, this intrusion into the Ek home was rude. And odd.

"What are you doing?" Luis asked when he reached the motorbike.

The one to Luis's left was short, paunchy, and had a bandit mustache. He said, "Yeah, who are you?"

"I live here," Luis said.

The one on his right was tall and stoop-shouldered. He had a receding chin and an acne-pitted complexion. He laughed and said, "I would never have guessed."

A pair of trash mestizos, Luis thought. Sixty percent of Mexico was a blend of Indian and Spaniard, descendants of Cortés and Moctezuma. These two, Luis knew the type. They spent ninety percent of their time trying to prove that they were ninety percent European rather than fifty percent Native Mexican. "What are you doing?"

"Those the only words you can speak, Indian?" said the fat bandit.

"What are you doing in Ho-Keh?"

"Look, Indian," said his partner, "the rest of your tribe isn't pestering us. Take a hint."

Luis took a hint. He took the motorbike's kickstand with his sandal and released it. The bike toppled, clattering on the rocks and caked limestone soil.

"Hey, goddamn you, fucking Indian!" The fat man was screaming, shaking a fist, but he did not advance. He had the cold, beady eyes of a bully-coward.

"Sorry, boss," Luis said, smiling. "I'm just a clumsy Indian."

Luis stepped aside so the fat man could right his bike.

"Shit, man, I paid good money for the custom paint job on the tank and the chrome was perfect. Now I got gouges and shit from this grit you knocked it down on."

"Lack of coordination, boss," Luis said. "What are you doing in Ho-Keh?"

The ugly gangling man slapped his scabbard. "A little whack across the forehead might teach him some manners. Maybe we should teach him some respect."

"Us Indians have thick heads, boss," Luis said, widening his smile. "You'd dull your blade."

"Shit, piss, fuck," said the fat man. He was spitting in his hand and wiping the side of the bike that had struck the ground. "It's gone on through to bare metal."

"I don't mind. I can sharpen it later on," said the ugly, smiling also.

"Draw it fast, boss, and do your business on the first swing," Luis said cordially. "Either way, your first swing will be your last."

The ugly wiped his brow. "Getting too fucking hot and too fucking late in the day for this shit, Indian. Working up a sweat in the heat, man, it's bad for the system."

The frozen smiles and the stupid, obscene, macho banter was water on the fuse, Luis knew. Nobody was going to die at Ho-Keh today.

Fat looked at Ugly in despair and said, "You see where anything's bent? Is the front wheel straight? I'll wreck the wheel bearings riding on a bent rim!"

"What are you gentlemen doing at Ho-Keh?" Luis persisted.

"Mr. Dugdale sent us to look at this little trail of yours,

see if it's wide enough and level enough that nobody snags themselves or trips and falls in the dark," Ugly said. "We're supposed to do what we can do and what we can't do, we're supposed to take measurements and notes for Mr. Dugdale."

Suppressing his anger, playing dumb, Luis asked, "Who is your Mr. Dugdale?"

"He's just a guy we work for."

"Who's coming to Ho-Keh to trip and fall in the dark?"

"I don't know, man. Mr. Dugdale, he's bringing gringos in for some kind of a thing. He didn't say."

"Did Mr. Dugdale tell you he had permission from us for you to measure so gringos don't fall in the dark?"

"I don't know. He didn't say he did, he didn't say he didn't. He paid us money to do what we want to do if you'd just leave so we could, man."

Fat was astride his bike, bouncing up and down. "The shock don't feel bent."

"Who is Mr. Dugdale? How do you know him? Where did you meet him?"

"Shit," Ugly said, shaking his head. "We'll never get done, you keep nagging us. Up around Cancún. We've known him. He's just a guy. I don't know anything else except he paid us cash in advance. What else you got to know? That's all I got to say. How about you go grind some corn or something so we can do our work?"

Fat and Ugly probably didn't meet him in a bar last night, Luis thought. Their association was of longer duration, though not very long. "You've worked for Mr. Dugdale on other jobs?"

Ugly slapped Fat on the forearm. "Un-ass that thing, man. We better finish before the middle of the afternoon. We don't, the sun's gonna melt you into a puddle of grease."

"Fuck you. I'll come when I'm good and ready," Fat said as he dismounted his motorbike.

"Good idea, boss," Luis said. "Hurry up or you'll miss your siestas."

"How far to the well?" Ugly asked.

"Cenote," Luis said. "Sacred cenote."

Ugly laughed. "Sacred bullshit. How far?"

"Not far," Luis said, suddenly inspired. "You gentlemen be careful and respectful at the cenote. I'm explaining this for your own good. Otherwise you're risking a curse."

They looked at each other. A smirking Ugly said, "Curse?"

Luis was remembering an old, old movie he had seen on television at Héctor's home. Egyptian mummies were annoyed at being unearthed. Later in the film, they came out of their wrappings and exacted vengeance. "I'm a modern man, gentlemen. I don't necessarily accept those stories. On the other hand, there is a lot that nobody understands."

"What stories?"

Luis was aware of no such afterlife vengeance in Maya cosmology, but he could not stop himself. "People who were sacrificed in the cenotes centuries ago. You bother them and they kill you for it. Bone by bone, they float up, assemble as skeletons and flesh and blood and bad tempers. You don't see them. You never know what hit you."

"Sacrificed virgins," Ugly said, grinning, grabbing his crotch. "They can attack me anytime."

"Not virgins," Luis said. "Captured enemy warriors and chiefs. Tough guys. You went to war in those days and you brought home important prisoners for sacrifice. My ancestors worshiped what nourished them. The earth, the sun, the rain. You had to keep the universe operating. Blood lubricated the machinery. Noble blood lubricated it the best."

"Crazy, stupid savages," said Ugly. "They didn't know nothing. You'd have to be an idiot to be scared of your curses, Indian."

"Crazy, stupid savages whose knowledge of mathematics and astronomy was the greatest in the world in their time," Luis said. "Sorry, gentlemen. I'm boring you, lecturing you on history. Go and do your duty for Mr. Dugdale."

They did, without a word, although Fat kept glancing back at his motorbike until he lost sight of Luis. Luis went into his house and located the Madonna tape, the earphones, and the barrettes. When he came outside fifteen minutes later, the mestizos and their scuffed Suzuki were gone.

8

That evening, Luis Balam met with Francisco Ek and three other Ho-Keh men in their thirties and forties. Though they were not the oldest heads of families, the elders such as Luis's father and the youngsters, the adolescents and newly married, deferred to them. They were mature and they were vigorous. When this fivesome reached consensus on a matter, it became Ho-Keh consensus.

It was overcast, with a high thin haze. There would be no rain, but heat and moisture hung under the cloud film, feeling like steam trapped in a boiler. Too uncomfortable to be inside debating an issue, regardless how briefly, Luis thought.

He asked them to the cenote, an appropriate spot. He had cracked the Bob Chance one hundred, investing it in Leon Negra and Corona beer, Coca-Cola, and Marlboros. Neither he nor Francisco smoked. Felipe Aguilar, Fernando Martín, and Diego Chi smoked like chimneys. Following obligatory drinking and smoking and small talk, Luis told his story.

He described the North American space agency theory, the supporting newspaper clippings, the smashing of a comet into Yucatán 65 million years ago, the fracturing of the limestone crust, the cenote ring, ash and smoke thrown into the atmosphere, catastrophic climatic changes, dinosaur extinction. He said he did not disbelieve the theory. What did he know compared to space scientists? He did disbelieve Vance Dugdale, who was no scientist. He disbelieved Dugdale's theory that North American tourists would bus out to a Maya village at night to look at plastic dinosaurs and listen to lectures. Dugdale, a posturing Desert Fox, has hidden motives, he said in closing, motives that are of no benefit to Ho-Keh.

Francisco Ek gulped his Corona, his Adam's apple bobbing. His eyes were wideset and Oriental. Francisco's hair was thinning on top; he compensated with luxuriant sideburns. He stared at his second cousin, and said, "What hidden motives?"

Luis was not as wiry as Francisco but wider in the shoulders. He was two months older and one inch shorter. Tiny differences had always counted between these men. They were either shortcomings or advantages.

Luis shrugged and said, "I don't know. I just don't trust him. That's what I'm telling you."

"You could be getting excited about nothing. The man will cut a few trees, move some rocks," Francisco said, sweeping a hand. "Not great damage to our land."

"That was what he said. What he would really do—" Luis shook his head. "I don't trust him."

"You sell to tourists, and you work with Cancún people, lawyers, police," Francisco said. "You are more familiar with that kind of person than I am. You say you don't trust Dugdale, I respect your opinion. The man isn't to be trusted."

Francisco is playing with me, Luis thought. He argues, then he agrees, seasoning his game with an insult. They had never come to blows, even as children. From an early age they had sensed that physical combat once commenced would not end without the end of a life. They had carried that instinctive common sense through puberty, meticulously avoiding rivalry for a woman. Should they have been hopelessly in love with the same girl, Luis knew, one of them and perhaps both would not presently be sitting on rocks, talking and drinking beer. "You can't trust a man, you don't do business with him."

"*You* do," Francisco said. "You do business with bad people every day of the week."

"They come, they go," Luis said. "They don't set up an exhibit in Ho-Keh."

"Your Dugdale and his tourists visiting us for this cultural theme park, we control everything, do we not? Our people who want jobs can be trained to work the Dead Dinosaurs Park. We can say no if Dugdale pulls a trick and kick him out whenever we choose."

"What he says, what actually happens, they could be the opposite."

"You went to Cancún when it was a greedy dream and helped your Mexicans build it, then you joined your Mexican police," Francisco said. "You brought home money. You bought clothes. You bought a radio. You bought a car. We stayed and never made the money. Now we can stay and make the money."

Mexicans, Luis thought. The Maya regarded themselves as Maya and Yucatecan, not Mexican. As far as stay-at-home Maya like Francisco were concerned, the Conquest had never occurred. *Your* Mexicans. Francisco considered

Luis a *mayero*, a citified Maya, no improvement on a Mexican.

"You had the opportunities I had," Luis said, angering. "You complain about my money and my car. You were too good for the Mexicans' money. Suddenly, you can't wait to take Dugdale's."

"Francisco is only saying that we should give it a try. It can't hurt us, not much," said Fernando Martín, a gentle man with slicked-down hair who worked erratically at an Akumal resort, bicycling in to wait on tables.

Luis looked at Diego Chi.

Diego puffed on his cigarette, measuring his words. Diego Chi worked the fields. He was short even for a Maya and seemed to be constructed of leather and steel cable. Diego had not to Luis's knowledge an iota of inquisitiveness about the world beyond his own.

He said, "My muscles and bones are feeling older than my years. My life is hard. I say that without complaining. I could go live the easy Mexican life. Hah! You would have to stick a gun to my head and march me to Cancún."

"You would have that easy Mexican life come to Ho-Keh?" Luis asked.

"Luis, I'm up in the morning for an hour before I can walk like a man, not a cripple. You are three years older than me and have a body that is fifteen years younger. I can happily accept the easy Mexican money if it comes to me, if I don't have to go out to them to get it."

"You're not smart if you don't listen to a new idea," Felipe Aguilar said flatly.

Felipe had mischievous eyes, bad teeth, and on a skinny torso a Los Angeles Kings T-shirt. He worked part-time for a cousin who owned a T-shirt stall at Tulum. Felipe

Aguilar wore new shirts home once or twice a week, and delighted in interpreting their meanings. This garment, for instance, was printed with the name of a famous North American soccer team that played indoors on a sheet of ice.

"Dugdale approached you, didn't he?" Luis asked Francisco.

"Who made it a law that Luis Balam and nobody else can be spoken to?" Francisco said. "We are not infants. We decide based on how good it is for Ho-Keh, not for us alone."

Francisco's words were soft, barely audible. They were dark and defiant. His fists were balled. Not for attack, Luis knew. Balled to conceal hands trembling in anger.

Luis scanned Fernando, Diego, and Felipe. They were smoking, drinking, looking at the horizon or at their feet. They were ready to adjourn.

Luis did not answer Francisco. He looked at his fingernails.

"Luis," Francisco said. "Would you come to my home for a minute? You would be doing me a favor."

Luis assented with a nod and began walking. Fernando, Diego, and Felipe exchanged relieved glances and stood fast, accepting the responsibility for disposing of the remaining beer and cigarettes.

Luis presumed the invitation was a form of apology. Francisco realized he had called Luis down too hard in front of the others. He and Francisco were intractable rivals, but they were not enemies. They neither liked nor hated each other. Their mutual respect was grudging and earned. Ho-Keh was too small for lingering problems.

"Is María feeling better?" Luis asked.

"I don't think she's worse. She's numb and has these headaches and a fever that comes and goes. I took her to that doctor on the highway by Xelha. He said maybe she was bitten by a tick or maybe she has a parasite. He said I could take her to Cancún City for tests he couldn't do. I said no. You're an Indian from a village, they treat you like a tramp. He gave me aspirin for her. María will be fine. She has been ill before. I have been ill. We've always recovered."

María Ek did not look worse to Luis, although there was a strain in Francisco's voice. María did not look improved either. Her eyes were heavy. She looked tired rather than sick. She was in her hammock watching television. She lifted her arm, smiled, and said a soft hello.

Luis was so stunned by the television set that he neglected to return her greeting. Several Ho-Keh homes, including his, had televisions, but a large-screen color model was a first. This TV sat on a wooden crate and had a screen that was at the very minimum twenty-five inches diagonally, a Panasonic in a sleek black cabinet. A lovely blonde green-eyed woman was shrieking at a handsome man with a jaw longer than Ricky's.

It was a soap opera produced in Mexico City, the staple of the nation's television. The blonde had delicate European features and a sharp tongue. She was the soap opera's slut-bitch-goddess, an exotic and immoral creature to be worshiped and despised. She was dressed in a tight, metallic dress and was informing the handsome man that he was less than a man. Luis found the typical Mexican male's dreamy adoration of the milky-skinned female masturbatory and disgusting, and he could not remove his eyes from her.

"Luis," María repeated. "Hello."

"What? I'm sorry, María," Luis said. He had never admitted to anyone that he regarded her as prettier than either of his wives. "Are you feeling better?"

"I am, Luis. The programs are in color. They're wonderful. I have a little pain, but the shows take my mind off it."

"I didn't know you had a set. When did you buy it?" Luis said, looking from María to Francisco, meaning *how* did you buy it.

Francisco motioned for Luis to join him at two chairs in the farthest corner of the one-room house. "I told my sons to go outside until you and I had talked alone."

Their two boys were a year or two younger than Esther and Rosa. With them gone and María's attention on her soap opera, they were essentially alone.

Francisco said, "I think you know I didn't buy the television. I couldn't buy it."

Luis did not reply.

"We've had it since last night. I think you know where it came from."

"Dugdale," Luis said.

"It isn't my TV set. It's for the whole village. I accepted it for Ho-Keh. It's in my home now because of María. When she's well, somebody else will have a turn. The people who have no television will get a turn before those who do."

"When I was here earlier today, nobody was around," Luis said.

"They were here, watching. Some people hadn't ever seen color. I hadn't seen color. María enjoyed the company."

"Dugdale bought you," Luis said.

"I deserve that. We're even."

"Did Dugdale come to you alone?"

"No. He had that guy who was out there today with him as an interpreter, the guy who looks like a weasel."

My friend Ugly, Luis thought. He was relieved that Ricky had not been in on it.

"It isn't my set," Francisco said again, dropping to a whisper. "I would have chased them away if it wasn't for María. My sons too, to tell you the truth. I'm worried they'll leave the village for rotten jobs in Cancún and get into trouble. Kids leave Ho-Keh, Luis. They want what the village cannot give them."

"I would have done the same thing in your position," Luis said sincerely, hoping that Francisco would quit saying it wasn't his set.

"I don't trust Dugdale either," Francisco said. "We'll watch him and his Dead Dinosaurs close. I promise we won't decide anything else without you. You'll be involved in everything from now on."

Luis took Francisco's proffered hand. Involved, he thought sourly. As an executive liaison.

9

Luis awoke with a rare headache and thought he was coming down with something. The throbbing dissipated in the morning and was gone by noon. He knew he had suffered no disease of the body. But maybe a disease of the ego had set his skull to pounding. Luis Balam had enjoyed the notion that in Ho-Keh's influential group of five he was slightly superior among equals. Last night had been a surprise in that respect too.

He forgot about it after lunch and worked at Black Coral with his babies. Business was spotty. Rosa sold matching silver necklaces to honeymooners from Charlotte. Esther sold black coral earrings to a Tulsa librarian. Luis sold nothing.

He haggled with a plump North American couple over rings. She was tall and walleyed, and protected lard-white skin with a baggy smock and floppy hat. The man came up to her chin. He was bald, and his face and dome were as red as bougainvillea. He seemed dazed by the heat and let her do most of the talking.

They tried on every ring in the shop. Their best offer

was pamphlets and salvation. They were evangelical missionaries, although they didn't immediately say so; like time-share condominium peddlers, evangelicals never identify themselves honestly until a foot is firmly wedged in your door. It was a standoff, not an unfriendly encounter, but no sale by either party.

Luis drove to Cancún and the InterPresidential. After his day thus far, an afternoon at the bullfights with Bob Chance was not a completely unpleasant prospect. Chance had been drinking, but he was not intoxicated. He did not bring a beer can with him and he chewed breath mints. He had showered, shaved, and was dressed in clean clothes—denims, deck shoes, and a T-shirt that proclaimed PARTY ANIMAL.

Mr. Bob Chance, lottery champion, was by Cancún tourism standards presentable. Luis thought his day was going to improve.

He was wrong.

They rode a taxi to the new Cancún City bullring. It was two years old, a three-tiered bowl painted beige and flamingo pink, the overwhelmingly popular color scheme of hotels and condos. Inside was a dirt ring and twenty rows of backless concrete benches that seated perhaps ten thousand.

Chance grumbled in the taxi that the hotel had soaked him thirty bucks a ticket for three bulls, but he cheered up at the sight of the vending plaza. You could get a cold brew, naturally. But a hot dog too. Chance couldn't believe it. He took three hot dogs and two beers to their seats. Luis, who did not trust what North Americans and Mexicans ground into sausage, contented himself with a cold Corona.

Luis had seen one bullfight in his life, one too many.

The first match of the afternoon was a repetition. Picadors on horseback and banderilleros on foot tormented the animal with darts and short spears. Then the matador, also on foot, danced and teased the beast before finishing him off.

Though it was the torrid height of the afternoon, the ring was two-thirds full. It was never too steamy for bloodlust and the matador was expert. The spectators roared their approval when he took the animal off its feet with a quick sword thrust to the neck, by acclamation awarding him both ears. Luis thought it was slight solace to the bull that its opponents were heavily dressed in clinging satin and sequins. That is, if it had the intelligence to comprehend and enjoy its enemies' heat exhaustion. Luis refused to enjoy the sport; to be caught up in the drama would be to yield to Mexicanness.

Chance stood. "Halftime, huh? Do they always end like this?"

"Unless the matador is careless and the bull is lucky."

"The upset of the century. I'll take the bull and give the points."

Luis looked at him.

"Football point-spread humor. I guess you'd have to've been there. Back in the good ol' days, Mikey's Sports Bar took a little action from its trusted regulars and I was known to lay down a shekel or two." Chance patted his stomach. "Hot dogs. For me they're like Chinese food. Scarf down a couple and ten minutes later you're hungry. To be on the safe side, I'll eat a couple more. Are we staying for the next two bouts?"

"Your choice," Luis said, following his plodding client down the stairs.

In the hot dog line, Chance said, "I don't know. In football, you can get the momentum and things turn around. Not in bullfighting. It's like Tampa Bay having to go up against the Redskins game after game."

Luis shook his head. "I don't understand."

"Hey, I thought you knew football. You about quoted that Super Bowl game verbatim."

"In the 1973 game the Redskins were good," Luis agreed.

"Well, they still are. Tampa Bay isn't. That's the point."

"I don't know Tampa Bay."

"As knowledgeable as you are, you should. They came into the league in 1976 and—"

"That explains it," Luis said. "Two years too late."

Chance looked at him.

The line progressed and Chance bought three hot dogs rather than two since they were small. He walked away from the plaza toward the taxi zone. "If it's all the same to you, Luis, let's bag it. I don't want to insult you locals, but bullfighting seems kind of dumb and pointless, although that matador guy has great lateral mobility. He'd have a shot at making it in the NFL as a free safety. By the way, what do they do with the dead bull?"

"Sell it for meat."

"Your basic triple burger deluxe. I slept on what I said I was gonna sleep on."

"You've made plans?"

"Kind of, but I don't know. Not yet. This outing, I appreciate it. It's swell. You're buying me time to think. It's damn hard to concentrate when you're worrying you'll be dead in five minutes. Your suggestion to draw up a deal with Mikey, it's starting to appeal to me. This lawyer buddy of yours, he's the best lawyer you know?"

"Yes." Ricky was the only lawyer Luis knew.

"You'd recommend him?"

"Yes. You're making promises on paper. He can do the papers to everybody's satisfaction."

"My other option, should you accept the assignment, is to escort me to the airport. Mikey shows, you babysit him till I'm on a plane."

"A plane to where?"

Bob Chance sighed. "That's the thing. To where? Mikey has my scent."

"Home?"

"And face the music like a man? Nah. Mikey doesn't hang me out to dry, Mom will. I'm the only child, you know. Mom had a turkey in the oven Christmas Day for her and me and assorted relatives. Then her baby boy splits with lotsa bucks and nary a word except half a dozen picture postcards."

"Mothers forgive," Luis said.

Chance simultaneously smiled and shuddered. "Mine holds grudges. Lemme tell you a story. On the Halloween I was in the sixth grade, me and Jimmy Harper across the street, we shoved a potato in Old Man Jenson's exhaust pipe. He lived on the corner next to Jimmy and gave us endless flak for cutting across his yard and for our balls going into his flower beds.

"The old coot starts his car the next morning and his muffler blows out from the back pressure. Man, it was super! We were seen and somebody rats us out to Jenson. He tells my mom and Jimmy's folks. They split the cost of the muffler, which was probably rusted out anyway, the crooked old bastard.

"My dad had been dead a year and Mom was raising me on a bookkeeper's wages, so, yeah, her share of the muffler was a hardship, but how come I still have to hear about the nineteen dollars and change whenever the subject is money?"

Luis had translated Chance's words literally. He had not been able to translate the nuances of the story or the scope of Chance and his mother's love and hatred for each other. "Mail your mother nineteen dollars."

Chance laughed bitterly. "And spoil her fun? That nineteen bucks is a nail in the cross I have to bear."

"Chance, you cocksucker!"

A man advanced between taxicabs in a manner not unlike that of the recently deceased bull. Luis compared them in shape, disposition, and gait. He was a swarthy Anglo in his thirties, with height and bulk similar to Chance's, but this man did not jiggle when he walked. Luis did not doubt that the gut straining his red T-shirt was as hard as a wrecking ball. His muscular and hairy white legs should have been concealed by long pants, not exposed in baggy plaid shorts. His feet were covered with an odd combination of striped socks and sandals. He was essentially neckless, had tiny dark eyes, and tightly curled brown hair.

"Jesus," Chance muttered. "Sweet Jesus."

"Mikey Smith?" Luis asked the man.

"Yeah. Who the fuck are you?"

Hands on hips, standing close enough for Luis to smell tooth decay on his breath and the sweat from his darkened armpits, Mikey Smith would have, in the low sun of morning or evening, cast a large shadow. Luis dared not remove his gaze from Mikey's and he could not see Chance in his peripheral vision. "A friend of Mr. Chance's."

"I'll clue you in, Pancho. This fat pussy ain't nobody's friend."

"Mikey, Jesus, please," Chance pleaded, well to Luis's rear. "I screwed up. I did a rotten thing. I'll make it up to you, I swear."

Mikey moved forward. "Fucking-A, you'll make it up. After I wipe the pavement with your fat face, goddamn straight you'll make it up to me."

Luis backpedaled and kept between the two men. "Calm down, boss. It's hot and you're sweating. You'll have a heart attack."

"Go bend a taco, Pancho. I got no quarrel with you."

"I said, Mr. Chance is my friend."

"Yeah, Mikey," Chance rasped. "Where I go, he goes. He knows karate."

Mikey Smith stopped. His face contorted as if he were about to sneeze, but he broke into hysterical laughter instead. "Oh shit, now I get it. You're Chance's bodyguard. Cheap sonofafuckingbitch. Three million bucks and he economizes. He hires himself a midget beaner to save his fat raggedy ass. You know karate or any of that other chink shit, Pancho?"

"No," Luis said.

"Wouldn't mean shit if you did, not to me."

"Three million spread over twenty years," Chance reminded him. "Yours and mine, Mikey. You and me, partners."

"I'll spread you over twenty years, Chance."

Mikey sidestepped remarkably fast. Luis stayed with him and raised his hands, not quite touching Mikey's chest.

"Come on, boss. Relax. Kill the man and you'll do a life sentence in a filthy Mexican jail."

Mikey looked at Luis's hands, then said, "Yeah, okay, you're probably right. I heard about Mexican jails. Money's what counts."

"Mikey, this is Luis Balam," Chance said, talking fast. "Luis has an attorney friend in Cancún City who'll draw up papers."

"Yeah?"

"Yeah, Mikey. No b.s. What can I say? I pictured this gigantic pile of money. It was like gold fever, you know. I couldn't help myself. But, hey, you set the terms. I'll sign for anything that's halfway fair. C'mon, Mikey, lighten up."

"Can't do no harm to talk," Mikey said. "Pay me what's fair, and extra for my aggravation and shit?"

"Absolutely, Mikey. No problem."

Mikey Smith extended a hand to Luis. "Okay, Chance, we talk. I'm calm and sweet as pie. I'm not some fucking animal. You make sense, you're fair, I'll listen. This shyster of yours, Pancho, you contact him, we'll have us a skull session. There'll be a finder's fee for you. Sound like a winner?"

Luis accepted the handshake and started to say, yes, it sounded good. Mikey jerked Luis forward, drove a knee into his midsection, and slammed a fist into the side of his head.

Luis landed hard on his knees, gasping for breath, unable to break his fall. His right ear rang, but he heard fragments, Mikey yelling, who the fuck you think you are, Pancho, some wetback hotshot con artist, you and your shyster writing it up in spick and fucking me royally?

Mikey kicked Luis's side, toppling him on the other. He continued yelling as he stepped over Luis, about how, yeah, him and the fat-assed dickless wonder would sign a deal, all right. He'd leave the fat pussy exactly three unbusted bones in his fat body, thumb and two fingers, so he could sign what Mikey put in front of him to sign.

Luis seized what he could, an ankle. Mikey jerked, cursing, dragging Luis along the pavement. Luis hung on, removing the sandal, peeling the sock. Inspired by Mikey's relish to break bones, Luis twisted his little toe and jammed it backward until it snapped.

Mikey screamed. Luis gave his foot a push. Mikey lurched, stumbled, and landed on his butt. Luis slowly regained his feet, aware that he hadn't crippled Smith. He had merely distracted him, buying himself a moment to recover. The price of the moment was dear: Mikey's rage.

The wronged lottery winner charged, howling in the language of a lower species, swinging wildly. Luis assumed a boxer's defensive stance and intercepted the blows. They landed with such force that Luis's forearms were driven into his face, staggering him.

Nose and cheeks stinging, he retreated. Mikey bore in. Luis swiveled his head as he backtracked. Should he stumble, Mikey would stomp him into a grease spot. They were attracting an audience. Luis noticed a man with two cameras, a North American tourist, shooting him and his adversary with one, motor clicking and whirring.

Mikey was maneuvering him into the parking lot. The surface there was unpaved, looser, treacherous. If he pinned Luis against a car the game was done. Their audience moved with them. The man with two cameras was in the lead, asking his companions if this didn't beat a bullfight for sheer excitement or what? The gallery was twenty or thirty or forty strong and growing, but where was his client, Mr. Bob Chance?

Nearing the front row of parked cars, Luis began circling to his left. Mikey was favoring his damaged right foot and turning on it would be especially painful. To Luis's disadvantage, he was reducing the space between him and Mikey, and the ability to avoid a mad lunge.

"Good strategy, Pancho," Mikey said, panting. "Thing is, I played the second half against Columbia Basin with a broken leg and the fourth quarter at Spokane with cracked ribs. A little pain, it don't mean shit to me."

Mikey's hands were flexing. Luis knew he was through wasting energy with wild swings. He'd seize Luis, hold him with an arm, and beat his face into hot dog sausage with the other, or wrap both arms around him and do what a boa did with prey.

The tourist with two cameras was pointing and shooting, explaining that they were settling a disagreement on either drugs or a señorita, one or the other. He was within reach and his strap was dangling. Luis grabbed the camera, a 35 millimeter with a long lens and a solid heft.

Mikey came at Luis. The tourist with one instead of two cameras cupped his mouth and called for *policía.* Between Mikey and Luis, inadvertently blocking, the tourist was flattened as if cardboard by Mikey's pursuit.

Luis swung the camera by the strap. It struck Mikey in the left temple. Camera separated from strap. Lens separated from camera body. Lens and body flew upward like a pair of pop flies. Mikey's eyelids fluttered. He landed flat on his face, dust roiling around his outline, reminding Luis of a building demolition.

Luis wanted badly to either sit or squat, but too many parts of his body hurt to move. He stood beside Mikey, like a statue, waiting for the police. The audience gave him a wide berth, though nobody was willing to leave and miss the final act.

Luis scanned the crowd for Bob Chance, but the only face he recognized was that of the man with one camera, who was vainly trying to reattach the lens and body of his second.

10

When Luis got back to Black Coral, his body was a headache from head to toe. He could move with reasonable confidence, albeit slowly. His pain was steady. No high-voltage jabs, no dizzying agony, no spitting of blood. Presumably, no bones were broken, but Luis had not the courage to endure a jolting ride in the Beetle to Ho-Keh.

He asked Esther and Rosa to please rig a hammock between poles in the rear of the shop so he could spend the night. They hung the hammock and gave him food, drink, ointment, and wet compresses. They volunteered to stay with him, to nurse him. He said, no, no, there is no place for you to sleep.

They argued, though feebly, for they were almost as angry with their father as sad for him. Though Luis was vague on the source of his injuries, Esther and Rosa knew too well what he looked like after a fight. While they loved it when Luis referred to them as his babies, they resented being treated as such. At nightfall, they inserted Luis and three Leon Negras in the hammock, wedging the beers between the woven mesh and a hip. Then they drove the Volkswagen home and had a better night's sleep than he.

Next day, by noon, Luis was becoming cautiously limber and his bruises were in full flower. He had visitors—Ricardo Martínez Rodríguez, attorney, and Vance Dugdale, king of the cultural theme park.

"Luis, you look terrible," Ricky said, clicking his tongue.

"Good day to you too," Luis said.

"You must be in considerable pain," Ricky said. "Everybody in Cancún knows of your melee. By felling that creature, you will be a legend. I am sorry for your pain. However, I am distressed too in regard to your abuse of Vance's employees."

Luis looked past Ricky at Dugdale, who was in the background, a detached observer. He was in slacks, Hawaiian shirt, wraparound shades, and visor. The top buttons of the shirt were undone. A gold chain nested in a tangle of graying chest hair. He had switched roles, it seemed, from Desert Fox to Pornographic Film Director.

Luis said, "Dugdale, you went to my village without my knowledge and bribed a man to approve your plan."

"Luis, please," Ricky whispered.

"You aren't in need of an executive liaison, Dugdale. Or a senior executive liaison. You just need a gatekeeper. Cheap labor like me. Someone to escort you into the village and maintain peace with the Indians. You take care of the rest."

"Luis," Ricky pleaded.

Hand on heart, Dugdale said, "Rick. Lu. You dudes are aces. Far be it from me to bring trouble. Vance Dugdale is no backstabber. Uh uh. Pure and simple, I made a mistake. I stepped on my own pecker."

"You brought a color television," Luis said. "You took

advantage of a good man whose wife is ill and bribed him with the television."

"Lu, the mood you're in, you're not gonna believe this, though it's the gospel truth. I thought a notebook had dropped out of my pocket at your cenote. I went back to hunt for it. As luck would have it, I struck up a friendship with your compadre, Frank Ick. The upshot is, Lu, I had this spare TV in the Jeep and one thing led to another."

Vance Dugdale sighed and lighted a cigarette. "I don't know what it is, Lu and Rick. Whenever I play the Good Samaritan, I box myself into a corner. I stick my neck out to help people and the situation blows up in my face like a trick cigar. Bummer."

"Who are you?" Luis said. "Where are you from?"

"Please, Luis. Please," Ricky said. "Vance, would you please excuse us for a minute?"

"Vance Dugdale can take a hint. I'll be up front, window shopping."

"Luis," Ricky said when Dugdale was gone, "I'm disappointed in you, I truly am. Quality employees are difficult to find and Vance's men are afraid to return to Ho-Keh."

"Trash mestizos like Fat and Ugly are not difficult to find," Luis said. "Keeping them awake to do their work, that's the difficult part."

Ricky shook his head. "Luis, that racist remark is beneath you. The fact remains, you vandalized a valuable customized motorcycle, challenged two innocent workers to a machete fight, and threatened them with a deadly curse."

"A curse?" Luis said.

"An ancient Maya curse, so Vance said. They were excited and Vance's Spanish, while impressive, cannot capture every idiom of a frightened speaker. Supposedly, skeletons crawl out of the cenote and pursue and kill the cursed individuals."

Luis shook his head. "No. Impossible. There is no such Maya superstition. In ancient Egypt yes, in Yucatán no."

"Luis, the bottom line is, you threatened the men."

"Not me," Luis said. "Those boys have large, cowardly imaginations. And Ricky, you were not in on Dugdale's television set bribe, were you? Please tell me you were not."

"No, Luis," Ricky said, looking at him. "You and I, we were together in my office then, remember?"

"Yes, yes we were," Luis said, relieved to read truth in his friend's eyes.

"The deal is done, Luis."

Luis did not reply.

"If the title of the park bothers you, Luis, if you feel Dead Dinosaurs is undignified, I will exercise my influence on Vance and insist upon a change. How does Ho-Keh Historical Monument sound to you?"

"Words don't change anything," Luis said. "Don't waste the effort."

"Obstructing the project isn't in anybody's best interest."

"Have you received your Havana dinosaurs? Or São Paulo dinosaurs?"

"No, not yet. Soon. Vance and I are attending to details today. That was the Mikey Smeeth person you fought with at the bullring, I presume. You were protecting Mr. Chance from him?"

"Yes and yes."

"Where is Mr. Chance?"

"Gone."

"Gone where, Luis?"

"Gone where indeed," said an entering Héctor Salgado Reyes. "Luis, you should be more vigilant in your shop area, especially in regard to your daughters' virtue. There is a gentleman wandering about, leering at them and your wares. He has the aura of a Los Angeles pimp."

"Inspector, that gentleman is Mr. Vance Dugdale, my associate," Ricky protested.

Héctor laughed. "Ah, your dinosaur king. Lawyer, do me a courtesy and chaperon your associate. See that his paws remain off the jewelry and the girls. I would be highly grateful. Luis and I are going to enjoy a confidential discussion. You might be saving his life. You know Luis and his temper. Should your associate touch his babies, he is a dead associate."

Poutily, Ricky began to protest, but common sense saved him. When he had marched through the tent flap, Héctor said, "Luis, you look like shit. You look like you had a fatal accident with farm machinery. You have my sympathy and to a lesser extent, my anger."

"Everybody visits me today to complain, Héctor. If everybody with a complaint was a customer, I would be rich."

"Do not be flippant, Luis. I am not unhappy that an officer came to my home yesterday, on my day off, and asked me to vouch for you and not to jail you. Oh no. And later, subsequent to your release, another officer came to my home and requested that I come in to assist in dealing with your fisticuffs opponent, who was terrorizing my jail staff and his fellow inmates."

"Thank you, Héctor. I mean the thanks sincerely."

"We are dear friends, so it was an insignificant inconvenience for me. You are party to a wild brawl with a gringo that attracts a huge gathering. Mr. Mikey Smith, we learn, is not Mr. Bob Chance's demented figment. The man has an extremely foul mouth, by the way."

"Smith hit me first, Héctor. He suckerpunched me."

"Luis, your opponents always hit you first. Sometimes they actually do. My concern is not the sensationalism or the health of the monster you defeated. Mr. Smith is an amazing specimen, incidentally. He made a physical recovery from your finishing blow to his head. There's a meaty gouge on the side of his skull. That and a swollen toe aiming in the wrong direction are the full extent of his injuries. The beast is impervious to pain.

"A mental recovery, I am not as certain. While I escorted him to the airport, he raved about his invulnerability. He described a cantina he owns in North America and the shrine on which is mounted the armored headgear of a football adversary. He alleges his bodily contact was responsible for splitting the helmet like a ripe mango. North American football, Luis, not soccer. I have watched the game on TV. He was boasting the impossible."

"Mr. Bob Chance claims the story is true, Héctor. Did you put Smith on a plane?"

"The earliest available flight. One way to Dallas, Texas. I made myself clear to the monster that he was unwelcome in the United Mexican States. He was an embarrassment and a troublemaker. I, in effect, deported him."

"Did he resist?"

"No," Héctor said, shaking his head proudly. "He was docile. I informed him if he returned to Cancún, I would personally be offended and not responsible for the consequences. He should not anticipate adherence to legal codes or basic human decency. He accepted my position."

"Mikey Smith may be a monster, Héctor, but he is a wronged monster. Chance cheated him out of one half of three million dollars."

"Chance's disappearance has cheated *me* out of one third of your gross earnings protecting him, my rightful commission."

"Chance went to his room?" Luis said.

"No, he did not. I have a tight surveillance plan in place, coordinated with a key InterPresidential manager. Chance is fabulously rich. He need not pack his belongings prior to fleeing. He can buy replacements. I will, however, nurture the slim hope that he returns for some irrational purpose."

"Chance set me up, Héctor. He used me to draw Mikey Smith out."

"No argument," Héctor said. "Smith did not confide in me, but I can easily believe he had pinpointed Chance as a guest of the InterPresidential."

"He followed us to the bullring. If I couldn't protect my client in a confrontation, we were at a public place and bystanders might. What is your opinion, Héctor, is Chance still in Cancún?"

"I would not hazard a guess. He is not a notorious fugitive, so my resources in locating him are limited to friendships and favors and luck. I cannot make a loud issue of Chance and pull my men off other duties. I cannot stage a manhunt and guard the airport and assemble roadblocks.

"I am upset, Luis. Our golden goose of proverb, obese and unaerodynamic as he is, the bird has quite possibly flown out of his coop. My stomach burns whenever I dwell on the fees we may have lost forever."

"Have you come up with anything on Vance Dugdale?" Luis asked.

"You have a gift for changing subjects, Luis. No, I have not. I do not have to inform you that Cancún and the Caribbean coast are booming, do I? The money attracts slick-fingered types by the multitudes. These jackals are so plentiful they are virtually an ethnic subgroup. I see Dugdales ten times a day, selling time-share condos, negotiating development deals with corrupt government ministers, picking pockets, and pimping their alleged sisters, who invariably are virgins.

"I am further upset, Luis, by the public relations problem I have regarding the camera you snatched as a weapon with which to dispatch Mikey Smith. The owner is a tourist agency honcho from Indiana, Indianapolis, who heads numerous and populous tour groups to Cancún. He books expensive lodgings in the hotel zone and never flinches at the price. You destroyed an extremely costly, professional-caliber Nikon and you rebuffed him when he asked you for compensation.

"I applaud your ingenuity in saving your own life and I deplore his greed in the face of an emergency, but you should not have totally snubbed him. He would have settled for a cheap compromise."

"I didn't rebuff him, Héctor. I just said *no hablo inglés, señor.*"

"Luis," Héctor said, sighing.

"A tourism boss ought to be smarter than to carry a camera without the strap around his neck. Isn't that a primary lesson to his customers on the dangers of travel? How to avoid the easy snatch and run? One of the rules of a safe and trouble-free trip? Besides, I didn't touch his second camera."

Héctor stood, smiled congenially, and wagged a finger. "Luis, you insist on being the fucking joker, fine. Come on. You gave me a surprise yesterday. Now I have a surprise for you."

Luis rose obediently and followed Héctor. Had they not been close friends, the congenial smile would have terrified him. They walked through the shop. Héctor winking and throwing a kiss at Esther and Rosa. Ricky and Dugdale were gone.

Outside, Héctor took Luis's arm, halting him. "Feast your eyes."

A slender young woman leaned on a fender of Héctor's menacing Dodge Dart, fanning herself with a handkerchief. She had olive skin, close-set green eyes, and an aquiline nose. Straight brown hair hung to her shoulders and a lacy blouse. Her ankle-length skirt was flowered and fringed. Should her strange clothing be available in Cancún boutiques (and it might well be for all Luis knew), it would be sized as "petite." She was a miniature North American and an average Maya.

Luis's initial impression was hippie. At next blink he knew hippie was inaccurate. She was not one of the antique North American bohemians who hitchhiked and mooched throughout Yucatán. She was too young, too clean, too clear-eyed. Not even the pitting of acne scars on her cheeks detracted from her extraordinary beauty.

"No raving beauty, is she, Luis? Poor homely girl. She doesn't even have a decent pair of boobs. Care to guess her identity?"

Héctor's congenial smile had spread into a congenial grin. His surprise would not necessarily be pleasing. "No."

Héctor tightened his grip on Luis's arm and started forward. "You are being too bashful. I shall be delighted to make introductions."

"I give up, Héctor. Who are you introducing me to?"

"The suspense overcame you, yes? She is Judith Maxwell-Chance, former lawfully wedded wife of Bob Chance."

11

Héctor took a step toward Judith Maxwell-Chance, then jerked Luis to a halt. He smiled at her and raised a finger. "One minute."

He turned his back to her and whispered, "Luis, exercise extreme caution. The lady is not entirely the puny and homely package she appears to be."

Homely? "What happened, Héctor? Did she insult your car?"

"Amusing. No, nothing happened except a little bossiness at the station. It's the things to come. Her name."

"What's wrong with her name?"

"It's hyphenated," he said, zigzagging the finger. "You have that dash intruding. Ladies up north hyphenate to tell their husbands that they are not the man. These modern ladies get to be the man too. Hyphenating ladies are aggressive, but not in ways pleasing to a man."

"An educational story. Why do I have to be careful?"

"I am placing her under your protection."

"Héctor."

"Luis, she is your client's wife."

"Divorced wife."

"Notwithstanding and irregardless, he is your client, she is your client. She has tremendous nuisance potential. She asks infinite questions. I am assigning her to you. She is forthwith your nuisance."

Before Luis could summon an objection, Héctor, graceful for a large man, wheeled and swept him toward the former Mrs. Chance, and made introductions with a courtly bow.

"Judy," she said, shaking Luis's hand. "No last names, okay? Mine seems to unravel Inspector Salgado."

Héctor's eyes widened innocently. "No, no. Doubtlessly a linguistic misinterpretation, Señora Chance."

"When you report a missing person in a strange town, you go to the police, don't you, even in Mexico?" Judy asked, looking at Héctor, then Luis. "Inspector Salgado referred me to you."

"We have not confirmed that Mr. Chance is precisely missing," Héctor said.

"Inspector Salgado says you are a private detective and that you're on retainer to Robert. What kind of retainer? Like a lawyer's on a retainer?"

While Bob Chance was Luis's age, Judith Maxwell-Chance was closer to Esther's. Her eyes were older, though; worry and suspicion and the heat were adding time. Up close, Luis saw that they were also slightly crossed, a characteristic of beauty to his ancestors. She was not Maya, nor an Indian of any variety he knew of, but she was blessed with classic Maya loveliness.

"Being available," Luis said.

"Super. That explains everything. You know about the Lotto money?"

"Three million Yanqui dollars," Héctor said, kissing fingertips.

"How did you trace Mr. Chance to Cancún?" Luis asked.

"Robert's mother phoned me on Christmas Day. I was shocked. We hate each other and hadn't spoken for months. I was afraid something bad had happened to Robert. She was just wondering if I knew where he was. I said if she thought he was with me, she was barking up the wrong tree. I don't know if she was relieved or not.

"She phoned again on New Year's Eve. She was half crocked. She's an off-and-on boozer. Like mother, like son. She said Robert had won the Lotto and taken off for Mexico. She'd received one postcard from Cabo San Lucas. I didn't know about the Lotto win. They don't make a big fuss out of a Lotto winner in the papers or on the news anymore unless you hit a biggie, like ten million."

"Three million is pocket change to gringos," Héctor said, wide-eyed.

"I didn't hear another word until the day before yesterday. His mother called and sounded really concerned about Robert. That might be a first for her. She admitted she had received postcards from here and there in Mexico. None of them said very much until the last card, which came from Cancún. He wrote that he was depressed and felt trapped and didn't know what to do or where to go from there.

"His mom said she'd fly down herself to blow his nose for him, except that thanks to Robert she'd been broke her entire life and couldn't afford a two-zone bus pass, let alone an airline ticket. I had to hear for the umpteenth time how she'd paid a neighbor nineteen dollars she didn't have to keep the police from locking Robert up when he was a child.

"If I wanted to make the effort, feel free, she said. If I caught up to him and he had a dollar or two he hadn't squandered yet, I ought to remember the unappreciated old woman who made it possible. Quote unquote. I'll miss a week of work and school, but we've had a terrible winter in Seattle. I can go for some sun. Mr. Balam, Inspector Salgado said you could find me a place to stay."

Luis looked at Héctor, who looked at his watch and said, "I am far, far overdue for an important law enforcement rendezvous. I shall be in touch."

Héctor bounded out of the lot, roostertails of smoke erupting from twin exhausts. Judy said, "Is he leading a drug bust?"

Luis smiled. "No. Héctor is overdue for lunch with his police friends. Certain Cancún restaurants feed them for free. What sort of place?"

"Cheap, on the water, and not a jillion people."

"I can give you sort of cheap and the sea. It is nearby and one hundred kilometers from Cancún. There are fewer people and no discos."

In his Volkswagen, northbound on the highway, Luis forestalled the inevitable questions by reporting in detail his business relationship with Bob "Robert" Chance and his fight with Mikey Smith.

"That's why your face is puffy and you're walking funny. Mikey Smith is a Neanderthal. He ought to be extinct."

"Like dinosaurs."

"Like dinosaurs. Mikey has the same charm and IQ."

"What killed the dinosaurs?"

"Dinosaurs—oh, I know what you're asking. I have a professor who's into that. They're saying a comet crashed around here somewhere. It's been in the paper. They're drilling and finding samples. Tiny glass beads in the soil and stuff, and that metal down lower in the ground, the metal you find in meteors, the metal that's at the right layer to date the comet or whatever it was."

"Iridium," Luis said.

"Iridium is it? You know all about—"

"Would you come visit Yucatán on the basis of the comet?"

"As a scientist, you bet. As a tourist?"

"Yes."

"No. What's there to see? You're a jillion years too late. The average tourist would be bored stiff."

"Mikey Smith had a right to be angry," Luis said. "Bob Chance cheated him out of his share of the jackpot."

"I thought we were talking about dinosaurs. Extinct creatures and Mikey Smith, that's close enough. Couldn't have happened to a nicer guy. Oh, I'd be mad too. Who wouldn't? I hope Robert paid you a ton of money. Fighting Mikey for him, protecting him, it wouldn't be worth it for any amount. Mikey's twice your size and crazy as a bedbug. You couldn't say anything against him to Robert, but I think Mikey was knocked goofy playing football."

Luis felt her stare. "I didn't fight Smith. He fought me. I fought to defend myself."

"Robert paid you a ton of money?"

"Not a lot of money to you. A retainer that is almost gone."

Judy laughed. "What do you mean, not a lot to me? Do you think I'm rich?"

Luis did not laugh. A beautiful North American woman and she was not rich? "Every North American who comes to

Cancún is rich. Your airline ticket would buy my family's food for six months and buy your former mother-in-law's bus tickets too."

"Sorry. I see where you're coming from. Insensitive of me. You won't shed any tears, but I work two part-time jobs and go to night school. My income falls under the official poverty level."

Luis turned to her. "You have no money for food and you came to Cancún?"

Judy patted his arm. "God, I'm sorry. We're really not communicating. After Robert and I broke up I moved back in with my mother. She wasn't too thrilled that I married him. We have our ups and downs, but we've struck a truce."

"What are your jobs?"

"I clerk in a convenience store and I shelve books at the local library. Your two jobs, detective and gift shop owner, that keeps you hopping, I bet."

"Three jobs. I also lead guided tours at the ruins. What do you study in school?"

"The -ologies. I love the -ologies. I'm going to be the first member of my family to graduate from college if it kills me, and it might. I have to quit fooling around and commit to a major pretty soon. After this quarter, I'll have the credits for junior status."

"What are these -ologies of yours?"

"Sociology, psychology, archaeology, anthropology. Stuff that's fascinating and doesn't require math. I'm a dunce where math is concerned."

"Anthropology," Luis muttered.

Judy Maxwell-Chance reached into the soft, zippered bag at her feet, her only luggage, and took out a scope and a tripod. "I travel light. These, undies, and Pepto-Bismol. Ornithology is my favorite. I wish I could figure how to make a living at it. For that matter, anthro and archaeology aren't terribly practical either, but I'll worry about that when I graduate."

Luis pondered the luxury of studying sciences that would never earn the student a cash income. North American tour groups devoted entirely to ornithology occasionally passed through. At the smallest provocation, a fluttering or a chirp, a column of men and women would stop suddenly as if sensing ambush and aim their scopes and cameras into the trees. What did these people do to earn money? "Bob Chance told me you ran and birdwatched. He didn't do either."

"Robert's form of exercise is bending his elbow and lifting his fork. His interest in birds is confined to fried chicken and the Seattle Seahawks football team. He lives and dies football, him and his beer-guzzling buddies who hang out at Mikey's Sports Bar. That's why Robert is in the jam he's in. I hear that his so-called buddies have a pool going. The closest to the exact day, hour, and minute when Mikey catches him wins the pot.

"Anyway, I'm in sunny, gorgeous Mexico and I'm going to enjoy myself. Thanks to some crazy gene nobody else in the family has, turn on a fifty-watt bulb and I tan. My mom says there's a pirate and a slave and who knows what else dangling on our family tree. I'm gonna bird and go home drop-dead bronze. Finding Robert is my number-one priority, but there's no reason not to treat myself until I do."

"Were you and Mr. Chance married long?"

"Two long years. It was a mistake, okay? Can we please change the subject?"

Luis nodded.

"Will you help me find him? I'll pay you."

"I can try."

"He ran like a scared rabbit while you and Mikey were fighting?"

"I didn't see him afterward. Héctor says he didn't return to his hotel room."

"Where are you taking me?"

"Just ahead. Akumal, a resort village. Akumal is 'place of the turtle' in Maya."

"Is this where those giant sea turtles come ashore to lay their eggs?"

"Not like in the past. Poachers and tourists have seen to that. You will like Akumal. It's headquarters for Mexican divers and snorkelers, but there are birds to watch and a beach to run on."

"What kind of birds?"

Luis had to think. "Birds. Pelicans. Do you like pelicans?"

"I've never seen a pelican except on film," she said, voice rising. "We're too far north. Are they brown or white pelicans?"

"They're pelicans," Luis said, taking the Club Akumal turnoff. "I have to ask you a question. Why did you come so far to search for a man you divorced?"

"What did Robert tell you about our divorce?"

"You were signing papers."

"Did he also tell you that I'd agreed to wait until after the first of the year to sign for tax reasons?"

"You argued."

"We fought. He made some promises that he broke. Little things regarding the separation agreement, but typical

Robert. I told him to go straight to hell. I thought it over later and decided, why be as petty and childish as he is."

"So you signed the divorce papers after the first of the year?"

"No. I was going to. Then his mother phoned me and I didn't sign the papers, period."

Luis stopped at the Club Akumal office. "Ever?"

"I could've signed and been entitled to fifty percent of his winnings. Washington is a community property state, but Robert would probably fight me in court, a big big hassle."

"You and Bob Chance are man and wife?"

"We are. Mikey Smith can take his half and I'll take half of Robert's half. God, I sound like a superbitch, don't I? Robert is in danger. He could be dead and I'm going on and on about money."

"Mikey Smith is out of the country," Luis reminded her. "Chance is frightened and in hiding."

Judy Maxwell-Chance opened her car door. "I don't love the big tub of lard. Maybe I never did, but I don't want anything to happen to him."

"I believe you," said Luis, who did.

"A part of me says, money isn't important to you. Forget demanding a quarter of three million. Take any semifair settlement he offers. The Judith Maxwell-Chance Scholarship Fund. Pay the rest of my college and I'll be a happy camper."

"What do your other parts say?"

"Take every penny I can. Robert skipped on Mikey Smith. Robert skipped on me too. Piss on him."

12

Luis installed Judith Maxwell-Chance in a single room at the hotel, which was almost as cheap as a bungalow and much cheaper than a condo. Judy's skyward fixation made the process inefficient, slippery. You couldn't hold her in one spot to finish a sentence. Luis was reminded of his babies when they were distracted by a delight. But this was when they were younger, and instead of a present or a scrambling iguana, Judy's delight was the random bird. Her eyes were turned upward, her mouth open in wonderment.

Gnatcatchers and flycatchers, she babbled. Tody-bills and swallows and orioles, I can't even identify the species of oriole. There, see, an acorn woodpecker hammering on a dead coconut tree. And why is it that tropical birds are in Technicolor? Before Luis could say he didn't know, they were on the beach, watching pelicans glide by, low and slow, *brown* pelicans, doing a flyby as if just for her.

Luis's neck was sore from the upward gaping and the sunlight was leaving him with afterimages. Luis, the tour guide, pointed out amenities: dive shop, palapa bar, pizza parlor, boutique, tennis courts, and the El Bucanero Ice Cream Parlor.

"No pirates, but they have twenty-nine flavors," he said.

"Roughing it," Judy said.

"At times. They run out of flavors and have just fifteen or twenty to offer."

Judy laughed and took his arm. "You have our sense of humor."

Luis did not think he was being funny, merely factual. North Americans thought the remark was hilarious, so he never failed to repeat it. Without fail too was his narrated tour of the bronze statue of Gonzalo Guerrero.

Atop a slab of limestone stood a man, lifesized and oxidized green, in Maya loincloth and headdress. At his side were two of his children. Seated behind him, nursing their third, was his wife.

"The first Spanish to come ashore on this coast shipwrecked in 1511. Every man except two died of disease or hunger, or were killed or later sacrificed. The survivors were enslaved. One eventually was ransomed to Hernán Cortés. The other, Gonzalo Guerrero, became Maya. He was tattooed and wore the earrings of a warrior. He married a Maya woman and had the three children on this statue. He became a warrior. In 1517 a Spanish crony of Cortés invaded the coast. Guerrero commanded the troops that defeated him. Cortés was very disappointed in Gonzalo."

"You're proud of your heritage," Judy said.

"You misunderstand. Guerrero was not Maya. He was a Spaniard conquistador gone native. I think the story is funny."

"That doesn't change the reality that you're proud of your heritage."

"I want to be proud of who I am, not who I was."

"Sort of heavy for a hot day," Judy said, taking his hand. "C'mon, I'll buy you an ice cream. When it cools off, I'm going for a run. Join me?"

"A run?"

"Not a serious run. I'm not accustomed to the humidity. Up and down the beach. A mile or two. It might loosen up your muscles and relieve your soreness."

"I don't run," Luis said, "unless I'm being chased. I have to go to the shop."

"Will you hunt for Robert with me, Luis?"

"I can try."

"I'll pay you."

"We'll find Bob Chance and he'll pay us both."

"Tomorrow?"

"Tomorrow," Luis said.

Luis headed for Black Coral. He hadn't gone a kilometer before Héctor's Dart filled his mirror. He was lying on his horn, waving out his window. The highway was shoulderless, so Luis stopped in his lane. Héctor, flasher flashing, stopped behind him. Motorists too unhappy at the inconvenience could discuss their grievance with Héctor while leaning on the Dart, feet spread, or if they were too persistent, at his jail.

"Luis," Héctor said, climbing out quickly, motioning Luis ahead of his Volkswagen. "We have a problem."

Héctor was a fleshy wick of perspiration and his teeth were clenched. Not good omens. Luis did not respond. He was in no hurry to learn the nature of this problem.

"Mrs. Chance," Héctor said.

"Mrs. Chance is no problem, Héctor. She has a room at

Club Akumal. Judy claims she is not Chance's former wife. She claims she is still—"

"Not *that* Mrs. Chance," Héctor said, voice cracking falsetto in desperation. "Our rich boy Chance is disappeared and these pretenders to the wealth won't quit announcing themselves to me."

As if cued, a woman in a tight, flowered sundress exited the front passenger seat of the Dart. She was tall and very white, Héctor's age plus several years. Roundly overripe in the hips and breasts, she was not otherwise fat. Her lips were as bright and as red as Héctor's blinking taillamps. Her long blonde hair, sprouting from dark roots, was as bright as silver and nearly as pale. The tropical climate was not agreeing with her, but she seemed to Luis less wilted than annoyed. She lighted a cigarette, glanced at her watch, sighed, and gazed absently at the jungle.

This woman, Luis thought, could be the mother or the elder sister of the soap opera slut-bitch-goddesses. He said, "Who is she? I know you're going to relieve my curiosity."

"The legally married Mrs. Robert Chance," Héctor whispered.

"No, you're mistaken. Judith Maxwell-Chance said she did not divorce Chance. They are legally married. I don't think she was lying."

"Somebody is lying, Luis. This lady is Mrs. Rita Trunkey Chance. She is not hyphenated, but is nonetheless formidable. She asserts that she married Bob Chance years ago and that they were not divorced by a court of law. She is not unattractive for a lady her age and she has tits. Were I Chance or any man I would be inclined to marry this woman in favor of the previous hyphenated and homely Mrs. Chance."

"Somebody is lying, Héctor. As you said."

"Luis, should you decide this Mrs. Chance is the liar, you are welcome to accuse her. I have not the courage."

13

After Luis had adamantly refused custody of the new Mrs. Chance, she asked him, "Okay to smoke?"

"Yes," Luis said. They were in the Beetle, windows down, en route to Cancún. Aside from removing the woman from the vicinity of Akumal and the other Mrs. Chance, Luis was uncertain what to do with her.

"Where I'm from, they're paranoid about smoking. People in offices have to go stand in an alley in the rain to smoke on their breaks. I'm business manager in a lumberyard. Of course you'd have to be the village idiot to light up in the yard. I smoke in my office so it doesn't matter. One of these years I'm going to quit just to get everybody off my back."

"Where are you from?"

"Not that it'll mean anything to you, Portland, Oregon."

"Portland, Oregon," Luis said. "Population 388,500 in 1972. Area, eighty square miles. Famed annual Rose Festival."

"You've been to Portland?"

"No. Is it far from Seattle, home of Bob Chance?"

"Nope. A four-hour drive. Are you a basketball fan? You bump into Trail Blazer fans wherever you go."

"No."

"Fine. Be the mystery man. No skin off my nose. What's Bobby's little wifey like?"

"Bobby?"

"Bob to you. He was my baby Bobby. I robbed the cradle with him like he did with his little Judy."

Luis did not answer.

Rita said, "Inspector Salgado played dumb too, hon. But Thelma gave me the full scoop."

Bob, Robert, Bobby? "Thelma?"

"Thelma. Bobby's mother. We hated each other's guts when Bobby and I were married. I took him away from her, him and her mothering chores. I even popped the question. I'm a few years older than Bobby and she thought I was an evil influence, corrupting her baby boy. Gimme a break! When we met I was a bartender at a tavern and he was fresh out of college, working at Boeing, drinking at the bar more nights than he wasn't.

"It was lust at first sight. We both had what the other was looking for. Damned if I remember exactly what that was, but we tied the knot in three months. Wasn't a lot longer than that before we split the sheets. We got along fine and dandy as long as we were between them. Then that got old too. We had us a terminal case of mutual incompatibility. He sure was cute, though. I was a cutie pie in those days too. Believe it or not, once upon a time I was a dairy princess.

"Thelma says Bobby's packed on the weight. Is it true that he's carrying a spare tire that'd fit an eighteen-wheeler?"

"Is he fat? Yes, he is fat."

"It has to be seventeen, eighteen years since Thelma and me spoke. I was surprised she knew where I was living. She phoned me out of the clear blue sky. Called me out of spite. I'll bet she knew all along me and Bobby never legalized the divorce and she was just waiting to drop the other shoe on somebody's head. The Lotto. This goon chasing Bobby he owes half the ticket to. Little Judy. Thelma filled me in on the whole ball of wax."

"When did she telephone you?"

"The day before yesterday. Thelma'd been looking to sink her fangs into Bobby, then he tips her off with a postcard. Thelma and Bobby, they have major problems."

"Yes," Luis agreed.

"Did Bobby lay his sad nineteen-dollar-muffler story on you?"

"Yes."

"Your cop friend acts like I ruined his day. I went to the police station right off the bat because that's their job, to locate missing persons, isn't it? Thelma said the goon was hot on Bobby's trail and he was in big trouble. I gathered from the inspector that he doesn't know Bobby's whereabouts. He was real vague. He said you're the person to connect with. You're working for Bobby as a private detective."

Luis wished he too could be vague. But he reported in detail his business relationship with Bob Robert Bobby Chance and his fight with Mikey Smith. He did not report knowledge of Judith Maxwell-Chance.

"So that's what happened to your kisser. You look like you were jumped in a dark alley. You telling me the full story?"

"Yes," Luis said.

"Thelma said she tipped the little wifey too. She shown her perky little face yet?"

With this woman, Luis thought, hyphen or no hyphen, better to be truthful now than attempt to lie yourself out of a lie later. "Yes. She has."

"Is she cute?"

"No more questions about her," Luis said, "and I will not report your arrival to her."

"Protective, huh," Rita said. "My, my. Well, little Judy has a major problem too. She can chop the 'Chance' off her name right now. She's not legally married to him."

Among the evangelical pests in Yucatán rummaging for Maya souls were the Mormons, young short-haired Anglos with white shirts and ties, riding bicycles, briefcases full of tracts dangling from their handlebars. Luis was aware of their polygamous past. Could Bob Chance be a lapsed member of the cult? "You and Chance have been separated for many years and not legally divorced?"

"I was already a two-time loser," Rita said. "I like men, but I was awful sick of husbands. I never got around to the time and expense of a legal divorce. I figured Bobby would get hot pants again and want to make an honest woman out of some poor dumb little gal. He could shell out for his freedom, far as I was concerned. Didn't hear a peep out of him."

"Chance married Judith while he was married to you?"

"Evidently so. Bobby wasn't a doer. Never put off till tomorrow what you can do next week, maybe. That was his motto. Hasn't changed a bit. Bobby married little Judy assuming I'd handled the divorce. Come to think of it, me handling *every* situation was my pet peeve with Bobby.

"Bobby's idea of marital responsibility was holding down a steady job and jumping my bones twice a week. Everything else was up to me. Hell, I even had to get the car serviced and cut the grass. He'd be taking a nap or watching football or out drinking beer with his buddies."

"You obviously hate Chance," Luis said.

"And came to Cancún to stake my claim to the money, to hell with Bobby?"

Luis shrugged, eyes forward.

"I'm a mean, bitter old broad who's capitalizing on a bad situation?"

"Are you?"

Rita laughed and slapped Luis's thigh. "The mean and bitter part is wrong. I'm having fun. I was saving for a trip to the Grand Old Opry, but after Thelma put this bug in my ear, I was on the horn to my travel agent in ten minutes booking a flight to Cancún. I tell you what, if I felt for an instant that Bobby was in danger, you'd be chauffeuring a kinder, gentler Rita."

"How can you be certain he isn't?"

"By the looks of you, you and that Mikey goon had some kind of alleycat brawl. Then your inspector took him by the scruff of his neck and stuck him on a plane. This town ain't big enough for both of us. Mikey's out of the picture, but Bobby's scared. Who the hell wouldn't be? Bobby is Bobby. He's curled up in the fetal position underneath a pool table in some beer joint. Trust me on this."

"If you say so," Luis said.

"Sorry to be so bitchy. I came down to Mexico for my chunk of the three mil. I won't b.s. you, but I'd definitely cry my eyes out if Bobby got hurt. I'll always have a special place in my heart for Bobby. A small place, but a place. He's that adorable puppy dog with the wagging tail you just can't paper-train."

"You'll have to stand in line for the three million."

"Isn't that the truth? I'm not greedy. Thelma, Mikey the goon, Bobby. I'm agreeable to a fair and equitable slicing of the pie."

"And Judith Maxwell-Chance?"

"How come my intuition tells me you're sweet on her? Listen, I don't know how long she put up with him, but anything beyond a weekend's too long. She's paid her dues. We'll throw a net on Bobby and haul him in. Everybody with a stake, we'll sit down like civilized human beings and hash it out. Gotta find him first, though. The inspector speaks highly of you as a person and a private eye. You available for hire to hunt Bobby down?"

"I already have a client on the case," Luis said.

"Gimme three guesses and the first two don't count. Little Judy?"

Luis didn't reply.

"Okay. None of my business. Results are what count. What I also need is a legal eagle to sort it out on paper for us. Having Bobby wrapped with a ribbon around him isn't worth diddley unless we have an agreement in black and white."

"A lawyer?"

"Yeah. Much as I hate shysters, you can't avoid them indefinitely, and this is one of those indefinitelys."

They were nearing the exit to Cancún Airport. Luis was inspired. "An associate of mine is a distinguished lawyer."

"A *Mexican* lawyer? He's capable of handling a deal this complicated?"

"Mr. Martínez is among the finest lawyers in Cancún, if not in all of Yucatán."

"A big-timer like him, how do you get an appointment without waiting a month of Sundays?"

"If he is at his corporate legal suite complex, we have an appointment."

The alley stairs creaked and the bar kitchen stank. Rita Trunkey Chance was unimpressed. "You sure this guy's a heavy hitter?"

"Ricardo is a humble idealist. He does not accept large fees."

"He's my kind of lawyer then. Hey, that's 'La Bamba' they're singing."

Luis went in. Ricardo Martínez Rodríguez was alone at his desk. His jaw dropped and he hurriedly shuffled sheets of paper.

"Did I interrupt?" Luis asked. "Were you expecting a client?"

"No, no, no, Luis. I had a—he left."

"You're flustered. Do you have a naked lady under the desk?"

"No, no. You and I, we should develop a communication system for appointments."

"Get a telephone, Ricky. Anyhow, since you do not have a client, I have a client for you."

Luis stood aside and ushered Rita in. "Mrs. Rita Trunkey Chance, may I present Mr. Ricardo Martínez Rodríguez. Mrs. Chance has an interest in the Chance lottery fortune, Ricardo. She requires legal services."

Ricky glided around his desk and took her hand, then kissed it. "I am at your disposal, Mrs. Chance. For legal services and whatever other services I am asked to perform."

Luis was no stranger to this predatory, breathless gaze of Ricky's. Rita, while not a young woman, was handsome. More important, she was blue-eyed and blonde. No machismo Mexican male could resist her exotic beauty, nor relent in his advances until the conquest was made.

Rita appeared to Luis to be equally dazzled by Ricky's exotic Latino beauty. She giggled at the double entendre and said, "You're coming on like you think I'm a rich gal, hon, but this gal hasn't seen a spare nickel lately, so don't be counting your chickens."

"Your wealth would be a bonus, a gift of the gods," Ricky said, escorting her to a folding chair and sitting on the closest corner of his desk. "The affiliation of you to Mr. Chance and the money, Mrs. Chance, you must apprise me in minute detail."

"It's incredibly complicated, Ricardo," Luis said. "Your favorite sort of case."

"The name's Rita, Ricardo. Your English is fantastic, you know."

Ricky, whose English was inferior to Luis's, said, "Your English is fantastic too, Rita."

They shared a laugh and Rita said, "Ricardo, I don't suppose they have *I Love Lucy* down here, but if you shaved that little cookie duster of yours, you'd be a dead ringer for Lucy's gorgeous hubby."

Hormonal discharge had blinded the pair to the world outside themselves. Luis took advantage of the sexual chemistry and sneaked out like a thief. When he arrived at Ho-

Keh it was dark. Men were unloading crates from a flatbed and lugging them into the cenote. Luis recognized Fat and Ugly but did not see Dugdale.

Some of the village men were outside watching the process, smoking cigarettes, drinking beer and soda, enjoying the slight cooling of nightfall.

"They brought in a tent like your shop tent this afternoon," Francisco said to Luis. "Except there are no sides to it. It's like a palapa of canvas instead of straw. For gringos in the darkness, it will pass as an authentic palapa. They put it up sloppy and crooked, but it's big. They can fit thirty or forty people under it."

Francisco looked tired to Luis. Haggard. "Are those plastic dinosaur parts in the boxes?"

"I don't know. Probably. The boxes were sealed," Francisco said. "The tourists begin coming tomorrow night."

Luis had no comment. He went into his house, where Esther was reading a Mexico City newspaper and Rosa had headphones on, listening to North American rock stars. He cocked a thumb toward the door. "What do you think of the dinosaur business?"

"I don't like strangers at Ho-Keh," Rosa said. "This is no different than if we sold jewelry out of our home, Father."

"A tourist threw this newspaper away at the shop today, Father," said Esther. "I'm reading an article that says the government is improving employment opportunities for Indians in Quintana Roo. If that were true, nobody in Ho-Keh would have to take money from the dinosaur man."

"My babies are smarter than we Ho-Keh men who decide things."

Later in his hammock, in the twilight separating waking and sleep, his groggy brain abruptly posed the question —what is a dairy princess?

14

Luis Balam searched for subtle and proper words. They were in hiding. The words he found were the bluntest. "Were you married before you married Mr. Chance?"

"No," said Judith Maxwell-Chance. "Were you married?"

"Yes. Twice."

"Divorced or widowed?"

"Divorced and widowed," Luis said.

"Oh dear," Judy said. "You have two daughters, Inspector Salgado said. They were the girls in your jewelry store?"

"Yes."

"They're lovely. I caught a peek of them while Inspector Salgado was speaking to you. Do they have the same mother?"

"No."

"They look like you. For half sisters, they really look like sisters."

"They are sisters."

"Your attitude is neat. To hell with the 'half.' I like

that! You're a family. How come you asked if I was married before I married Robert?"

Because, Luis thought, I have lost more than words. I, a detective, have lost control of two questions designed to produce an answer. One question asked and the investigative technique has degraded into a conversation. On to question number two, presented without tactics or finesse: "Was Mr. Chance married before he was married to you?"

"Nope. And, I know, marrying a confirmed bachelor pushing forty, I should've had my head examined. Please, let's leave it at that. Why did you ask me if he had a prior marriage?"

Luis looked away.

Judy twisted and leaned toward him. "What's the matter?"

Luis could superbly deceive those deserving of deception. His face was a talking mask. But with the innocent he was stupidly transparent. He pointed and said, "We are five minutes from the cutoff to Cancún Island. We'll begin the search for Bob Chance at Bob Chance's room."

"Didn't you tell me that Inspector Salgado had Robert's room under tight surveillance?"

"Héctor has been very busy and things go wrong. Even a rich man might risk returning for a few favorite belongings."

"Like his football videotapes and a six-pack," Judy said. "You may be right, but you can't really believe he'd be sitting there."

"I don't believe, I don't disbelieve. Bob Chance could know that Héctor kicked Mikey Smith out of Mexico. At the least, he could have slipped through the surveillance for a few minutes. He could have paid somebody to close their eyes."

"And accidentally left a clue to his destination while he was in his room for a few minutes?" Judy said.

"A mystery clue," Luis said, smiling. He loved detective movies and TV shows where the criminal dropped a matchbook cover or a careless remark that led the detective hero to him. "We might have luck."

"Robert had luck. Look what luck's done for him."

Luis again parked discreetly on Kukulcán Boulevard opposite the Cancún InterPresidential. Out of the Volkswagen, Judy paused to gawk at the structure.

"What do you see?" Luis asked.

"My impression? Las Vegas. Or what an archaeologist discovers after he's gobbled some wild mushrooms he shouldn't have eaten."

"Is that a bad impression?"

"Not good or bad. Not for me. Not that I could afford ten minutes' rent on a broom closet in here. Not sour grapes either. I love Akumal. This morning at the beach, a royal tern—"

"Come on." Luis spotted a break in Kukulcán's manic traffic, clasped Judy's hand, and took her across.

"I thought you didn't run."

"When it is a choice of run or die, I run."

"Brr," Judy said as they entered the lobby, striking the wall of chilled air. "Your blue uniform and clipboard. You're dressed like an exterminator going in to give an estimate. I guess you have your reasons."

"Protective coloration," Luis said in the elevator. "Same as the birds you watch have. Sometimes I carry a bathroom plunger into these wonderful places. An Indian on his way to unclog a toilet is not suspicious."

He knocked on Chance's door. Nobody answered. Luis pressed his ear to it and heard a waterfall. A couple in swimsuits, towels draped on shoulders, walked by, observing them with mild interest.

Judy said to Luis, "I trust you on the roaches, Fernando, but can you get rid of the scorpions too?"

The couple turned their observation to each other.

Luis knocked again. The hallway was now vacant. He took Chance's duplicate room key out of his pocket and turned it in the lock.

"God, where did you get hold of the key? And where's the tight surveillance that was supposed to be on Robert's room?"

"To answer the first question, I am a detective. The second, I can't answer."

Luis switched on the lights and quickly closed the door behind them.

Judy held her nose and said, "Yucch."

Luis scanned an unchanged scene of putrefying litter and dirty clothes. "You tidied and cleaned up after him when you were married?"

"Sure did. I had it in the back of my mind from the outset that he was attracted to me because I was young. The day I packed and moved out, I felt guilty as hell. I felt like a mother deserting her son."

What attracted you to him? Luis barely stopped himself from asking. The TV was on, tuned to nothing. Volume on the electronic snowstorm was set high—his raging waterfall. Red VCR lights blinked. He ejected the 1983 Super Bowl. The cartridge was very warm.

"That's Robert's speed," Judy said. "Fabulously rich in Mexico on a fling, and he hides out in a hotel room staring at old football games. Brr brr. The lobby was cold. It's frigid in this ritzy dump. Luis, do you know what you're looking for? The mystery clue?"

He did not know. He paced the room uneasily, swiveling his head. "Yes. The mystery clue."

"Do you see any evidence that Robert came back after your fight with Mikey?"

Luis was not enough of a criminologist to differentiate day-old filth from week-old filth. "Not yet."

In the main room was the bed, a nightstand, a table, and four chairs. But for an ashtray, the table was empty. He went into the bathroom. Used towels were randomly scattered. Toiletries too: uncapped toothpaste, shaving cream, disposable razors, a twelve-pack of condoms sealed in cellophane, cologne, stick deodorant.

"Well?" Judy said from an edge of the bed.

"No."

She opened and closed the nightstand drawer, and got up. "Not even a Gideon. I'll check the closet. Robert would pack a few things."

"I will do it," Luis said, moving to the closet.

The hollow-core sliding door resisted. Luis pushed. Prone on the closet floor was the source of the resistance, an overweight man squeezed into the space as if extruded. His eyes had the milky sheen of a fish past its prime. Taped to the side of his face was a patch of gauze. His lips were parted, revealing sharp yellow teeth.

At the instant of death, Luis thought, Mikey Smith was being himself, shouting a profanity.

15

Inside Bob Chance's room were Inspector Héctor Salgado Reyes of the Quintana Roo State Judicial Police, an anguished Cancún InterPresidential Hotel assistant manager, Judith Maxwell-Chance, Luis Balam, and on the bed as if lying in state, covered by a sheet, Mikey Smith.

Héctor's men were at the door, forming a barrier to the hallway, which was clogged with the morbidly curious. Héctor was leaving it open for the litter bearers and the examining doctor. Eyes upraised, the manager was asking, why me, why is this happening in *my* hotel, on *my* shift. When he was done pestering God he asked Héctor what a gringo tourist lady was doing at a murder scene, no place for a lady. I'm indirectly involved, bozo, she said. He asked Héctor what an Indian in a parking valet uniform was doing at a murder scene. Héctor told the manager to be careful with the Indian talk, that he personally was half Zapotec.

The manager was small, bordering on delicate. He wore tight slacks, pointed shoes, and his hair slicked straight back. He said he didn't have to be careful, this was *his* shift, *his* hotel. An arm and a camera thrust above the doorway mob like a periscope, the camera whirring and clicking, a voice saying that he had a fast lens and fast film and that they should turn out fine without a flash. Héctor then thrust up his arms and said that was it, close the goddamn door, the medicos could fight their way through these ghouls like we had to.

The manager said *he* would decide if and when to shut the door. The guests already knew there was a murder. Secrecy would frighten them. Was the killer still prowling the hotel?

Héctor took him by the collar and asked if he desired to depart via the door or the fucking window, his choice. The manager screamed from the door that it was an outrage and that Héctor owed him the twenty dollars regardless. Héctor made reference to the manager's mother and asked the officer pushing the manager into the crowd to please shut the door securely behind him.

"I suppose at this juncture, Luis, you are dying to criticize my surveillance plan," Héctor said.

"Not me," Luis lied.

"You promised that twink twenty bucks for what?" Judy asked.

"To notify me the instant Bob Chance was observed on the premises, Señora Chance. He insisted that Bob Chance never returned to the premises, a ridiculous assertion."

"Robert is a jerk, but a killer, uh uh."

"Excuse me, please," Héctor said. "Mr. Chance and Mr. Smith are—were mortal enemies. Mr. Smith is dead in Mr. Chance's room and Mr. Chance is unavailable to clarify the circumstances."

"I'm not telling you how to do your job, Inspector, but

putting a hotel manager in charge of monitoring Robert's room, well, maybe that wasn't too professional."

"I should have had my officers cruising the halls on the long shot that Chance would return?" Héctor said with exaggerated patience. "Not that I enjoy a surplus of manpower. Nevertheless, gringos harbor an unfortunate stereotype of Mexican law enforcement personnel. They would check out of the hotel in masses."

"I can't imagine why."

Luis shot Judy a glare that startled her.

"Sorry," she said to Héctor.

"Apology accepted. I admit a degree of fault. I could have spared perhaps a man in plainclothes to monitor the hotel, outside and inside. But who would have dreamed that this greedy manager and his underlings could not have observed the entrance of a gentleman as—forgive me—conspicuous as your former husband."

"Not former," Judy said. "Not divorced. Husband, period."

Héctor looked at Luis.

Luis nodded at Héctor, then at the television. "Whoever killed Mikey Smith inserted a football tape and played it at high volume."

"To muffle the sounds of violence. Mr. Chance, this husband of yours, is an avid North American football fan, is he not?" Héctor asked Judy.

Arms folded tightly against her bosom, she said, "Robert and about fifty million other macho American males whose idea of a good time on Sunday is cold beer and the New York Raiders. I repeat, brr. Can we pretty please raise the temperature up above freezing?"

Héctor sighed wearily and adjusted the thermostat. "North American football noise to drown out the act itself. Conversion of the room into a meat locker to mask the inevitable decomposition. Clever, efficient premeditation."

"Not by Robert. He couldn't premeditate anything. That big teddy bear couldn't organize a trip to the beach. And c'mon, kill Mikey? Mikey barged in on him, Robert would faint dead away."

Translation of "big teddy bear"—not the literal, the actual—soared over Luis's head. Whatever the true meaning, he didn't like how Judy said it. Spoken in affection, he thought enviously.

"I agree with Judy, Héctor. You should have seen him outside the bullring. He was like a child, he was so frightened of Smith."

"Ah, but Mikey is dead in Chance's room. Mikey and Chance are mortal enemies on account of three million dollars. Chance, meanwhile, is gone. It is a situation—what is that North American expression?—a situation that looks like a duck and smells like a duck and quacks like a duck is invariably a duck."

Luis removed the sheet from Mikey Smith's face. "Héctor, first you have to determine cause of death."

Héctor laughed. "Natural causes, yes? Mikey felt death coming on, gained entry to Chance's room, crawled into the closet and died like a jungle animal skulking into the wilderness to await his demise."

"Héctor, where is his mortal wound? Other than the gauze covering the side of his head where I hit him with the camera, there is no visible injury, no tears or holes in his clothing, no bloodstains on the carpet. Look on the opposite side of his head. A pinkish bald spot. A handful of hair was pulled off? I don't remember the spot. Mikey Smith and his temper, he could have done it himself in his rage."

Héctor said, "Señora, do you wish to go into the hall while we puzzle this out? As we do, Mr. Smith must be unveiled, so to speak."

"No, I've seen blood and gore. I used to volunteer as a candy striper in a hospital," Judy said, though her eyes were on the floor.

Héctor said, "That is your decision. Why should my recommendation matter? It is that kind of day. I have a suspiciously dead gringo in my jurisdiction. Gringos stuffed into closets of luxury hotels, this is not the experience you write into a guidebook. This is not a desirable Cancún moment. There will be for me the nightmare of Mexico City tourism ministers and United States of America Embassy employees and the paperwork."

"It is possible Mikey Smith had a fatal heart attack as he prepared to kill Bob Chance. Chance panicked. He dragged him into the closet and ran."

"Oh yes. It is possible too, Luis, that the Mexican national soccer team will win the World Cup."

"Mikey is a Type A, but uh uh. Robert cashed in his lifetime supply on luck when he cashed that Lotto ticket. For what it's worth, you'll never convince me Mikey died of a heart attack *or* that Robert murdered him."

"Luis, did you search the remainder of the unit?" Héctor asked.

"For mystery clues? I did. The bathroom is the only other room."

They excused themselves and examined it together. No mystery clue leaped out of the clutter. Héctor frowned at the sealed condom package, rotating it in his hand, and said in Spanish, "So sad. A man as lavishly rich as King Solomon and he can't get laid."

"He would if he could. He had too many worries."

"Oh, that," Héctor said, shaking his head. "Even sadder. Tragic."

Judy was rummaging through the closet and dresser.

"Mystery clues?" Luis said.

"Underwear that should be disposed of by the EPA and a slice of pizza. Pepperoni, but don't quote me."

"Had he packed?" asked Héctor. "Are essential belongings gone? The bathroom is generously stocked with personal hygiene articles."

"Let me look some more and think. Robert isn't exactly *GQ* material. He wouldn't have any problem traveling light if he had to."

"Murder fugitives generally place their wardrobe low on the priority list," Héctor said.

Judy turned to him. "Hey, look, you know, go ahead and prove it. All you've got is a body."

Héctor looked at Mikey Smith. "Luis, see, he was bursting into a snarl when he died. Mr. Smith is an excellent contradiction to the myth that a person is peaceful in death."

"Is Smith snarling because snarling is normal for him or is he angry because he knows somebody is murdering him?" Luis said.

"Anger comes naturally to him. Luis, you planted the idea when you speculated on a heart attack. As I reconsider, I cannot discount the dreadful possibility that injuries inflicted by you in the fight resulted in his demise."

"How?"

"Don't be defensive, Luis. I am merely playing devil's advocate, preparing for a hypothetical line of interrogation. My layman's theories are these. He succumbed to an infection. A blood clot dislodged."

"I indirectly killed him?" Luis said, shaking his head, forcing a smile.

"I am not a doctor or a judge," Héctor said with a helpless shrug.

"No way," Judy said. "You could run Mikey Smith over with a locomotive and he'd hop up and brush himself off. Somebody, somehow, murdered him."

"The gauze and tape are clean. The gauze was not changed too long ago. Let's see what is underneath," Luis said, tearing the dressing off.

"Luis, you are tampering with pathology evidence—oh my fucking goodness!"

Centered in an area of bruising and scabbed tissue was a small hole. Blood surrounding the hole was congealed. The underside of the gauze was decorated with a brownish-red ring. Luis said, "Gunshot?"

"Yes," Héctor said, addressing Judy. "Two years ago, in Playa del Carmen, I investigated a homicide. The investigation was a cut and dried foregone conclusion. I arrived at the scene and the murderer was sitting in a cafe, drinking a beer, smoking a cigarette, ashtray and beer bottle and smoking pistol on the table. A hysterical woman, his wife, was kneeling by the side of the victim, her lover.

"The passenger ferries at Playa del Carmen go to Cozumel Island. The wife and husband and lover lived at Playa. The wife and lover would take separate ferries to Cozumel and rent a room, then catch separate ferries home.

"On the last day of the victim's life, they became brash

and careless. The husband was a laborer and had informed the wife that he would be working down the coast around Tulum all day. They might work late, in which case he would sleep in his car. The wife and her lover thought they were in love. They regarded their presence together in public to be as forbidden and rare a fruit as the fruit they savored in their rented rooms.

"So they rode the same ferry home. Witnesses on the boat reported that they held hands. They decided to risk a drink at a romantic cafe with a view of the Caribbean. That's where they were when the husband came up behind them and pressed an automatic pistol to the side of loverboy's head. The husband had suspected them for weeks and his Tulum job was a lie. He was waiting."

"What kind of sentence did the husband get?" Judy asked.

"He is in jail for a while."

"A while? Not twenty years, not ninety-nine years, not life?"

"He could have killed the woman who cuckolded him too, señora, but he did not. He only killed the man who seduced her."

"Talk about compassion," Judy said, rolling her eyes.

"The man is being punished."

"Well, he sure learned his lesson."

"My belated point is, on the Playa del Carmen case, the loverboy's wound was an identical twin of Mr. Smith's wound. On the autopsy they extracted a twenty-five-caliber slug from his cranial cavity. This is a tiny, tiny weapon, a favorite of sneak thieves and sissies. I have two or three identical weapons in the trunk of my car. A similar slug, I deduce, ricocheted within Mr. Smith's thick skull."

"Fired by whom?" Judy said. "Robert never owned a gun in his life. Even if he did and had the nerve to use it, he'd quickdraw it out of his pocket and shoot himself in the foot."

"The tape and gauze are clean, Héctor," Luis said. "Would Smith allow the killer to rip loose the gauze and fire his gun?"

"It would be like pulling a jaguar's tail," Héctor thought out loud.

"The killer crept up behind Mikey, shot through the gauze, and later replaced the dressing," Luis said.

"To temporarily confound us agents of justice. No gauze in the bathroom?"

"No," Luis said.

"I will double-check."

While Héctor double-checked, Judy said, "No. I can't picture Robert taking gauze with him. Anywhere. I used to go crazy because he'd forget to carry a hankie."

Héctor returned. "I shall begin at the hotel pharmacy. Our killer, Bob Chance or whoever, bought gauze somewhere."

"Make that killers. Plural. And I don't mean the second guy was Robert."

Judy had their attention now. She patted the tabletop and continued, "Three chairs around the table. Fourth up against the wall."

"Not conclusive," Héctor said. "The chairs are on casters. They could have been rolled hither and yon in complete disarray during and after the murder."

"There's no disarray. The arrangement of chairs at the table is the most orderly part of the room." She picked up the ashtray. "And how about this?"

"How about an empty ashtray?"

"It's empty, Inspector, but it's dirty. It's been used recently. I don't think Mikey smoked and I know Robert didn't. That was *one* bad habit he never got around to acquiring."

16

What now? Judy said. Nothing now, Héctor said; this is a police matter. I mean about Robert, us locating him, Judy said. He is party to the police matter, Héctor said. Wait a second, Judy said; Robert is harmless, and that ashtray— Is likewise a police matter, Señora Chance.

Luis broke in and struck a compromise. We'll leave you, Héctor, if you will meet us for dinner tomorrow evening and divulge what you've learned, the gauze and any other mystery clues. Deal, Héctor said; where? Your choice. The aforementioned Playa del Carmen restaurant. Early dinner. Has to be, so my appetite isn't spoiled for regular dinner with my family later on.

Sick, Judy said. Nostalgia? asked Luis. Great seafood, Héctor said; the fish doesn't stink and they feature a policeman's discount.

In the car, Judy asked Luis to drive her back to Akumal. "Since progress has ground to a halt, I might as well take the rest of the day to unwind, me and my field guide and my binoculars."

"We have to stay out of Héctor's way," Luis said. "Everywhere we went to look for Chance, we'd bump into his men. We will sort of honor the deal."

"What do you mean, sort of? And where exactly would we bump into his men? Do you have an idea where Robert is?"

Her eyes were wet and her nose was so runny she sounded as if she were talking underwater.

"I'm sorry," Luis said. "What did I say? I am sorry."

"No, no, not you," she said, patting his arm. She blew her nose and composed her speech. "It's an accumulation of everything. When Robert and I were married I considered Mikey and Mikey's Sports Bar a rival, like another woman. My self-esteem went even further down the tubes. Here was a fat, loud jerk who was more attractive than me."

"No, not so," Luis said, very nearly adding that nobody was more attractive than she.

"Right. Not so. I grew up a bit and came to realize that Robert was the problem, not me. The thing is, I always thought of Mikey Smith as a gross, disgusting animal until I saw him dead. Nobody deserves what he got. He was a human being and somebody took his life. Nobody has that right. And that nobody isn't Robert."

"I agree," Luis said.

"You do, really? You weren't just backing me up with Héctor in there to be a nice guy?"

"Chance attacking Smith is unlikely," Luis said. "That blood sport they have in England? Chance attacking Smith is like a fox turning on the dogs."

"Hounds. Or like a hemophiliac attacking a vampire." She laughed and blew her magnificent nose. "The inspector will do his job, I know, but I think he was patronizing me when I pointed out the dirty ashtray."

"There are five billion people on the planet. Half of them smoke."

"Sure, but one of them was in the room with Mikey Smith. Maybe Robert too, but no matter what he said about the chairs, there were three people in that room."

Luis shrugged. "Probably. Bob Chance included."

"Oh, God!"

Luis passed a slow-moving truck with plenty of space to avoid an oncoming Nissan sedan—two or three car lengths and one entire second.

"What?" he said.

"Jesus, do you always drive that way?"

"What way?"

"Don't go 'what way.' The driver had gold front teeth and a string tie. I *saw* them."

"He missed us," Luis said.

"That was considerate of him. Getting back to 'sort of' honoring the deal and bumping into Héctor's men, Luis, please clarify."

"The police will be covering obvious places. Car rental agencies, the airport, hotels, bus stations."

"Where does your 'sort of' come in to the equation? Where do we look for Robert?"

"I have an idea or two, I'll look into some things," said Luis, who had neither ideas nor things to look into.

"Such as?"

Luis turned at Club Akumal. "I'd rather develop these ideas and things first."

"Okay. When?"

Luis hoped he had sounded mysterious and competent. "We can go out in the morning."

"Okay. Where to?"

"It depends on what I can develop."

Luis stopped at Judy's hotel. She opened her door. "Thanks again, Luis. As early as you like is fine with me."

She was out and gone, quickstepping up the stairs to her room. Blue jeans. Frilly blouse, low-cut in back. Silky skin. Hardly a pockmark or a pimple. Good shoulders. Narrow hips but ample buttocks, perfect handfuls.

Depressed, Luis exited, bound for Black Coral. She hadn't invited him to stick around, he a non-birder, to birdwatch with her. Had she said she was going for a run, he might have said, need some company? Might have.

Instead he pondered imponderables:

Where is Bob Robert Bobby Chance?

Should he, Luis Balam, introduce Judith Maxwell-Chance to the existence if not the person of Rita Trunkey Chance?

Did Bob Chance kill Mikey Smith? Was Bob Chance in his hotel room when someone else killed Mikey Smith?

Does Judy like him?

What is a dairy princess?

Does Judy have a North American boyfriend?

Who dirtied the ashtray and/or aligned if not sat in three of four chairs?

Was Chance still alive? Was he still a client, dead or alive?

Why does Judy Maxwell-Chance hyphenate? Why did she marry the man with whom she hyphenated?

Where did Vance Dugdale's crated plastic dinosaurs come from so promptly? From Cuba or Brazil, whichever, why were they delivered when promised? Such efficiency was disconcertingly un-Mexican.

Judy had patted him on the arm *twice;* were the pats significant?

Why would Bob Chance, so paranoid that he barricaded his door against housekeepers, grant entry to Smith? Impossible, out of the question!

But then, how did Mikey Smith enter? Door, hinges, latch, and jamb should have been torn off, flat on the carpeted floor of Chance's $200-plus room.

What would it be like to have three million dollars? A disputed partner dead. You the murder suspect pursued by the law and two wives, who will ultimately own the three million?

How could Judy possibly make love to Chance? How could she have that gelatinous bulk on top of her?

When Chance set him up to battle Mikey, was it merely one act in an entire drama leading up to Smith's ultimate death?

Luis, who never got headaches, was getting his second one in three days. Black Coral had its usual depressing ratio of browsers to buyers. Luis hung around, helping his babies, who didn't need it.

When they had the shop to themselves once more, Luis told them about his day. He was atoning for his machismo after the Mikey Smith fight, and they would hear it soon enough anyway by word of mouth. Their initial reaction was horror, followed by analysis.

"Are you positive your Mr. Chance didn't kill Mr. Smith, Father?" Esther said.

"I am. Héctor isn't."

"The woman Inspector Salgado brought to you, Father, is she his wife?" Rosa asked. "Does she think he's innocent?"

Luis said that Judy Maxwell-Chance thought Robert Chance was innocent, but that he didn't know whether or not she was his wife, and neither did she. He introduced Rita Trunkey Chance to the conversation.

"He's a bigamist?" Esther said in wide-eyed amazement.

"He's a bigamist because he's a coward," Rosa said. "He's afraid to tell anybody the truth. That is why I think he's alive and safe."

"Because he's afraid to tell anybody the truth?"

"No, because he's a coward who never grew up. He'll flee from everything and hide under something."

"If he's alive," Esther said.

"He's alive," Rosa said.

"Was Chance in the room when Smith was murdered?"

They looked at each other, then Esther said to her father, "He was. He had to let Smith in. Another person killed Smith for him because he could not do it himself."

"Good logic," Luis said. "So who was the killer and where is Chance?"

"You're the detective, Father."

"Good answer," Luis said. "When I find the killer I'll find Chance."

"Yes," Rosa said. "The killer didn't murder Chance. Only Superman could have moved that huge body out of the room."

"Agreed," Luis said. "And Superman would have moved Smith too."

"It is possible he didn't flee," Esther said.

Rosa thought for a minute and nodded. "The killer could be kidnapping him or protecting him. Or he might have taken Chance away to kill him. Solve your case, Father."

Luis kept Black Coral open longer than normal, much longer than necessary. Travelers on Highway 307 were going to and from, not cruising trinket shops, and Luis stayed open an hour after nightfall. He was stalling, in no rush to attend the gala opening of the Dead Dinosaurs Park.

He and his babies sat out front and watched passing vehicles, speculating on their destinations. Esther and Rosa imagined illicit rendezvous of star-crossed lovers and smuggling runs in and out of Belize. Luis leaned toward tardiness (the speeders) and boredom (those speeding even faster), two Mexican epidemics. Esther and Rosa said he was being an old poop.

They loaded their trays of merchandise into the suitcases Luis had bought on the cheap in Cancún City. Tourists in the hotel zone were shamed into upgrading at pricey luggage boutiques and the shabby yet serviceable discards found their way to the city, where they could be had for a pittance.

They loaded the Volkswagen and as they bumped along the Ho-Keh road Luis marveled once more at Hitler's people's car. The Beetle was bottomless. Filled with his daughters and his wares, Luis could still see out half the windows.

"Father, the younger Mrs. Chance, is she a North American Indian?" Esther said.

"She says not."

"She looks part Maya. Don't you think she's beautiful?"

Luis yawned and said casually, "I suppose she isn't terrible-looking."

Luis observed in the mirror his girls looking at each

other, suppressing giggles. He suppressed a sigh, reminded again how transparent he was, and he a master private detective.

At the clearing, Luis could see a glow from the cenote. Unloading with the girls, he could hear the portable generator that powered the lights, a roar competing with boombox mariachi. He could not see silhouettes of plastic dinosaurs. He had visualized tiny heads on tall, snaking necks, mouths agape in the agony of impending extinction.

A forlorn bus with rusting wheelwells was parked at the foot of the path. He walked out to the instant canvas palapa that looked slipshod and fake even at night. Incandescent bulbs dangled around and under it like Christmas lights strung up in haste. Most of Ho-Keh was there, along with twenty or thirty visitors, Anglos of predominantly older years.

The villagers were not receiving employment training. They were observing in bewilderment as elderly, white-haired North Americans rhythmically pumped the handles of slot machines. Those not on the machines were crowded around a roulette wheel overseen by Fat and a blackjack table presided over by Ugly. Fat and Ugly were wearing sombreros.

That Luis was not totally surprised did not mitigate his rage. He took deep breaths, balled his fists, told himself to remain calm. The air was ripe with gasoline fumes from the generator, tropical vegetation, and cigarette smoke.

He scanned faces. Francisco was looking in the other direction. Fernando, Diego, and Felipe were bunched at the perimeter, behind Fat, mesmerized by the erratic movement of the ball bearing around the roulette wheel. No Ricky. Where was Ricky? Vance Dugdale, king of the cultural theme parks, was servicing a line, taking cash and doling out cans from an ice chest at a table in front of the generator.

He went up to Dugdale, who was not wearing a sombrero. He was in tight slacks, Hawaiian shirt unbuttoned to the navel, and several clunky gold necklaces. His look of the evening, thought Luis: 1970s Degenerate.

"Lu. I was concerned you weren't gonna show. Rick evidently stood us up, that heartbreaker. Gotta have your *mucho primero* staff at your side, or what's the use."

Dugdale was dispensing beer and premixed cocktails, winking at Luis, grinning a cheek-cracking grin, displaying a keyboard of teeth that was an almost irresistible temptation to Luis and his balled fists. "We have to talk, Dugdale."

"Gimme a sec, Lu, till the line peters out. Customer service is our motto."

Luis took him by a flaccid bicep. "Now."

"Hey, in a sec, okay?"

Luis squeezed harder.

Dugdale's cheek-cracking grin became a teeth-gritting grin. "Lu, *compadre*, I'm experiencing some mild discomfort, okay. Some fingertip tingling. Let's not be silly, Lu."

"We can talk or we can stand like this until you feel some gangrene," Luis said.

"Is he a cop?" said the next customer in line, an oldster whose red nose clashed with his yellow golf outfit.

"No way, José," said Dugdale. "No sweat. Like I guaranteed, security is a given. Another strawberry daiquiri for the missus, sir, and a Dos Equis for yourself? Ow!"

The customer looked at Luis and said, "That's all right. We're not as thirsty as I thought we were."

Luis escorted Dugdale around the generator to the far side of the cenote, beyond most of the noise and glare.

"Where the hell are we, Lu? Hey, a person could get lost out here. Stanley and Livingstone could get fucking lost out here."

Luis smiled. "A person could."

"Lu. Come on—"

"Where are your plastic dinosaurs, Dugdale?"

"Lu, I was planning on explaining. I explained to Frank and, well, he's not thrilled and who can blame him, people naturally resisting change as they do, but we had us a big-time glitch."

"Glitch?"

"A situation that didn't go according to the ol' game plan. The shipment from São Paulo has been delayed in transit. The culprit is bureaucratic customs and tariff shit I don't *comprehendo.* So, in effect, we got us your basic blessing in disguise.

"You see, Lu, I kind of overestimated in cerebral terms how excited tropical tourists would be about a historical, educational concept. Especially these old coots who saved for their cruise and expect to have themselves a fling. This is why gambling as a transitioning tool is *perfecto.*"

"Cruise? Transitioning?"

"Cruise ships. Bluehairs, Lu. You gotta love 'em! They're taking the vacation of their life, out there in international waters in the ship casino. They come ashore, buy their schlock souvenir shit from the locals—no offense to you and your fine coral jewelry establishment, Lu—then what? You turn seventy and your window of depravity narrows.

"They get a mild taste of the wild life on the ship, those one-armed bandits and whatnot. Their appetites are whetted. I have connections. I book them out here, exclusively the geezers, a whisper outta the side of the mouth. An innuendo, that's my brochure, Lu. They love chump-change gambling, Lu. They eat it up. Safe sin is what it is.

"That old goober in there dressed like a banana sweating the cops? He's assuming I'm paying you off. You got a zillion different police departments in Mexico. It's incredible. They're all doing their own thing, so who do you bribe? And when you do lay a bribe on, how can you trust them? Corruption is an insidious thing.

"No bribes in our situation. No need for bribes, Lu. The cruisers come ashore for the day at Cancún or Playa del Carmen or Cozumel. One-day stops, that's the key. We recruit on the spot. Bus them out, bus them back. They sail in the A.M. There's no time for loose lips to sink *our* ship."

"Transitioning?"

"Said it once, Lu. I'll say it again. You're a damn quick read. I was transitioning to my transitioning, as it were. The gambling is a teaser, a narrative hook. Draws them out, then we zing them with apocalyptic history. When the props and the dioramas go on line, the slots will be in the background and the tables will be gone. We need the gambling now for the overhead, but as soon as my ersatz dinos steam in, they're the bottom line. We'll be supplying fun on two separate levels and the priority is the cultural. You have my word of honor."

Luis said, "I don't believe you."

"Lu, Frank and I went through this scene. Top on my list of things to do tomorrow is scrounge up a satellite dish for Frank and his Panasonic, put a smile on that grumpy face.

"Yeah, the customs and tariff glitch made me look bad, but, whoa, no excuses. The buck stops here. I'm committed to the program we initially agreed on, you and me and Rick and Frank, and you're my executive liaison and whatever else you want to be in the organization, Lu, you can be whatever you want to be!"

"Who are you? Where do you live? Where do you come from?"

"Lu, I'm a citizen of the earth. What's an address and a résumé prove? Lu, Lu?"

Luis walked back toward the fun.

"Lu. Come on. I thought we just smoked us a peace pipe."

Luis skirted the palapa. He did not want to see or be seen. He came upon a visitor five meters from the head of the path, an elderly man urinating.

"Oops, caught me in the act. This isn't sacred ground or anything I'm taking a leak on, is it?"

"I don't know. It's too dark."

The man laughed nervously. "Well, you gotta go, you gotta go. This speakeasy you have here, it's fantastic."

"Speakeasy?"

"That's what your honcho with the Don Ho shirt says it is, except the gambling's what's illegal, not the booze, though I wouldn't lay odds he's operating with a valid liquor license. You know, you guys really ought to install facilities."

"Facilities," Luis said. "I'll work on it. I'm the senior chief executive liaison."

"Good boy, but I'll miss out on your portable potties. We're off for Jamaica bright and early in the morning. Pissing in the weeds in the middle of the night leaves a lot to be desired."

"You are in no danger. Usually Diego Chi captures his snake before nightfall," Luis said.

"Huh?"

"Diego Chi keeps a boa constrictor in his corn crib to make a meal of the rodents who come for a meal," Luis said truthfully.

"You've got to be kidding," the tourist said.

"It escapes constantly," Luis lied. "Diego has a restless snake."

The tourist's miniature waterfall dried up.

"The poisonous varieties that live out here in the jungle, you shouldn't worry. They're sluggish at night unless you step on them."

"Holy shit!"

Luis tramped through the brush to the path, saying, "Have a nice evening, sir."

17

"What is a speakeasy?"

"It's a—this is long before our time—an illegal saloon in the 1920s, during Prohibition. You snuck down stairs and said 'Sam sent me' and they let you in or they didn't. I'll bet those were exciting places. How come you asked?"

"What is a dairy princess?"

"You win a beauty contest for farm girls, you're a dairy princess. Big boobs, tiny brains. Don't get me started on beauty contests, Luis," Judy said bitterly.

Luis made no reply. He decided that the proper moment to introduce Judith Maxwell-Chance to the existence of Rita Trunkey Chance lay in the indistinct future.

"It's my turn to ask weird questions," Judy continued. "Why does this boat have to go so fast on this beautiful, smooth water and make it feel like it has potholes? And why do you act like you're pissed at me?"

The boat was the Playa del Carmen to Cozumel ferry. Cozumel, thirty miles long and nine miles wide, was Mexico's largest island. Ferries made the eleven-mile shuttle throughout the day. Luis said, "They're usually behind schedule, so if they go too fast they won't be quite as late."

"That makes great sense, but that doesn't explain why we're going to Cozumel and why you're so gloomy."

"My ancestors, the women, made the voyage to Cozumel in dugout canoes to worship Ix Chel, goddess of fertility. Later, Cortés came but he didn't stay long. He sailed up to Veracruz to conquer the Aztecs, who were a much softer enemy than us Maya. Later still, pirates like Henry Morgan and Jean Laffite used Cozumel as a staging area for their raids. In World War Two, your Army built the airstrip and your Navy operated a submarine base and trained divers. Cozumel has a rich history."

"Luis."

"Cozumel is renowned today for tourism and div—"

"Luis."

"Diving. Because of the reefs, snorkelers and scuba divers love Cozumel as much as they love Akumal. Tourists love the shopping at San Miguel, Cozumel's town. Cozumel looks like real Mexico. Cozumel doesn't have Cancún's fake glitter and the prices are lower if you are a good bargainer."

"Luis, please cut the tour guide routine, okay? You were developing ideas on Robert, you said yesterday. Do you think he might be in hiding on Cozumel?"

Luis fielded the easier question, explaining that he was not angry at her and his gloominess was the result of last night's deception at Ho-Keh. Out spilled Vance Dugdale, Ricky Martínez, Francisco Ek and his supporters, and the plastic Dead Dinosaurs from Brazil that were actually slot machines from who knows where.

"So that's the reason you asked me what killed the dinosaurs."

"Yes."

"That joker and his gambling scam is a country mile off the subject of Robert, but it's outrageous."

"Yes, it is."

"What this Dugdale is doing is illegal?"

"Extremely."

"He's asking for trouble. Dugdale's pretty clever recruiting customers from cruise ships that leave the next morning, but a jungle casino won't remain a secret for long."

"Trouble for us. Probably no trouble for Dugdale. He'll disappear, then reappear next week or next month at another village to sell his Dead Dinosaurs."

"Police?"

"Police. Maybe the army too. I don't know. They would love to teach us Indians a lesson."

"This man, Francisco, who is kind of a co-leader in your village, can you talk to him?"

"I'll try. It's better that he comes to me."

"I don't understand why he's going along with this Dugdale sleazeball."

"It's complicated," Luis said.

"I'm really sorry, Luis, but I'm also confused. What does Cozumel have to do with anything?"

"Dugdale is a mystery man. I have a business friend on the island. He knows things. He can maybe tell me the origin of Dugdale's gambling equipment, so I can trace Dugdale from it. Before I can satisfy Ricky and Francisco and my friends that Dugdale is no good, I have to find out who he is."

"Wait a sec. Luis. I thought we were searching for Robert today."

Luis pointed out the window. "What's that bird, the white one with the black head?"

"A royal tern. What do you care?"

"It's a beautiful bird, Judy. You have given me an interest in birds."

"Getting back to Robert."

"My business friend is Alejandro. I buy my black coral and ninety percent of my other stock from Alejandro. He gives me the best wholesale prices on the coast. Alejandro buys and sells many things. He meets many people. He may know Dugdale. He may also know Chance."

"Sounds like a bizarre character, but him knowing Robert, that's really unlikely."

"Unlikely, I'll admit. Impossible, no. You don't know Alejandro. Besides, you can see sights and, remember, we are having an early dinner with Héctor. He'll have news for us on his investigation."

"I'm not holding my breath, but I'll play along," Judy said, sighing. "Who exactly is this Alejandro?"

"I'm not completely sure myself. He owns a small factory that makes jewelry from the black coral divers bring up from the reefs. As I said, he buys and sells too. He's a silent partner to some of the vendors you'll see in the market."

"Is he, you know, shady?"

"Dealing in stolen property, you mean?"

"Yeah."

"There are rumors. You can't believe whatever you hear."

"But you could be dealing in stolen property?"

"No, not me," Luis said. "I pay Alejandro for everything."

"See no evil," Judy said. "Are we going to his office?"

The ferry had docked and passengers were lining up to disembark. Luis said, "Alejandro has no office. He's in and out of his factory and at the market. His office is his brain. He never forgets anything. A merchant owes him money from a transaction two years ago, when Alejandro catches up to him, he'll adjust the debt for inflation and exchange rates, and tack on interest. In his head. He won't be off five pesos."

"How do we find him?"

"He'll find us."

They walked off the boat, across the *malecón* directly into the bustle of cafes, shops, and a handicraft market choked with tourists.

"Convenient," Judy said, going into the market.

"Yes. They take plastic and real money. You can buy ceramics from Oaxaca, Héctor's home state. Hammocks from Yucatán State. Glass, weaving, wood carvings, you name it."

Judy paused at an alcove dedicated to hand-tooled leather purses. "Alejandro won't notice us, Luis. Business is booming. He'll be too busy counting his money."

"Alejandro has no schedule. He likes to keep track of what's selling and what isn't. He likes to keep track of his partners. They can't steal as much from him if he makes unpredictable appearances."

"Well, still, with the hundreds and thousands of people in town, we're a needle in a hay—"

"Luis, holy sheet! Your face. Da side you stopped da truck with looks worser'n the other, and you ain't got a good side, you ugly little focker."

Emerging from behind a curtain hung between flimsy partitions was a tall Mexican with muttonchop sideburns and a face as long and homely as the most miserable street dog's. He had clothed his scrawny body in chinos and a University of Florida T-shirt. Dangling in the corner of his mouth was a Salem, which he chain-smoked.

On one partition hung velvet paintings of voluptuous Maya maidens who strongly resembled the young Sophia Loren; on the other hung velvet paintings of Elvis, who strongly resembled Alejandro.

Luis shook Alejandro's hand. "I had an accident. Speaking of ugly."

"Luis accident-prone. Sheet. I hear tell of da fight. You beat sheet out of gorilla that jump on you. You world-famous, mon. Your name da jaguar. You lived up to jaguar. Who's ugly? Me or da fine art?" said Alejandro.

"Flip a coin," Luis said. "Alejandro, this is my friend Judy."

Alejandro bowed at the waist, a gesture as off balance as it was courtly. "Luis's friend is my friend."

"What language is he speaking?" Judy said. "I didn't pick up five words."

"Alejandro speaks Alejandro language, mixed-up English, Spanish, and West Indies dialects."

"How does he do business, how does he communicate with his customers?"

"With a pocket calculator and emotion. He punches in a figure and smiles. They punch in a figure and he reacts like he's been shot. And so on. He's colorful and fun and sharp."

"Mon, quit fockin talking about me. You come to buy? I got you 'mazing price on lapis lazuli. No sheet."

"No."

Alejandro lighted another Salem from the one he was smoking. "You and da lady good friends?"

"Yes."

"Go shop, go lonch, go fock?"

Luis's cheeks burned. "No."

"I think I'm picking up Alejandro language," Judy said. "Did the lapis fall off a truck and does 'fock' mean what I think it means?"

Alejandro looked at her. "Smart lady. You look Mayan. You Mayan?"

"Seattleite."

"Alejandro, we need information," Luis said.

"You ain't Mayan," Alejandro said to Judy. "You belong to dem Indians up north dat John Wayne killed off?"

Judy laughed. "My pirate and slave genes."

"Da fock she say, mon?" Alejandro said to Luis. "She don't make no sense."

"Information, Alejandro."

"*Free* information?" he asked in horror.

"Casino gambling equipment. Slot machines, roulette wheels, card tables, where would you get your hands on that stuff?"

"Casinos ain't legal, mon. You got your sports betting parlors in Cancún, but no Las Vegas sheet. No can do."

"I'm asking about the equipment, not casinos."

"You can own it in your home, you don't open to the public. Like dirty pictures, it ain't illegal till it be found on you. Why you asking?"

Luis was not about to reveal last night's experience at the cenote. Alejandro's stream of information flowed in every direction. "Just curious."

Alejandro smirked. "Curious. Sheet."

"I need to know if somebody on the coast bought gambling equipment recently."

"You need to know who the somebody is?"

Luis nodded.

"Focker owe you money?"

"More than money," Luis said.

"This stuff's 'round. Rich gringos buy condos and villas on the Carib. Don't matter what part of da world dey in, dey got to have dese playrooms." He looked at Judy. "What you call dem?"

"Rec rooms," she said. "Rumpus rooms. Dens."

"Yeah. Yanquis buy pool tables, neon beer signs, and game machines, like dey got a real cantina dey don't got to leave home to go to. Maybe Papa home pretending to carouse keep Mama happy 'stead of Papa gone doing the carouse for real."

"Recently that you're aware of?"

"Luis, you a pushy focker. Not recent. Last year guy built condos up by Cancún. Not Cancún, but up by. *Mucho dinero* condos, mon, no time-share sheet. Punta Paraiso, he name it."

"I've seen it," Luis told Judy. "Big and fancy. They have walls and a guard gate."

"Big and fancy as the Cancún InterPresidential?" she asked.

"The building isn't as big, but they say the condos are huge and go for half a million dollars and up."

"Da builder buy da machines, stick dem in da model unit playrooms to make da gringos drool and sign da papers. He bought machines and tables for two or three units. Biggest buy I hear of recently."

"How long ago did the builder buy them, Alejandro?"

"One year."

"That's not very recent," said a discouraged Luis.

"You want I lie and say one week, one month, mon? Make you happy?"

"No. Where did he buy them?"

"Roundaboutly from Cuba."

Luis thought of Ricky Martínez's Havana-São Paulo slip and his "Vance is seeking further capitalization."

"I know roundaboutly," Judy said. "Are you saying the Cubans don't sell them directly in this area?"

"Smart lady," Alejandro said. "Cubans on da *malecón* and in da bars and shops, scare da sheet out a da Yanquis. Tourism all through. Nah, da things come down from Veracruz. You know Veracruz, up on da Gulf Coast?"

"I don't follow you," Luis said. "Cuba is manufacturing slot machines and selling them to Mexico, shipping them in at Veracruz?"

Alejandro closed his eyes and shook his head slowly. "Sheet no, mon. Da gaming devices is thirty-five or forty years old. Dey been around. When Castro marched into Havana and ended da party, da sheethead, he ended da girls and parties and gambling. Da girls and machines and partiers and gamblers what could, escaped Cuba. Castro, mon, he ain't *no* fun.

"Da equipment was available and da condo king bought dem from Veracruz or not Veracruz and installed dem in da Punta Paraiso model unit."

"Thanks anyway," Luis said, extending his right hand.

Alejandro jerked his out of range. "I ain't done yet, mon. Dey got stole."

"How long ago?"

"One month. Story is, da thief was a gringo salesman who got fired and had keys he'd made. Just stories is all dey is, sheet folks repeat to me."

"Are there names in the stories repeated to you?"

"No. You da detective, Luis. You want name, you go sleuth da name."

"Thank you once more, Alejandro. A final question. Have you heard of anyone importing big plastic dinosaurs from São Paulo, Brazil?"

Alejandro cackled. "No. Dat da stupidest thing I ever hear."

"You know of Luis's fight," Judy said to Alejandro. "Do you know Robert Chance, the man who was with him?"

"Dat da gorilla?"

"Different ape," Judy said. "Luis was protecting him from the gorilla."

"No. He da guy with da gambing equipment?"

"No," Judy said. "Robert Chance has his own gambling problems."

18

"Was I hearing things or did your spacey friend say your name was jaguar?"

"Spacey?"

"Yeah, you know, as in beamed down. Space case. Alejandro could be from Mars or Jupiter. You yourself don't know who he is, where he's from."

Luis smiled and raised two fingers. "Balam is Maya for jaguar. It is a common Maya surname."

Their pear-shaped mestizo waiter acknowledged Luis by walking slowly to the bar. He had to serve Indians, but he didn't have to like it. The owner of the restaurant, one of Playa del Carmen's finest establishments, was his uncle. The greedy bastard had said that everybody's money looked the same. This being the case, thought the waiter, any uppity Indian *will* show me the color of his money for each and every round. No bar tabs. Especially for this Indian, talking English, him and his rat-faced woman, a crossbreed who dressed like a *gringa.*

"Do I really look Maya, Luis?"

"You do. Forget your slave and pirate genes. Climb your family tree and you may be surprised. What are those tribes in the north who fought John Wayne in movies? Apaches and Comanches."

"Me, Native American? Come on. I've been described in ways I won't repeat, but never as Native American. Come to think of it, maybe I am. There are scientists who claim every native of this hemisphere descended from as few as four women who crossed the Bering land bridge. That's a tidbit from an -ology class I took last quarter."

The waiter brought their drinks, his third Leon Negra, her second margarita. Luis counted out the money methodically, exact to the peso. The soft, plump half-caste refused to speak to or make eye contact with him or Judy. He would see a tip from Luis when Luis saw snow falling on the Caribbean.

"We could be family," he said. The Leon on an empty stomach was speaking for him. One more, he knew, and he might be adding a suggestion of incest.

Judy sipped her margarita, flicked a grain of salt from her lower lip, and said, "I know you're going to be pissed, but I have a confession to make. After I'm out of school, I'm going to save up for a nose job. Before I save for a car or furniture or anything, I'm getting my schnozz fixed."

"You would ruin your nose," Luis said grimly.

Judy laughed. "Was something lost in the translation? Are there plastic surgeons in Mexico who do nose jobs?"

"There are plastic surgeons in Mexico City who do nose jobs exclusively," Luis said. "Mexicans love and hate you North Americans. They love and hate your movies and music and cars and your European faces."

"Not mine. Not love, anyhow."

"They would die in a minute if they could be reincarnated as light-skinned, blue-eyed blondes. They can't change their eye color and skin color, but they can change a big Mexican nose into a small North American nose. The rich people pay plastic surgeons thousands of dollars for a small, pretty nose. The poor people pay ten dollars for a plastic invention. Thousands and thousands have been sold. The inventor is rich. You stick these plastic splints up your nostrils. Instantly, your wide downturned nose is a wide upturned nose."

"You're kidding," Judy said.

"No."

"You say Mexican like you aren't Mexican."

"I am Maya before I am Mexican. I don't feel Mexican. People in Yucatán, whether Maya or mestizo or European, we feel we are Yucatecan before Mexican." Luis touched his nose. "This nose is as big as yours but not as pretty. The Mexico City plastic surgeons should pay the Aztecs and Zapotecs and Mixtecs and Maya and every Native Mexican a royalty for every nose job. This is our nose they are cursed and blessed with."

Judy smiled.

"You have a beautiful nose, Judy."

She laced her fingers around her margarita glass and stared into it.

Luis caressed her fingers and said, "Please don't change your nose."

"You're divorced and widowed," she said, looking up, flushed. "Tell me about your wives."

Luis did not want to, but by asking personal questions she was giving him the opportunity to quiz her on hyphenation, marrying Chance, and current love interests. Fair was fair.

"Esther is by my first wife. I went to Cancún in the

1970s to work construction. Cancún Island was brush and sand then, but the boom was beginning. There was much work. Too much work. I didn't come home to Ho-Keh often enough. My wife met a man from a neighboring village. Evangelical missionaries had converted him. He converted my wife. They ran off to his village. The man didn't want Esther, so my wife left her with my parents while I was in Cancún. The man and her live together as stupid, happy Pentecostals. They go into trances at church services. Some of their friends in North America have died handling poisonous snakes because Jesus wasn't paying attention and didn't protect them. They have four children of their own.

"Rosa is by my second wife. I was working again at Cancún, coming home every third or fourth weekend. I was so greedy for cash money I didn't learn from my mistakes. Six months after Rosa was born, while I was shoveling sand into a cement mixer and pounding nails, earning a wage, my wife died of a fever."

"Luis. I'm sorry."

"I stayed in Ho-Keh from then on and raised my babies, but I couldn't overcome my love for cash money, a wage. I joined the Traffic Police, the Tránsito. I worked out of Tulum City. Héctor was my boss."

"Was it a secure job?"

"As secure as a job in Mexico can be. So why did I leave the police?"

Judy nodded. "Why did you leave the police?"

Luis drank from his bottle and said, "I told this story to Bob Chance too. A long story. A rich man in a fancy car was drunk and speeding. He hit and ran over a Maya family on a bicycle, killing them. He didn't tap his brakes, didn't slow down to see what he had struck. He bought out of the trouble, but I wouldn't stop the investigation. I was fired. Héctor couldn't save the investigation or my job. If he had tried any harder he would have been fired too. Héctor has seven children."

Luis spoke faster, blurting it all out before he lost his nerve, "How did you meet Chance? Why did you marry him? Why did you hyphenate your name?"

"Meeting Robert is *not* a long story. Were it a long story, had I used my brain, I wouldn't be here. The margaritas are delicious, but, wow, what a kick. Is your tequila stronger than we have back home? Brilliant question, Judy. How would you be expected to know? Well, anyway, were you aware that Robert worked at Boeing?"

"The jet airliner company. He planned engine production."

"Him and a jillion others. Robert was a tiny cog. He sat in a little cubicle."

"He mentioned the cubicle to me. He gave me the impression it was a prison cell."

"A lot of people are worse off than he was. I worked there six months in the mailroom. I married Robert and quit Boeing soon thereafter because he wanted me to be a little hausfrau. I hated the job, but the money was good. We separated and I tried to get back in."

She made an undulating motion with her margarita. Foam lapped over the rim.

"Oops. Aerospace work is like a roller coaster is what I was demonstrating, slob that I am. They'd lost airline contracts and were laying off, not hiring. Where was I? Okay, I worked in the mailroom in Robert's department. I'd deliver twice a day. Printouts, memos, directives, flow charts. You can't comprehend the paperwork, Luis. They say the paperwork necessary to build each airplane would overload it and it'd be too heavy to lift off the ground."

"And you met Chance delivering his mail?" Luis said, coaxing the story along.

"Yeah. Lucky me. As they say, one thing led to another."

Héctor stormed into the room just then and sat at their table. His face was the color of bougainvillea. Luis knew better than to ask what was wrong. Only Héctor could safely defuse one of his own florid rages.

"What's wrong, Inspector?" Judy asked. "There's steam coming out of your ears."

"What's wrong?" Héctor said through clenched teeth. "What's wrong? The cops in this town are petty, shit-ass crooks is what is wrong."

"The one-way streets?" Luis said.

"Good guess, Luis. That is why you're such a splendid detective."

Luis knew better than to reply.

"One-way streets?" Judy said.

"They change the direction of the signs and write traffic tickets on gringos and innocent Mexicans. This cop tries to write me a ticket. *Me.* Five North American dollars or fifteen new pesos. Pay him on the spot."

"Didn't they know who you were?"

"New cop. He was told to get everybody. I identified myself. He went and got his sergeant. No problem, but I sat there thirty minutes starving to death because this dumbass baby cop doesn't know how to steal correctly."

Thirty minutes longer would have been great, Luis thought. Judy's story was developing.

"You never ever did a sign switcheroo?" Judy asked skeptically.

"Héctor is so angry because he devised the system in Playa del Carmen," Luis said. "He is the father of the scheme."

"If you cannot perform with consummate professionalism, you should not wear the uniform. No further comment." Héctor glanced at his watch and snapped his fingers. "We must order quickly."

Their indifferent, pear-shaped waiter materialized instantly. He distributed menus and waited obsequiously at Héctor's side until orders were given. He rushed to the kitchen and returned with chips, salsa, and fresh drinks. The absence of a check was conspicuous.

"Not that I'm complaining, but why did we have to order so quickly?" Judy said, munching a chip.

"It is five-thirty," Héctor said. "We Mexicans customarily eat our main meal at lunchtime. We have a small supper, but rarely before eight. Therefore if I eat this meal too late, I will spoil my regular supper at home and insult my wife."

Judy digested Héctor's logic in silence as their food was served. Héctor had selected grilled fish and freshly baked rolls. Judy and Luis followed Héctor's lead in kind, though not in quantity. Luis would have preferred black beans and tortillas, but he did not wish to seem a disagreeable guest. He and Judy finished dinner and nursed their drinks while Héctor demolished a second basket of rolls.

Contentedly sipping a cup of coffee, Héctor said, "On to the agenda of the Smith murder."

Luis snapped his fingers. "I had completely forgotten."

Judy giggled and tapped his shin with a sandaled toe.

"The murder has generated a tremendous uproar," Héctor said. "Major shareholders are of course *chilangos* and they are beside themselves and otherwise incredibly displeased. Gringos murdering gringos in their showcase hotel, such activity does not stimulate business growth."

"Who?" Judy asked.

"*Chilangos* is a term for Mexico City residents," Luis explained. "Much money in Mexico flows to wealthy *chilangos.* Cancún money is no exception."

"You and the inspector said that cheelongo word like you had a mouthful of doggy doo. What's the problem?"

"I have overheard North Americans speak of your Washington, D.C., inhabitants."

"Okay. Enough said. Gotcha."

"May I proceed? Thank you so much, Luis. Progress has not been dramatic thus far, but we have gathered snippets of information. The late Mikey Smith, for example." Héctor crossed himself. "I am loathe to insult the dead, but Mr. Smith was a dishonorable man. After his solemn promise to be deported, Mr. Michael Smith limped off his airplane at Dallas-Fort Worth and caught the next available flight back to Cancún. His precise subsequent movements have not been ascertained thus far. He was seen at the hotel by employees; however, he and Mr. Chance, or at least men who strongly resemble them, were seen separately. The facts are unclear, should they be facts at all."

"Fortunately for the human race, not many people could be mistaken for those two," Judy said. "Was your assistant manager buddy in on the sighting?"

Héctor shook his head, saying, "No. You can be a cruel

woman, señora. Your cruelty is no doubt a byproduct of hyphenation."

Judy smiled and squeezed a meaty wrist. "Sorry, Inspector. Cheap shot. Did the gauze clue pan out?"

"We canvassed every pharmacy in the hotel zone and those in the city within a practical distance. We underestimated the number of pharmacies and the volume of bandages and dressings they sold. Overindulging gringos are not only afflicted by sunburn and the shits. They recreate with reckless abandon at beach volleyball, jet skiing, parasailing, and tennis. Abrasions and bruises are countless."

"Nobody remembered selling a package of gauze that evening?" Luis said.

"Nobody remembers to whom they sold what. Business was brisk and frankly—do not be offended, señora—one North American looks the same as the next."

"I guess Robert is still your prime suspect then."

"We are most anxious to locate and interview him."

"Are you close to locating him, Héctor?"

"No. Bob Chance is gone. Vaporized. He is totally unseen and unheard of since the murder."

"What about the man who dirtied the ashtray, the third man in the room?" Judy asked.

"We are exploring that and all contingencies, señora," Héctor said unconvincingly.

Luis thought of Esther's commentary on Bob Chance. *Another person killed Smith for him because he could not do it himself.* And Rosa's. *The killer could be kidnapping him or protecting him. Or he might have taken Chance away to kill him.* He retained those thoughts and instead asked, "Has there been an autopsy?"

"Sensationalism has bumped Mr. Smith to the head of the line. A formal report will be days and weeks forthcoming, but I have connections. I am informed that the slug is as I deduced, a small-caliber sissy bullet fired at point-blank range."

"Approximate time of death?" Luis asked.

"Because the room was an icebox, uncertain at this point," Héctor said. "Preliminary guesses are that he could have been dead as long as twenty-four hours."

For no good reason, Luis related to Héctor the Dead Dinosaur inaugural.

"Casino gambling?" Héctor said.

"A transitional tool according to Dugdale," Luis said.

"Oil surges through his veins, Luis. Put a stop to him and his funny games."

"I'll try," Luis said.

"Try extremely hard, my friend," Héctor said. "Otherwise the boots of hell will stomp through Ho-Keh."

"I know."

Héctor grinned. "Luis, where you're sitting, he sat where you sit."

"Who?"

Héctor made a gun of his hand and stuck the barrel, a finger, in his ear. "Loverboy."

19

"I never noticed," Judith Maxwell-Chance said. "You don't have seat belts in your car."

"I never noticed either," Luis Balam said.

"Are you, you know, okay, Luis? I'm a little tipsy from the margaritas."

Luis stifled a yawn and said, "Leon Negra has barely any alcohol."

"Liar. I'm not implying I don't trust your driving, but this highway isn't lighted."

"Oncoming drivers can't see any better than we can, Judy."

"God, what does that mean?"

When Luis stopped laughing he said he didn't know what that meant.

When Judy stopped laughing, she said, "Swell. You're drunker than a skunk."

"No I'm not. My mouth is dry and a headache is coming on."

"Then you're hung over already. Well, that's a relief.

What's so urgent that we have to go up to Cancún City tonight and see your lawyer?"

"Ricky Martínez is not my lawyer," Luis said. "He is a lawyer I do detective work for."

"He's also the bozo who got you tangled up with that Dead Dinosaurs gambling creep."

"Yes. He is."

"And it's important that we see him immediately?"

"I have to remove Dugdale's gambling operation from Ho-Keh."

"And Ricky the lawyer can help?"

"He can help if he wants to help, and I will insist to him that he wants to help. He may know who Dugdale is and where he lives. Ricky can go to Dugdale and convince him to leave us alone or he can take me to him and I will convince him to leave us alone."

Judy moved her seat backward, pulled up her legs, wedging her feet up against the glove compartment, and said, "If you crash us into something, I'll be my own air bag. Might just as well visit your attorney buddy. We're at a standstill as far as Robert is concerned."

Thinking of Rita Trunkey Chance and desiring to please, Luis said, "Who knows, Ricky could possibly supply a mystery clue on Bob Chance."

"How so?"

Mystery clue. Luis knew that he was, if not drunk, certainly unsober. Eyes aimed straight through the windshield, he lifted a shoulder.

Judy lowered her feet and twisted to face Luis. "What's the matter? You're acting weird, like you were when you asked me if Robert had been married before."

Luis could not prevent himself from divulging the fact that Bob Robert Bobby Chance had been previously married. He could not prevent himself from describing his brief experience with Rita Trunkey Chance.

They traveled five kilometers in utter silence before Luis said, "I'm sorry."

"Don't be. You're sweet for telling me. Robert and his witchy mother concealed it. I could have gone for years without finding out."

"Perhaps Rita Trunkey Chance is lying," Luis said.

"Do you think she is?"

"No."

"Me neither. Robert's pushing forty. Odds are he was married. I don't remember asking him if he were married, but I must have and he must have said no and I must have taken his word for it. Robert seemed so much the confirmed bachelor. Did he tell you he had a first wife?"

"No. I am not sure he knew he was still married to her."

"Probably not. He expected her to do the divorce and it didn't bother him that he didn't see any papers. That's Robert's style of handling responsibility. Bury his head in the sand."

She started laughing as tears streamed down her cheeks. "Crazy, huh? I'm happy I'm not married and never was, and sad I'm not married and never was."

Luis touched her arm gently, then her leg, and said nothing.

"Not to come on too mercenary, but I guess I'm out in the cold on Robert's Lotto winnings. Rita's always been his wife, so I never was his wife. She's entitled and I'm out of luck. The Judith Maxwell-Chance Scholarship Fund is down the tubes. I absolutely positively have to catch him and take him home."

"What?"

"Bigamy's illegal, you know. Robert's going directly to jail, the bastard. Do not pass go, do not collect two hundred dollars."

"This Rita woman impresses me as a reasonable person. She may not object to you receiving a share of the money."

"What someone says and what happens when the papers are signed are two different things. Is your Ricky Martínez pretty sharp on American marital law?"

"Ricky is not sharp on Mexican marital law."

Judy laughed and blew her nose. "My mouth is dry and I feel a headache coming on too. Is that a market up ahead on the right?"

"It is."

Judy dug a wad of pesos out of a pocket, gave it to Luis, and said, "The last thing I need right now is a hangover. If you'll go in for a six-pack, I'll buy."

"I can pay," Luis said.

"No," she said, closing his fingers around the money. "This is your private detective retainer."

In that case, Luis said, slamming on the brakes. The market had no Leon, but their Corona was cold. Judy asked Luis for a detailed description of Rita, then asked again, requesting clarification on details such as the difference between hair and root color, estimated age (please say over fifty, Luis, please), and approximate number of pounds (or kilograms) overweight.

"Wait a sec," she said, clapping her hands. "Is she the

dairy princess? Is she the reason for the dairy princess questions?"

Luis nodded, smiling.

"I'll bet she was elected when they hauled the milk to town in horse-drawn wagons. In those big metal cans they sell in antique stores for ridiculous prices. God, scratch that! Being half looped and feeling sorry for myself is no excuse. Retract your claws, Judy. Well, let's not retract them entirely. Luis, you unloaded this middle-aged dairy princess on your attorney buddy. I didn't think you had a mean bone in your body."

"Ricky was overwhelmed by her light features. Mexican men have a weakness for the fair-skinned blonde. The *güera.* To have such a woman is—the status is beyond comprehension."

"You too, Luis?"

He looked at her. "I told you, I am not Mexican. I am Maya. And no *güera* possesses your beautiful nose."

She drank from her Corona, inverting the bottle, raising air bubbles. "We won't be barging in on them, will we? I'm not ready for that scene."

"I doubt it. I introduced them two nights ago."

"Ricky loves them and leaves them, huh?"

"He loves women for the pleasure they surrender to him. In the morning he despises them for the pleasure they surrendered to him. In the night they are queens, in the morning they are sluts."

"A swell guy. Soul brother of guys I've encountered in my own limited experience with the male of the species."

"Ricky is not a bad person."

"You don't have to defend him to me, Luis. Supposing Rita hired Ricky to represent her in a claim against Robert for the Lotto money. Would they still be together professionally if they went to bed and Ricky dumped her in the morning?"

"He can hate her, but he will be her devoted lawyer for as long as she pays him."

"Or as long as she promises him a percentage of a settlement?"

"Yes. Ricky loves incentives."

"And Rita might have a line on Robert and pass the news along to Ricky?"

"Maybe."

"And the cow maybe jumped over the moon too. But what have we got to lose?"

Luis parked in front of Ricky's apartment house, a nondescript, two-story, cement-block building in an unfashionable Cancún City neighborhood. The place was substandard, a construction of sand and graft.

"Are you coming?" he asked.

"Nope. Better I stay in the background, I think. Rita could be in there doing lawyer things with him if they aren't doing the other."

Ricky answered the door in his bathrobe. The room was dark and his hair was mussed. "Luis. We should in the very near future develop the communications system for appointments I alluded to at my office."

"I interrupted you? I'm sorry."

"You did not interrupt anything. It is late."

"Late? It's eight o'clock, Ricky. Normally you're splashing yourself with cologne and clipping your nose hairs, readying for a night at the discos."

"Pardon me for not being amused, Luis. I have been ill.

I've had a severe touch of a virus. I wasn't in the office yesterday or today."

"I am sorry," Luis said, walking in. "May I come in for a minute? I will be as brief as I can."

"By all means," Ricky said caustically. "My home is your home."

Ricky's home consisted of a living room, bedroom, minuscule kitchen, and a bathroom with unreliable and foul-smelling plumbing. It was palatial to Luis. It was also pathetic. Luis would not have lived in such a dwelling if you made a refugee of him and brought him in at gunpoint.

Ricky devoured the North American men's magazines that encouraged his urbane notion of himself. They published centerfolds of women with their legs spread and articles on improvement of seduction techniques.

Ricky obeyed bachelor pad decorating recommendations he could not afford. The secondhand chrome and glass tables were, respectively, rusty and clouded. The mirror screwed into the ceiling above his bed was precarious; Ricky was constantly shaking plaster dust from his sheets. Hanging on the living room walls were an odd mix of framed prints. Flowers, Renaissance paintings, and seascapes. Of late, his magazines advised sensitivity.

Glad to be in the dark. Luis sat uninvited on an armless vinyl couch. "You are representing Mrs. Chance?"

"I am. Yes I am. A wronged lady who deserves restitution."

"Where is she now?"

"Why ask me? I put her up in a hotel near my office. I am not her companion."

"Not even that evening?"

"That evening. Of course," Ricky said with a smile in his voice. "I have influenza. I've lost most worldly contact for the past thirty-six hours."

"You haven't heard that Mikey Smith was murdered?"

"Oh, yes, Luis, I am cognizant of the Smeeth homicide. A horrible, brutal thing. I haven't lost all worldly contact. I am attuned to events. Have the police captured your client Bob Chance yet?"

"No."

"And this was the man you referred me to in the civil matter. Fortunately I did not follow up. He's dangerous, Luis. He could have killed me too."

"You're a lawyer, Ricky. You shouldn't try and convict a man before his trial."

"My worldly contacts inform me that you again committed psychological terror at Ho-Keh, Luis. First Vance's workmen, then a customer. But Ho-Keh and Vance are the purposes of your visit, I presume."

"You presume right. What customer?"

"The man taking a leak in the jungle. Your stories of snakes. Vance says the man has been unable to pee since. His subconscious mind links urination and snakes. Vance says our reputation could suffer and that we could be sued."

"Ricky, are you attacking me in advance to deflect my attack?"

"That could be one interpretation," Ricky said after a pause.

"How could you do it to us?" Luis said. "Do you realize what the police and the army will do? And don't say Dugdale's gambling speakeasy can be kept secret."

"I won't, Luis. I won't. My sole defense is that Vance

assured me the gambling phase is temporary, until the cultural props come in from Brazil."

"A transitioning tool."

"Yes. You understand."

"I understand too well. The transitioning has to end. Now."

"Vance is doing his utmost—"

"Now, Ricky. And who is Dugdale, by the way? Where is Dugdale?"

"Luis, please don't shout. The walls are made of paper."

"Ricky, you told me in your office that Dugdale was seeking 'further capitalization' for expansion. Who is he begging money from? And why? To buy television sets to bribe Maya men with sick wives?"

"I don't know, Luis. Vance is occasionally vague."

"Where can I locate him?"

"I honestly do not know, Luis. Vance comes to my office. He makes appointments. He says that future planning for Dead Dinosaurs keeps him on the move and a fixed base of operations is not practical at this point in time."

"So you could not locate him if you had to?"

"Not precisely."

"Not *precisely?*"

"In a certain context I am able to contact him, since he contacts me frequently."

"Ricky, we've been friends for a long time. Please stop the lawyer talk. You must have some idea how I can contact Dugdale."

"I swear to the Virgin of Guadalupe I do not," Ricky cried.

"I have to see him."

"You'll hurt him," Ricky said.

Luis did not reply.

"Luis, I swear. Next time Vance and I meet, I will persuade him to eliminate Ho-Keh from the Dead Dinosaurs Parks circuit."

"What is Dugdale, Ricky? He was the Desert Fox. What is his alter ego today?"

"Please, Luis."

"What do you know about the Punta Paraiso condominiums?"

"That gringos wealthier than God live in them."

"Does Dugdale speak of them?"

"I don't recall. He may have."

"The Punta Paraiso builder brought Cuban gambling machines in from Veracruz and put them in the model units to attract buyers."

"That is news to me, Luis."

"A month ago the slot machines and gaming tables were stolen."

"Oh, Luis, first Vance is a gambling gangster. Now he is a burglar. May I return to bed? My influenza is relapsing."

Luis got up and felt his way to the door. "Go to bed, Ricky, and recover so you can do the right thing."

"I will, Luis. I promise."

Luis walked out knowing that one portion of Ricky's promise would be kept. He would return to bed. The smell of cigarette smoke and perfume was too dense to be lingering from the night before last.

20

"Well?" Judy said.

"Nothing," Luis said.

"On locating Robert or your Dugdale creep, neither one?"

"No."

"Was the dairy princess with him?"

"I did not see her in the apartment," Luis answered truthfully. "He was ill."

"Will Ricky use his influence to boot Dugdale out of your village?"

"He promised he would try."

"You sound unconvinced, Luis. You should have leaned on him a little. Not hitting him or anything, but when you're upset you get moody, and you can really be intimidating, you know."

"Ricky is my friend."

"I've got a creative idea to contribute. For a change. What kind of a huge humongous hassle is it to phone long-distance from Cancún?"

"To Seattle?"

"Yeah. Robert's mother. Maybe he's contacted her."

"The cheapest method is to call collect. Your telephone companies charge less than ours. Ours has branches in the bus station and airport and in Cancún City. You can use pay phones too."

"I don't mean cheap. I mean fast and reliable."

"For fast and reliable, add luck and prayer to the fee."

"Great."

"The big hotels are the best. Their switchboards can get you right through, fast and reliable, but they charge a fortune for the service. Tourists see the surcharge added to their bill when they check out and they faint."

"Money is no object if you aren't paying. Do you still have the spare key to Robert's room?"

"I do, and I like your creative idea," Luis said, pulling the trunk release and getting out. He put on his Tránsito shirt and name tag.

"You carry your protective coloration with you, huh?"

"I never know when I will need it. You can take the clipboard."

Judy buttoned a shirt button Luis had missed. He kissed her. She kissed him back, pushed off, and stepped into the car, saying, "I almost said, stop it, I'm a married woman, but I'm probably not."

"Then don't say stop it," Luis said, getting in.

Judy took his hands from her and guided them to the steering wheel. "You're distracting, Balam. You really are. Drive. We have a creative idea to explore before we forget what the idea was."

In the subarctic InterPresidential lobby, Judy shivered and said, "Oops. I just thought of something. It didn't occur to me. The room may already be occupied by a new guest."

"No. No matter how loudly they beg to rent their two-hundred-dollars-per-night room, Héctor won't release the crime scene so quickly."

"I just thought of something else," she said at the elevator. "How do we pay for this? They have to be on computers. We can't call and say charge it to Robert Chance. I still have a credit card, but he probably canceled it. Besides, everything considered, he's probably no longer registered in their system."

"Two choices. I bribe the desk clerk or I intimidate him."

"I'm sorry I said you intimidate people, Luis," Judy said as they entered the room. "You don't have to prove anything to me."

"Saving money is always sensible," Luis said, picking up the phone.

Judy wrote Mrs. Thelma Chance's telephone number on a piece of hotel stationery and looked around. "The same. And, dammit, there's the ashtray. They didn't even take it in for fingerprints."

Luis identified himself in loud, gruff, profane Spanish as Inspector Salgado conducting official police business. The clerk took the number and said yes sir, yes sir, one moment.

Luis handed her the receiver. "Jesus, it's already ringing. Mom? Mom, it's Judy."

Judy whispered to Luis, "The old witch hates me calling her Mom. She was always Mrs. Chance to me. Mom, it's Judy. I'm in Cancún. Hi."

Luis went to the refrigerator. The gods had provided two cold cans of refreshment, although they were a brand of North American light beer. He popped the tops and gave one to Judy, who smiled and winked, having fun.

"Where? A Cancún hotel. No, I'm not with somebody, not how you're saying it. Has Robert reached you?

"Oh, it's for you to know and me to find out. Swell, Mom. Your secret's out on Rita Trunkey, by the way.

"Uh huh, uh huh, the dairy princess. Naughty, naughty of you, Mom, to conceal her and her undivorce from me.

"Yes, Robert is a big boy. So why'd you send two wives down here to the big boy? To stir things up and avoid responsibility? Like son, like mother.

"Don't hang up, Mom. The money, remember the money. We can cooperate like adults, can't we?

"Mikey Smith. Uh huh. Wasn't that terrible. How'd you know? Did Robert—?

"Oh God, detectives? The Seattle Police Department? Doing an assist for the— Mom, don't say 'spick.' It's not a nice word. The Mexican police asked the Seattle police to interview you. No, I'm sure they didn't treat you like a common criminal.

"No, Mom, I'm not calling you a liar. They were probably just frustrated because you couldn't help them find Robert and you thought they had an attitude.

"But you have heard? When?

"Yesterday. Uh huh. Not ten minutes after the cops left. So you weren't lying to them but don't you think you should—

"Uh huh, they can go to hell for treating you like a common criminal. What did Robert—he called twice?

"You wouldn't accept the charges? Jesus, Mom. He phoned again in ten minutes. He said he was spending his last twenty bucks on the call. C'mon.

"He was serious? You're positive? Well, you know Robert better than I. He blew every penny, huh? Not every penny? He promised you he'd pay you back. When?

"Mom, stop crying. The money's not all gone, okay. Just this year's. He gets the same amount for the next nineteen. Remember? Cheer up. What did he—

"Do I think he killed Mikey? Of course not.

"You don't think he'd have the backbone either. Well, that isn't exactly how I'd put it. It would be a moral thing with him too. You know that. We're pretty certain Robert was there when Smith was killed. Him and a mystery man. Did he tell you what happened?

"Mom, didn't you even ask him? Didn't the subject of Mikey Smith come up?

"He was too busy begging you to send him money? And you wouldn't. How come I'm not surprised? Did he say where he'd be if you changed your mind?

"He'd call you, don't call him. Good thinking for a fugitive. Did he say anything?

"Mom, I'm not yelling. Where was he? At a big-deal ruin where they had a big-deal event coming up soon. Uh huh. He'd be coming and going. What else?

"Mom, I'm not interrogating you. And you don't have to yell. Was Robert with anybody?

"He had a one-track mind set on money. Mom, he's your son. He's desperate—

"Who skipped out, who had no intention of even paying back the nineteen dollars you paid but couldn't afford to replace Mr. Jenson's muffler. Mom, have you been drinking?

"What's all my fault?

"You've got your nerve.

"Well, kiss my ass too, Thelma."

Judy held the dead receiver and said to Luis, "You know that's the first time I ever had the nerve to call her Thelma."

21

"Luis, you aren't feeding me drinks and beer to get me drunk and seduce me, are you?"

Luis smiled.

"Sleeping with a client, isn't that a conflict of interest or unethical or something?"

"No," Luis said. "I'm a detective, not a doctor."

"Well, we aren't going to, bub. Not here. I don't care whether they changed the linen or not, this is Robert's bed and there was a dead man laid out on it, need I remind you. C'mon, sit up."

Luis sat up, encouraged that *not here* wasn't a synonym for *no.* Not in English, not in Spanish, not in Maya.

"I'm only laying down for a minute. I'm woozy and it's your fault and Thelma's. You gave me this beer and Thelma drove me to chugging it. I'm not used to drinking. Jesus, the room's spinning. The room or the bed, I'm not sure which."

"Hang a foot out to touch the floor."

Judy did what he said. "Hey, the spinning stopped. Is this the wisdom of an experienced drinker?"

"Ancient Maya wisdom," Luis said. "Inscribed on temples."

"I've got to be crocked. I can't tell if you're kidding me. Too bad putting the brakes on the room can't help my other problem."

"What problem?"

"Get me out of this joint into some fresh air or I'm gonna lose my dinner."

Luis's speedometer needle tickled one hundred kilometers per hour. Windows down, the gale did not sober them up, but it kept them awake.

"Is Chance out of money?"

"Thelma was confused and she was confusing me. Yes, he had a reserve, no, he was dead broke. Yes, he would repay a loan, no, she wouldn't have to wait for next year's Lotto check. Who knows? It wouldn't be the first time he lied to his mother."

"Chance is with your third-party cigarette smoker?"

"That's my hunch. Thelma's big-deal ruin with the big-deal event, what could Robert be talking about?"

"There are important ruins within a day's drive of us. Large ruins like Chichén Itzá and Uxmal put on sound and light shows for the tourists at night. Music blasts from speakers all over the place and colored lights flash."

"Historically accurate?"

"No. They're soap operas. Love and war and virgins offered to the rain god. The tourists love them."

"Don't be an old poop. They sound like fun. Are they regularly scheduled?"

"Every evening in high season. A show in Spanish and a show in English."

"Not qualifying as a big-deal event then," Judy said. "Not how Thelma impressed me this function was, not that special."

"What day is it?"

"Lemme think. March 17. Get me home soon, Jeeves, or the day will shortly be the eighteenth and I'll turn into a pumpkin."

Luis looked at her.

"Your English is super, but it ain't that super. Is a holiday coming up?"

"A holiday and the vernal equinox."

"The first day of spring."

"Yes. The temple of Kukulcán at Chichén Itzá is a pyramid. The Castle. *El Castillo.* Each of its four sides has ninety-one steps. Add the platform on top and you have three hundred sixty-five. Kukulcán was an astronomical structure. The sun dictated how it was built.

"On March 21 and 22 and at the fall equinox, September 21 and 22, the sun darkens the north face except for a jagged strip of sunlight on the side of the steps. You see a glowing snake slithering down the temple steps to the base, a serpent's head. Kukulcán means feathered serpent in Yucatec Maya."

"Wow!"

"Thousands of visitors come to Chichén Itzá for the equinox. You want to be there, you want to stay at a Chichén Itzá hotel, you have to make reservations months in advance.

"The spring equinox is much busier than the fall equinox. March 21 is Benito Juárez's birthday. It is an important national holiday."

"I've heard of him. Once upon a time he was a famous general or president?"

"Yes. In the last century. Benito Juárez is Mexico's only Indian president. He was pure-blooded Zapotec from Héctor's home state, Oaxaca. Juárez was a champion of the people and much beloved. Many Mexicans celebrate his birthday. They go places for the holiday."

"Places like Chichén Itzá. Can we go, Luis? This might be our best shot."

"We can go. Chichén Itzá is three hours out of Cancún by Beetle, two hours by tour bus. I am an amateur maniac on the road. Tour bus drivers are professional maniacs."

When they arrived at Akumal, Judy was asleep, resting against Luis's shoulder. He awakened her by tracing a finger along her impressive nose. In her room, they nestled on her bed, fully clothed but for their sandals.

"Luis, you really want me just for the sake of wanting me?"

"Yes, Judy."

"God, that's sweet. No man ever wanted me to just, you know, want me. There was always an ulterior motive."

Chance's ulterior motive? Luis dared not ask for fear of breaking the spell. Before he could congratulate himself on his judgment, Judy was snoring.

Luis sighed and rolled back onto his pillow, hands behind his head, staring at the ceiling, considering his next move. He could do the despicable and take advantage of a comatose woman. Or he could lie quietly beside her and also sleep.

As it was, he could do neither. He could not paw her and peel off her clothes. He would hate himself for the remainder of his days. Nor could he sleep on this soft bed. It was spinning, it or the room. Luis hung out a foot and touched the floor. His cure was flawed; the room (or the bed) spun in the opposite direction.

Luis curled up on the floor. It was tile, hard and cold and exceedingly uncomfortable. The room did not spin at these icy, torturous depths, however. Eventually he slept.

In the morning. Was it morning? Light in the room. Water running. A storm. This was the dry season, but it rained in the dry season too. The dry season was drier than the rainy season, which was wetter than the dry season. Was he actually out-of-doors? Then the rain began dripping on him.

Stiff and disoriented, Luis groaned and rotated, looking up for the sky or a roof leak. Judy was standing over him, wrapped in a towel, giggling, wringing her hair out on him. "Your turn. The water's fine."

Luis showered, diverting half the water into his vile, parched mouth in a vain effort to quench his thirst. After the warm shower, he took a cold one. He felt barely improved, though encouraged that he might survive. He sloshed and spit a mouthful of Judy's toothpaste, wrapped himself into a towel, and went out to find Judy in bed, her towel prominently draped on a corner of the headboard.

Luis climbed into bed with her. She said, "If you're wondering what's going on, I wouldn't last night because I had to be sure it wasn't the booze and beer."

"It isn't?"

"Come here."

Afterward, she said, "No man's ever said I was pretty.

They never cared enough about getting me into the sack to use a line on me. Don't look at me like that, Luis. My experience is limited, okay, but I am a married woman, sort of. Hardly anyone's ever wanted to go to bed with me is what I'm saying."

"You are pretty. Me saying you are, is that the reason you are welcoming me in your bed?"

"One of the reasons. I like you a lot. I'm lonely. I'm horny. I'm thousands of miles from home. Et cetera."

Luis smiled but didn't reply.

"It's tough for you to say you like me too, huh?"

"I am Maya, but some Mexicanness is inside me."

"Machismo?"

Luis nodded. "We can't express our feelings and we expect perfection and purity in the women we care for."

"Well, Mexico doesn't have a patent on it, believe me. 'Women we care for.' I think you expressed your feelings whether you realize it or not. How about we go for a run?"

Luis was up on an elbow. He closed his eyes and collapsed onto his pillow. "A run?"

"Exercise oxygenates the brain cells we didn't kill last night."

Luis laid a hand on her thigh. "Weren't we just oxygenating?"

Judy removed the hand. "C'mon."

On the beach, padding along, Luis wondered how he could oxygenate when he could not breathe. Judy said, "How do you know so much?"

"About what?"

"Everything. The vernal equinox thing, for instance. And you seem to understand what oxygenating means, and I'm not certain I do."

Partly speaking, partly gasping, Luis told of his 1970s Cancún self-education.

"You made a textbook out of an old World Almanac and memorized it?"

"Not entirely. Portions."

"Okay, what's the capital of the state of Washington?"

"I don't know."

"What's the sales tax rate in the state of Washington?"

"As of July 1, 1973, four-point-five percent."

"Jesus."

"Why did you marry Chance?"

"He asked me. I figured that he was my one chance at marriage. Pun intended."

"Did you love him?"

"I usually liked him. Robert's likable, as in a cocker spaniel."

"Not lovable?"

"That's pushing it."

"Why—did—you—hyphenate?"

"Self-loathing. Hating myself for being so desperate as to settle for a man simply because he asked me. By retaining my maiden name I was giving me back to me."

Luis staggered to a halt and bent over, hands on knees. "Stop. Can we go birdwatching instead? I would very much love to birdwatch now."

"Too late in the day. Best time's in the morning. We stayed in bed too long being naughty. I have a creative idea, thanks to oxygenation."

"Tell me," Luis said, still doubled over, gulping for air. Tell me anything that will keep my mind off my churning stomach, he thought.

Judy sat on the sand, stretching, right fingers to left

toes, left fingers to right toes. "Dugdale's Jeep, you know, that he brought Ricky Martínez to your shop in when you met him?"

Luis was upright, hands on hips. "Yes."

"You said Dugdale rented it somewhere in Cancún, didn't you?"

"Yes."

"It was a super-duper deluxe model with air-conditioning and everything, right?"

"Yes."

"Well, how many rental outfits would have a rig like that available?"

Luis breathed deeply and saw fewer stars than a moment ago. He might survive oxygenating, just maybe. "Not many. Not many at all."

22

Cancún car rental agencies were scattered in the city and at malls and hotels on the island. They were also clustered at the airport, in the terminal and nearby. In the unlikely event a tourist could not find a selection of rental cars without assistance, the hordes of time-share hustlers could also steer him to their favorite agency.

On a street corner, Luis accosted a young Mexican man who was closely following a group of visitors, smiling and chattering and offering the best deals in Cancún. The visitors were ignoring him, so Luis knew they had been in Cancún for at least a day, veterans of no less than twenty such encounters. The hustler was visibly alarmed by the Indian blocking his path. His expression indicated his next word could be *policía.*

Luis stuffed a ten-peso note in the shirt pocket to which a CHARLIE nameplate was pinned, and said, "Carlos, I'm buying five seconds of your time. Where should I look for a fully equipped rental Jeep?"

Charlie/Carlos was relieved that he was being neither panhandled nor mugged, and recommended the airport.

Luis and Judy began there, had no luck inside the terminal, but got lucky at their fourth stop outside, an agency two blocks from the terminal on a pocked dirt road. It consisted of a chain-link fenced lot and a one-room office. In the lot stood a mix of Beetles, Nissan Tsurus, and utility vehicles—Jeeps and Geo Trackers. In the office was a mestizo clerk as short as Luis and twice as round.

"Candy-apple red, chromium wheels, air-conditioning, like new. Of course I remember the unit," cried the clerk. "That Jeep is the flagship of our fleet. I beg you, where is it?"

"I don't know," Luis said. "Show me your rental papers. Maybe I can recover it for you."

The clerk squinted at him. "Maybe? You said you were a detective. Didn't the manager hire you?"

"Your boss is not my client. I'm hired to find the man who rented the Jeep. I locate the man, I'll locate your Jeep."

The clerk wore a Stetson and a string tie. The tie was held together by a silver cattle head. A wishful Texan, Luis thought pityingly.

"I am not authorized to release that information."

Luis shrugged and looked at Judy, then at the wall clock. "All right, we'll go. You can recover your own Jeep. Unless the renter becomes bored and drives it into the Caribbean for fun. Or strips it and sells the parts. Time passes and anything could happen."

"Like having a couple of drinks and then taking bets on how far out in the water they can go before it stalls," Judy said, nodding.

The clerk raised a hand. "No. Please wait. I will lose my job unless the vehicle is recovered soon and undamaged. I committed a terrible error when I rented the unit out. I accepted cash for a deposit instead of a credit card."

"Why is money so awful?" Judy asked. "Nothing spends like cash."

The clerk sighed. "Cash has no identifying numbers. Cash cannot be spent beyond the limit in hand. I can max out a customer's credit card to make good his obligation. That and the insurance will customarily cover our loss."

"Why did you accept cash?" Luis asked.

"I very seldom do," the clerk said, perusing a filing cabinet. "This customer was newly arrived. His credit cards were in his luggage, which had been delayed in Houston. He seemed sincere and convincing, so I relented and against my better judgment accepted dollars."

Some of that better judgment went into your pocket for relenting, Luis thought. "But you did check identification and confirm a local address?"

The clerk withdrew a manila folder and rolled his eyes, suffering a fool. "Naturally."

"Good," Luis said. "We'll be sure to mention you to Mr. Dugdale when we see him."

The clerk opened the file. "Dugdale? Who is Dugdale? Mr. Martínez signed for the vehicle and his associate paid the cash."

Luis could not summon a response.

"Ricardo Martínez Rodríguez, Cancún City attorney. Mr. Martínez is the man's attorney and senior business adviser. He is legitimate, isn't he? So I thought. I attempted to contact him. He has an address, but he is never in. He has no telephone. This attorney, his name is not familiar to me. What kind of lawyer has no telephone and has an office above a bar?"

"Mr. Martínez is among the finest lawyers in Cancún, if not in all of Yucatán," Luis said.

"Splendid," the clerk said morosely. "Just bring home the unit, please, or your lawyer or some other lawyer can defend my manager on a murder charge."

"So much for creative ideas," Judy said as they turned off Highway 307 at Punta Paraiso.

"You had a good idea," Luis said. "Dugdale just had a better idea. Perhaps Ricky will listen to me the next time we have a conversation about the cultural theme park impresario."

"You can ask him yourself tonight, can't you?"

Luis just remembered that he could. Tonight was Dead Dinosaurs' second night. "Would you like to come?"

"Uh huh. With you, on a date, mixing pleasure and business?"

"Yes."

"What should I wear?"

"We can return to your room and you can try on different clothing."

"I traveled light, remember?"

"You can still model for me."

"Lecher."

The half kilometer from highway to beach property was paved, a rarity. Usually the roads to beach property were potholed limestone, dusty or muddy, depending on the season.

A low brick wall and a tall wrought-iron fence centered by a guard shack and gate protected Punta Paraiso from ordinary humanity, while allowing a partial view. No visitor need come calling who was not suitably envious. The architecture was a sprawl of asymmetrical townhouses—red tile roofs, gingerbread stucco, and deeply polished wooden shutters and doors. Every unit was beachfront, of course.

"My oh my," Judy said.

"*Punta* means 'point' in Spanish and *paraiso* means 'paradise,' " Luis said. "The coastline juts out a bit for the point. As for the paradise, that's up to the individual."

"I'd take it. Wouldn't you?"

"I've never thought of whether or not I would. It's too impossible. Unless you're wealthy, like a—"

"Go ahead and finish. I know what you were going to say. Like a Lotto winner."

"Like a Lotto winner," Luis said.

"Unless you're a retard who blows your winnings."

The gate was of railway crossing design, a solid timber raising and lowering on a concrete and steel base. Luis gauged the beam as quite adequate to stop a Volkswagen. The guard showed no inclination to raise it. He was muscular and unsmiling, dressed in crisp khaki. He looked to Luis like a Boy Scout with a mean streak.

"They aren't hiring," he told Luis. "They filled the janitor job."

"I'm not applying. I'm a detective. I want to see the manager about some stolen property."

"What stolen property?"

"Property stolen from him, not you. It's his business, not yours. Call him."

The guard went into his shack, taking his time, salvaging his manhood. Judy said, "You've got a chip on your shoulder the size of that crossbar. What's the matter, Luis?"

"He's the kind who doesn't respect anyone he isn't

afraid of. He was ready to spit in my face, but he didn't know if I could have him fired. How would you react if he told you the maid job was filled?"

"Okay, okay. I just asked."

The guard replaced his telephone receiver deliberately. Mouth tight and eyes elsewhere, he lifted the gate, and waved Luis through, raising three fingers and pointing to the left. They drove on brick as smooth as pavement, past rainbow landscaping, a tennis court, a putting green, and a swimming pool.

Luis counted condominiums and people. Roughly fifteen units and no inhabitants in sight. He surveyed the driveways. Mercury Grand Marquis, Chevrolet Suburban, Chrysler LeBaron—favorite luxury vehicles in Yucatán, each new and costing in excess of his lifetime income. But there was only one for every three condominiums. Either everybody was off having picnics on their yachts or sales were slow. At the end of the complex was a satellite dish and a string of cabins that Luis assumed to be the servants' quarters.

Number Three was the third unit from the far end. A light-skinned Mexican in tan pleated slacks and a red pullover stood at Three's doorway, arms folded. He had European features and blonde streaks in a thick, blow-dried head of hair. He looked to Luis like the North Americans who came to Cancún primarily to golf.

"That's a fifty-dollar haircut in Seattle and I'll lay you money the sun streaks came out of a bottle," Judy said.

The manager ignored Judy and shook Luis's hand, a salesman's distasteful obligation, neither offering nor requesting a name. "I don't normally receive visitors without an appointment. Paco said you were in possession of stolen property belonging to me."

Judy was staring at the manager and Luis didn't like it. He had the sleepy good looks of a crooner or a gigolo, but the demeanor of a dead fish. Maybe he saved his smiles and personality for serious real estate prospects. Luis looked around and said, "A scenic, luxurious place you have. And deserted."

"The subject is stolen property?" the manager said. "Our security is excellent. Our owners haven't complained of items missing. What property?"

"Yes, Paco is a tough guy. No doubt he does an outstanding security job," Luis said. "There are no 'for sale' signs. Are your owners sailing or on a shopping expedition to Cancún?"

"We don't have 'for sale' signs," he said, as if Luis should have known better. "Our clients view the available homes on an appointment basis."

"Business *is* bad," Luis said. "Sorry."

"Recessions are out of my control. The stolen property?"

"Which is the model unit?"

"Number Three. This one. As I said, I don't normally receive—"

"Slot machines," Luis said. "A roulette wheel. A card table."

"Come inside."

Luis and Judy accepted the less-than-gracious invitation and followed him into Three. The living room alone was twice the area of Black Coral. Full width, floor to ceiling windows faced white sand, blue sky, and bluer water. They stood on shag carpeting centered on a floor of gleaming marble. Walnut and brass ceiling fans lazed, but an unseen and unheard air conditioner was doing the real work. The furniture complemented the hacienda exterior. Of heavy wood and geometrically patterned cloth, it was somebody's idea of Aztec modified by Hernán Cortés's interior decorator. Where was the architect from? Luis wondered. Mexico City? Los Angeles?

Judy was admiring the wall art: Indians at war and at ceremony and in solitary contemplation.

"Original oils and signed prints," said the manager. "We're flexible in terms of including the art and furnishings in the purchase price."

"I love the horses," Judy said. "They're beautiful."

Every Indian nation in the hemisphere must be represented, Luis thought. Except the Maya. He said, "The Spaniards brought horses. We didn't have horses."

"False advertising," Judy said to the manager.

"Do you have those things?" he snapped at Luis.

"I can have those things for you."

"The price?"

"Vance Dugdale."

The manager sat in a chair and smiled. "Pardon me for not fainting from shock."

He didn't invite Luis and Judy to take seats. Luis preferred to stand anyway, but couldn't leave a snub as is. He took Judy's hand and they sat on a half-kiloton sofa across from the manager. A massive wood and glass coffee table separated them. Overlapped on it were glossy magazines. They looked earnest and literate, specializing in Judy's -ologies. There were monuments on the covers, not celebrities.

"Dugdale stole your things."

"You confirm my suspicions. Recover the gambling equipment and I'll pay you a reward. No questions asked. The gambling motif was great fun for the recreation room. Unique and exciting. Eventually this unit will sell, but it would have sold already if the items had not disappeared. Prospects were drawn to that room and we were more than willing to include everything at no extra charge. The equipment was old and virtually irreplaceable. The government frowns on the importation of gambling paraphernalia."

"Very generous of you, boss. Unfortunately, Dugdale is elusive. What can you tell us about him?"

"Nothing significant. He worked as a commissioned salesman for me for two months. No sales. His listed address was in Cancún City. We had disagreements and I fired him. After the things vanished I went to the address. It was a fake. It was the police station."

"Dugdale has a sense of humor. Any other information on him?"

"Virtually none. Salesmen come and go. They walk in, you give them a tryout. On big-ticket sales, you need a gringo to sell to a gringo. They don't trust us Mexicans or they don't think we're competent to consummate a large deal. You have to have a Dugdale or two around to counteract the prejudice."

"Why did you fire him?"

"I couldn't pin it down to a single reason. Aside from no sales, I simply didn't trust the man. My mistrust apparently was justified. My judgment in hiring him was bad. The man had no class. His style is the interval ownership condo, not luxury full-time housing."

Interval ownership, Luis thought; a Cancún euphemism for time-share. The manager had an "interval ownership" background too.

"You went looking for him when?"

"Two days after I fired him, the rec room was cleaned out. I assume he had a key made."

"How did he get by Paco?"

"Paco claims he never returned, but every man has his price."

"What's in your recreation room now?"

The manager led them along a wide hallway. Judy paused to ogle a bathroom bigger than Luis's house and a hot tub that could accommodate Héctor's entire family. The recreation room was bigger than the bathroom and Luis's house combined. A Tiffany lamp hung above a pool table that outweighed his Beetle. Also in the room was a shuffleboard court, a pinball machine, and Pac-Man. Behind the wet bar were neon beer signs: Miller Lite, Budweiser, Corona.

"A generic rec room," the manager said sadly. "The rich Anglos had similar furnishings in theirs two homes ago. We had to improvise quickly. We are not impressing anybody."

"A shame. Anything else missing besides the gambling stuff?" Luis asked.

"Only a TV set."

Luis and Judy looked at each other. "Please describe the television."

"A twenty-five-inch Panasonic, as I recall. Black cabinet."

"Can you provide us a serial number?"

"Yes. Come to my office."

On the way out, the manager paused in the living room

and removed one of the magazines on the coffee table. "Good reading. I don't suppose Dugdale once touched them, all the hours he spent showing this unit."

"No class," Luis said.

"None," said the manager. "An article in this issue is especially fascinating. Did you know that sixty-five million years ago, a comet struck the Yucatán and—"

23

Luis dropped Judy at Akumal. There would be no modeling. He had duties. She had a siesta to take; when in Rome, she said. She kissed him almost long enough to postpone obligations and local customs.

Luis went to Black Coral, rehearsing en route excuses to feed his babies. They were of an age when they accepted their father, an adult unmarried male, now and then fluttering off and alighting in other than the family nest. They presumably would accept the nest of Judith Maxwell-Chance, whom they liked and approved of although she was North American. What they would not accept was their father failing to inform them in advance of his fluttering. Esther and Rosa would be angry and worried.

Luis pulled into Black Coral, aware that his lies would be inadequate. But his babies were neither angry nor worried. They were not there. Black Coral was as the sign painted on the tire across the front tent flap proclaimed: closed/*cerrado.*

Luis, angry and worried, went to Ho-Keh, punishing the VW on the access road. Esther and Rosa were home, glum and red-eyed, but not because of their father's misdeeds. Wordlessly, they took him, one by each hand, to Francisco Ek's home.

Luis felt queasy. He knew before they entered what awaited them. Francisco's home was illuminated by four candles on tall candlesticks. They were stationed in the center of the room, corners of light to a table within. On the table was a human form wrapped in sheets. A lidless coffin lined with silken cloth stood on a lower table in front of María's body.

Friends and neighbors came and went, paying their respects to the Ek family. Francisco stood stoically against a wall with his two sons, receiving condolences. Luis noticed the Panasonic television set facing an adjacent corner. As if Luis were not sufficiently guilty for tending to selfish physical needs when he should have been home, he topped his self-hatred with the thought that if the candles were a little brighter and if he could sidle a little closer, he might be able to read the serial number on the TV's placard.

Luis loved María Ek like a sister. What was he doing to himself and her memory? What were the Chances and Dugdale, the promise of Judy's love, and pie-in-the-sky money from lottery winnings and dead dinosaurs doing to him?

Luis turned around before his babies or Francisco could see him and dried his eyes on his shirttail. He felt a gentle elbow on his arm. Francisco. Luis followed him outside.

Francisco led the way to the cenote. To the palapa. To slot machines and gaming tables protected by plastic trash bags. To cigarette butts and plastic cups and beer cans and a miscellany of other litter. To a Dead Dinosaurs Park that was not cultural or scenic or educational. Or clean.

"I'm sorry," Luis said. "Sorry about María. Very sorry."

Francisco went to Dugdale's ice chest and removed two beers. "The last. A miracle. These were destined for us."

Luis could not disagree with fate and destiny. He thought for an instant that the fictitious spirits with whom he had abused Fat and Ugly did indeed exist. They had claimed María Ek as payment for this sacrilege. Ancient curses equated to fate and destiny; somebody inevitably paid for despoiling the cenote. He brushed away the thought, popped the top of his beer, and said, "When?"

"Yesterday afternoon. The boys were with me in the field. We came home and discovered her in her hammock. The television was on. Her face was serene. As far as I can determine, she felt no pain and was watching a soap opera she enjoyed."

Luis read nothing in Francisco's Oriental eyes. He was not through grieving; no good man could be, and Francisco was a good man. Tears, keening, whatever his emotions, Francisco Ek's mask would not crack in the company of any person, particularly Luis Balam.

"Hadn't the doctor told you that a tick or a parasite caused her illness?" Luis said.

"Yes. The same doctor examined her body yesterday and told me that a tick or a parasite had killed her."

"Are you willing to accept his opinion?"

Francisco sipped his beer and measured his words. "María didn't have an accident and she wasn't murdered. She could have had cancer or a bad heart. Who knows? I don't. That doctor doesn't. If I had money, I could buy an expensive autopsy in Cancún City. But I wouldn't let her be violated even if I had every peso in the world. We bury my María tomorrow."

The Maya feared being buried alive, so the deceased lay like María for a day before the funeral. Luis felt the practice was backward until one day at Black Coral the subject of death was broached with a customer, an Englishman. Luis forgot the impetus or context of the morbid conversation, but he recalled the man saying that in the Victorian era his countrymen were buried with bells.

"Dead Dinosaurs is scheduled tonight," Luis reminded him.

"Dugdale came to Ho-Keh earlier. I told him we couldn't do it tonight. He said he was sorry about María but we couldn't cancel. He said he'd already sold tickets to the cruise ship tourists."

"He's selling admission tickets?"

"He said he had not planned to until the park became entirely cultural. But, he said, increased overhead forced him to. He said he was in a cash-flow crunch. He speaks in strange words that have no solid meaning. He offered me money. I refused. He bribed me once. Not again. He spoke of a satellite dish. I repeated to him that we couldn't have tourists in the village tonight. He said we had no choice. He said he was looking out for us. He said it was in our best interests not to cancel."

"Why?"

"Some tourists would be angry. They would feel cheated. They would complain. We would have the police in Ho-Keh."

"Dugdale is threatening us," Luis said.

"Yes, he is. As he threatened us, he smiled and spoke softly and called me Frank, like he was my friend."

"Did he mention the legitimate cultural equipment, the plastic dinosaurs and dioramas?"

"I asked. He said some smaller pieces had arrived in port. If he had time he would bring some of the materials out tonight."

"Which port?"

"I asked. He started talking about other things. He talked about how rich Ho-Keh and I would be."

"Was Dugdale alone?"

"No. Somebody was driving that red Jeep. A big man. I couldn't see his face. The windows were too dark. Luis, do you want the television? I don't want it anymore."

Fat as a chauffeur, Luis thought. "No, but I would like to see the serial number."

They returned to Francisco's home and took the TV outside. The serial number matched the one given them by the Punta Paraiso manager.

"Stolen?" Francisco said.

"Yes. I'll take it back to the owner."

"I'm not surprised."

"Francisco, are we permitting the tourists in tonight?" Luis asked. "I'll abide by your decision."

Francisco Ek looked at Luis with his cold, black Asiatic eyes. "Dugdale gave us no choice. We have to have Dead Dinosaurs. We do not have to like it."

He hesitated, then continued, "And Dugdale does not have to like it."

24

In early evening the sky emptied. Water sheeted on the highway. Strobelike lightning ignited and thunder boomed as if it were the sound track in a war movie. The VW's windshield wipers were overwhelmed, and Luis drove more by memory than sight. In fifteen minutes it was done. Steam wisped from the pavement and the air smelled like damp laundry. Chac, the Maya rain god, had given a preview of the rainy season soon to come.

Luis went to Héctor's apartment in Cancún City and invited, cajoled, and begged him to attend tonight's Dead Dinosaurs session. Luis was worried what Francisco might do in his present state of mind. If anybody screamed *policía*, it was preferable to have friendly law enforcement readily available. Further, the evidence against Dugdale on theft of the television was leverage to put him out of the cultural theme park business. Fast.

Héctor said he was off duty and Luis said apologetically that he knew he was off duty. Héctor said, then why the hell should I go out to your isolated, remote village and smugly observe gringo tourists pissing their money away when I can stay home and enjoy my children racing around these four spacious rooms like lunatics and my adoring wife, Carmen, bitching at me. Luis said he would see to it that Héctor had free run of Dugdale's ice chest and Héctor rose to his feet saying that Luis drove a hard bargain.

They picked up Judy at Akumal. She looked drowsy, a sleepy bug in the corner of one eye and her hair hastily brushed. She yawned, exciting Luis even further. He wished they could go upstairs to her bed, never mind the outside world, never mind their troubles and responsibilities.

Riding in the rear as they headed to Ho-Keh, elbows resting on the front seats, Judy related to Héctor her conversation with Mrs. Thelma Chance, mother of Robert.

Héctor groaned. "Our client, Luis and Señora Chance, he is broke and totally without funds for the remainder of this calendar year?"

"Broke or nearly broke," Luis confirmed.

"Robert was never a whiz with money, but it takes talent to squander one hundred and eight thousand dollars in three months," Judy said. "Since you insist on the *señora,* I'll call you Inspector, okay? Inspector, Luis and I think Robert may be at or near Chichén Itzá."

"Yucatán State is out of my jurisdiction," Héctor said in a happier voice. "Mr. Chance's mysterious disappearance from the immediate area is, therefore, explained."

"Robert didn't kill Mikey Smith."

Héctor sighed. "The man is a pauper. Does it matter if he is Jack the Ripper?"

"Jesus," Judy said, settling back, shaking her head.

Luis changed the subject, describing their visit to Punta Paraiso.

"Dugdale steals televisions?" Héctor said. "I am shocked."

"I have matching serial numbers, Héctor. If you become bored, arrest him."

"On the basis of the word of a pretty-boy condo shark? Really, Luis."

Luis told them of María Ek's death.

"I'm so sorry, Luis," Judy said. "And that creep Dugdale insists on going ahead with his casino night?"

"He does."

"The man is evil incarnate, Luis," Héctor said, crossing himself. "A demon."

"Take him into custody, Héctor. You and I, we can interrogate him."

"We can roll your little car over his legs, back and forth, until he is inclined to talk candidly and truthfully," Héctor said. "Then we can sacrifice him according to the custom and methodology of your ancestors."

"All right," Luis said. "Yes."

"Tearing the victim's beating heart out of his chest with a flint knife, was that not the technique of choice, Luis?"

"Late. Following our Classic Period, but prior to the Spaniards. The Toltec came down from Mexico and took over Chichén Itzá. They favored the knife. Some Maya in the Classic Period, 250 A.D. to 900 A.D., preferred to sever the head."

"Oh, decapitation has much to recommend it, Luis."

"I'm not hearing any of this," Judy said. "Uh uh. You guys are unbelievable. While he may deserve the worst, where I come from, we have due process."

"Should the contents of Dugdale's ice chest not be of high caliber, Luis, I shall shoot him in his due process."

Luis turned. "Héctor isn't serious, Judy. Unfortunately."

She winked at him. "Could've fooled me."

"I am unofficial tonight," Héctor said. "I am a guest, on the scene to drink and gamble. I refuse to torture criminals when I am off duty."

They parked next to the same forlorn bus. Judy pointed at the TV and said it looked like it had been caught in the monsoon. Luis said he had forgotten to take the set with him, and Francisco, evidently, had forgotten to move it indoors. If somebody reminds me, he added, we can return it later.

Judy said, "Still dripping wet. They turn the thing on in their jillion-dollar model condo, that should be interesting."

"The television will be clean for them," Luis said. "Please wait here a minute."

Luis looked in at Francisco Ek's. The house was crowded. The majority of those keeping the vigil were women. He saw Esther and Rosa. He saw his mother and María's sister. He did not see Francisco.

They went to the cenote. The scene was a reenactment of opening night, but there was no Vance Dugdale. No Ricky either. Fat and Ugly staffed Dead Dinosaurs by themselves. A clumsy and churlish skeleton crew, they made change, tended bar, and ran the roulette wheel. The card table remained covered. No Ho-Keh people were present to receive employment training. The crowd was bigger; Luis estimated forty-five to fifty, a fairly equal mix of oldsters and young honeymooners. Boombox mariachi throbbed. Cigarette smoke clung in the hot, windless humidity like a dirty blanket.

Luis scanned for Francisco Ek.

Judy said, "This is gross. Tacky. It's like casino night at some men's lodge."

Héctor pushed through the crowd to the ice chest and helped himself.

"Any trouble from Dugdale's employees?" Luis asked.

Héctor smiled. "None whatsoever. The boy with the bad posture and smallpox complexion glared at me. The evil eye. I glared at him in reciprocation. We shared a moment of mutual disrespect. He does not know me and I do not know him, but I know what he is and he knows what I am."

"What is he, Héctor?"

Héctor gulped his drink, a piña colada, and said, "He is a future customer of mine. I am familiar with the type. He is petty and stupid. By the grace of God and dumb luck he is not already in jail somewhere for bungling a crime that would pay him less than the humblest honest job."

"Speaking of crime," Judy said. "Aren't we breaking the law just by attending this little gathering?"

"Interpretation of criminal behavior is inexact, señora."

"Okay, but suppose we're raided."

Héctor laughed. "Then I place everyone under arrest instantly and retroactively."

Through a crack in the tall North American mass, Luis glimpsed Francisco's head bob up to the rear of Ugly. The strung lights flickered.

The generator.

"Don't move," he told Judy. "Take Héctor's hand."

Luis pushed his way toward Francisco. Ugly's fists came up. Luis swept them aside with an arm, saying, "Not you, boss, not now. Get out of my way."

Ugly jumped aside and Luis vaulted his table just as the generator coughed and quit. Lights winked out. "Guadalajara" strummers and crooners droned into silence.

Luis raised a hand, fingers spread, a centimeter from Francisco's chest, not touching, knowing better than to touch.

The visitors fell as quiet as the generator and music. A bird squawked. A fleeting breeze rustled the vegetation. An animal called, a rasping growl. Jaguarundi? Luis wondered. Or a raccoon.

"Jesus H. Fucking Christ," somebody muttered, somebody isolated in the deepest, darkest jungle.

"Nobody panic, ladies and gentlemen," Héctor yelled. "Technical difficulties. The festivities are done for the night. Any of you with cigarette lighters, flick your Bics."

Dead Dinosaurs lit up well enough to forestall panic, but not well enough for anyone to really see. Luis was reminded of a nocturnal Christian religious celebration.

"You two boys in charge of this fiasco," Héctor boomed. "Report to me. We shall organize a procession to the bus."

"What about my money?" demanded an elderly male voice. "The wheel was spinning on my lucky number."

"Your lucky number is sixty-nine," said an elderly female voice. "That isn't on the damned wheel."

The crowd roared.

"That's his *age.* Get your minds out of the gutter," she said. "How he drinks and smokes, he should of croaked years ago."

The crowd laughed again. Luis whispered to Francisco, "What did you do?"

"Dirt in the gas tank."

He had higher drama in mind than a clogged fuel line, Luis knew. "Then?"

"I hadn't decided. Where is Dugdale?"

"You came through the brush, not from the village?"

Francisco didn't answer.

"He isn't here, Francisco. You have my word. I haven't seen him. His two trash mestizos are in charge."

"I gave this nightmare life, Luis. I am the one to kill the nightmare."

"You killed Dead Dinosaurs, Francisco. You killed the monster by killing its power."

"Dugdale," Francisco said.

"We have Dugdale on the run," Luis lied. "Héctor is with me. Inspector Salgado, my friend with the State Judicial Police. I brought him to arrest Dugdale, who must have been tipped off."

"The gambling machines, are they also stolen?"

"Yes. Stolen from the same place as the TV set. Dugdale was a condominium salesman. He stole from his bosses."

"Are you taking the machines to the owner along with the television?"

Luis paused, thinking. "No. Killing the machines kills Dead Dinosaurs for good, doesn't it? Should those plastic dinosaurs even exist, they will never leave Brazil."

"Lead the gringos out, Luis. And thank you."

Luis found Francisco's hand. "Wait for daylight so you don't hurt yourself. Your sons and your family and your friends need you tonight."

Héctor had organized a procession to the bus, a strange

necklace of lighter flames and cigarette embers. He came to Luis, saying, "Your friend, the widower, he is who made your eyes come out of your head?"

Francisco was gone. "Yes."

"He sabotaged our cultural experience, yes? Where did he go?"

"Don't worry, Héctor. The trouble is finished."

"So are we," Héctor said, giving Luis a wad of money. "I confiscated the proceeds from Dugdale's pair of losers. Consider it a donation for funeral expenses and the children's education, should they go to school."

"Thank you, Héctor. Francisco will thank you."

"Less a nominal commission, of course."

"Of course."

"Señora Chance is standing by at the bus to ensure that the passengers board safely and Dugdale's boys do not wander off. She suggests we follow the bus to its destination and subsequently follow Dugdale's boys. Luis, no. I am not playing detective on my free time."

Luis removed as many cans from the ice chest as he could carry and said, "Come along as an observer, then. We'll do the detecting."

Héctor removed as many cans from the ice chest as *he* could carry and said, "What are we waiting for? We shall detect and observe our hearts out."

Luis gave the money to Francisco's older boy. They trailed the bus in the Beetle, Luis intermittently regretting Judy's idea. The bus was as slow as the Christian Messiah's encore and its exhaust was asphyxiating.

Eventually it pulled into Playa del Carmen, stopping by the docks. Fat and Ugly walked away. The majority of the tourists headed for their ship in obvious relief. A few trailed

Fat and Ugly, speaking angrily. Freed of their dark jungle hell, they were feisty, demanding admission fee refunds. Fat and Ugly responded with epithets in Spanish, middle digits, and instructions in broken English to go after Dugdale, the boss.

They mounted Fat's custom motorcycle and rode out of town, heading south on the highway. Luis followed. Fat and Ugly turned at the Punta Paraiso access road. Luis went on by.

"Well?" Judy said.

"We should have a look," Luis said. "We should have a conversation with them."

"Think Paco will let us in this time of night?" Judy asked.

"We can ask."

In the back seat with his liquid cargo, Héctor patted Luis on the shoulder, and said, "Take me home first, driver. A can or two of this coconut drink could render my Carmen romantic."

"It won't spoil, Inspector. You'll be missing the fun."

"Nocturnal confrontations are never fun, señora. Home, Luis."

25

On the first portion of their trip to Cancún City, Héctor was chatty, discoursing on love and the abundance of healthy vitamins in canned fruity booze. He snored seismically during the second forty kilometers. Luis unloaded him with difficulty and manhandled him to the door of his apartment. Héctor awakened sufficiently to let himself in. Luis was grateful. Carmen would take one look at her husband and would not be in a romantic mood. A nonassaultive mood, if Héctor were lucky.

Southbound for Ho-Keh, to pick up the television, their pretext for calling late and unannounced at Punta Paraiso, Judy asked about María Ek's death. Luis told her what little he knew. She fell ill, she died.

Judy left the subject in silence for ten kilometers. Luis thought he knew what was stewing inside her head. The telepathy of lovers. She was appalled that people should merely die. In this day and age, in this technological world community bursting with medical advances. The Third World Syndrome. The pity of it all. The utter waste, the tragedy.

Luis had been lectured by North Americans on the

Third World Syndrome. Education, motivation, and foreign aid, these were the keys. There was no reason for people to live like this, no excuse. On every aspect from sanitation to tardy buses to siestas. You can turn it around; all you have to do is want to.

Senseless death was the ultimate insult to modern civilization. An X ray, an antibiotic, and María would be up and about, scrubbing laundry and frying tortillas. Maybe it was that easy, maybe it wasn't. Luis didn't know. Didn't people sometimes just die? At every funeral did not every presiding holy man pronounce that the deceased's time had come? Every god introduced to Luis in his life had standing reservations on high for their chosen.

Evidently his brain waves were broadcasting to Judy, because she did not transmit through her mouth a Third World Syndrome editorial. Instead, she asked, "Do you believe in an afterlife?"

"Me as an individual man or the Maya people?"

"Okay, a two-part question."

"The ancients saw the world and the afterworld as layered squares. There are thirteen layers above ground, including the world we live in. There are nine underworlds. Each of these layers is presided over by a god. We Maya have gods for everything. The layers up above are good. They are full of light and happiness and good food. The underworld layers are dark. They are cold. They stink and are dangerous."

"Heaven and Hell," Judy said.

"Yes. We made our conversion easy for the Spanish. It wasn't like they had to torture a completely new faith into us. Cortés came to Mexico for the gold. That we can understand. The friars came along on his heels to convert us to

Christianity. I will always understand a man who tries to take my money. I will never understand a man who tries to take my soul."

"The Maya are Catholic?"

"We are like anybody. We can be anything. Some of us are Catholic. Mexicans have their own brand of Catholicism. The Virgin of Guadalupe was a dark-skinned lady. We Maya have our own version of Catholicism. We blend our ancient beliefs with what the Vatican teaches.

"Many Maya stick entirely to the old ways. Others are sold a god by evangelical missionaries, who claim there is but one god, and despite it being the same god as the Catholic god, their god is the only god. These sects and cults, the Baptists, the Mormons, the Pentecostals, the Jehovah's Witnesses, *their* same god is the only god and everyone else's god is false. Those people confuse us."

"You as an individual man, Luis?"

"Me?"

"Don't be cute. Do you or don't you believe in an afterlife?"

"I don't think that far into the future."

"You aren't a believer?"

"I am a secular humanist."

"What's that?"

"I am not sure. Missionaries approach me. I tell them I'm a secular humanist. They shrivel and skulk off like they've seen the devil. And you, Judy? As an individual woman."

"Me?"

Luis laughed. "Do you or don't you believe in an afterlife?"

"I'm like you. I'd rather procrastinate until the grim reaper is tapping on my door."

"You aren't religious?"

"I'm a doubter. I'm a skeptic."

"You don't believe there is a god?"

"Yeah? Where's he been keeping himself?"

"Himself? Don't modern hyphenating North American ladies argue that God is a she?"

"Well, they're wrong. A woman wouldn't have screwed things up so badly."

At Ho-Keh they loaded the television into the Beetle without breaking it. The Panasonic was no longer dripping wet, but it felt dewy, the plastic cabinet slippery as a fish. Luis smelled corroded metal and mildew. The village was dark and silent. His people were in their hammocks, either asleep or quietly sobbing for María Ek. From the cenote came the clinking of metal on metal and stone on metal.

Paco was not on duty at the Punta Paraiso gate. A bicycle missing its front wheel and tire leaned against the guard shack. Paco's night replacement came out of a chair inside the shack, stifled a yawn, and raised a hand. This guard's khaki was wrinkled, the shirt spilling over his belt. He was twice Paco's age, twice his weight, and had half his hair. He looked to Luis like Héctor on his worst days. Héctor's tomorrow morning occurred to him as an accurate comparison.

In broad daylight, their vulgar affluence in no jeopardy, Punto Paraiso management had assigned an aspiring Nazi who would be pleased to give an intruder a bad day. At night they selected the Cisco Kid's Pancho. The Third World Syndrome proven valid, Luis thought.

"Is the manager in, boss?" Luis asked.

"He is gone for the day. He lives in Cancún."

Luis cocked his thumb toward the back seat. "This is his television that was stolen. We recovered it from the thieves. The manager asked that we return it immediately, as it is important for the ambience of the model unit."

"Who are you?"

"A private detective. I was hired to do what the police cannot or will not."

The guard peered inside the car and squinted. "Who is she?"

"My secretary."

"You can leave the TV with me."

"No, sorry, boss," Luis said. "My orders are to take it directly to the model unit."

"I don't know nothing about stolen TVs," the guard said, shaking his head. "You can't go in."

"What is the story on the bicycle?" Luis said, stalling, thinking. "Yours?"

"No. Belongs to a maid. Indian girl." He winked at Luis and cupped his hands at his chest. "Young and cute, built good for an Indian. Her first day on the job and she gets a flat tire. Juan and Ernesto, these two groundskeepers, they was coming in and offered to fix it for her. The three of them, they went on in with the tire to the employee cabin where the boys live. They said they got bicycle tools in the cabin."

"Juan and Ernesto, were they riding in on Juan's custom motorcycle?"

"Ernesto's motorcycle, not Juan's," the guard said. "Ernesto loves his cycle like no man ever loved a woman. You know Juan and Ernesto?"

Luis returned the wink. "See, boss, I was kind of working with Juan and Ernesto on this case."

The guard laughed. "Them? They're laborers, not detectives. They ain't smart enough or honest enough to be detectives."

"I said 'kind of,' " Luis said. "You're a smart guy, boss. I don't have to tell you how those boys were kind of working with me, do I?"

"You don't?" he said, nodding but asking the question.

Luis winked once more and lowered his voice. "Those boys, between you and me, they tipped me who they sold the television to. I recover the thing—you do not want to know how—and the manager pays me and I pay them something and when I say how cooperative you've been, boss, maybe they'll pay you something."

The guard brightened, but said, "I don't know. I don't know what I ought to do."

"Well," Luis said, stroking his chin thoughtfully, "think of it like this. Why would I bring the TV out at night when I am fairly certain the manager is gone for the day, a fact which you have confirmed?"

The guard frowned in thought.

"You know, don't you, boss? Juan and Ernesto, my boys, I go to them. They accept the TV from me. They're probably suspected of stealing the set. Can you imagine? I give it to them and, honest boys they are, they tell the manager of my visit and give him the television. Everybody is happy."

The guard looked at his watch. "Ten minutes. Can you be in and out in ten minutes? Please."

Luis said he could, absolutely, and they went under the raised barrier. Judy asked how "bullshit artist" translated into Spanish. Luis smiled, parked at the model unit, and unloaded the TV.

"You can wait right here, Judy."

"Expecting trouble?"

"They aren't very nice. I'm leaving the car so I can surprise them."

"Yeah, but aren't we just talking? Isn't information the reason?"

"Yes. We came to talk."

"Incidentally, why are we talking to them?"

"Information on Dugdale."

"As of tonight, isn't his Dead Dinosaurs Park scam history?"

"It is, but Dugdale has to hear the words from somebody's mouth. Mine. He has to hear from somebody that he is unwelcome in Ho-Keh. Me."

"Logical, I guess. Juan and Ernesto can point you to Dugdale. And speaking of those two fine young men, they're repairing that girl's flat tire. That's sweet of them. Maybe they aren't Boy Scouts but they're doing a good deed. So what's the problem?"

"All right," Luis said. "Stay behind me, stay quiet, and walk on your toes. We must not spoil our surprise."

"My macho guy," she whispered, pinching a buttock. "These worker cabins don't look too bad."

A single row of half a dozen units, they were faced with matching gingerbread stucco, arches above their doors, and tile roofs. Luis said, "The developers won't spend any money to house the gardeners and handymen who live here. It'll be like a movie set. You're seeing the best."

At an end unit, Fat's custom motorcycle was up on its kickstand. A bicycle rim and uninflated tire lay beside it.

The lights were out in every condominium and every cabin except theirs. Luis did not understand rich people any better than he understood missionaries. The wealthy spent fortunes on their homes, but were never in them. He did understand the absence of the cabin laborers; they were out drinking their meager wages.

Luis heard whimpering. Juan and Ernesto's door was ajar. Luis walked into a single room that smelled of perspiration and sewage. On one of two cots was a young Maya woman. She was on her back, *huipil* hiked above her waist, torn panties around one ankle. She was sobbing and writhing, desperately holding her legs together. Blood trickled from her mouth. Ugly was above her, pants at his knees, twisting and cursing, one hand on a breast, the other on a thigh, prying her legs apart and himself between them.

Fat leapt off the other cot, where he had been sitting, enjoying the show. His pants were on, though unzipped, presumably awaiting his turn. There was a chair between the cots. Draped over the back were their scabbards. Fat withdrew a machete and lifted it just as Luis slammed into him, gripping his wrists. Momentum toppled them onto the empty bunk. They rolled to the floor on the opposite side, Luis landing hard on the floor.

Luis had glimpsed Ugly's head turn, had heard his curses increase in volume. Ugly was preoccupied, but that would not last. Luis knew he had to finish Fat quickly, before Ugly joined the fight. While soft and flabby, eyes glazed as much by terror as anger, Fat was on top, feeling as heavy as he looked, having the advantage of fifty kilograms and gravity.

Fat pushed and jerked his machete hand, trying to wrench free for a killing blow. He was keening, eyes wide, spittle bubbling. Adrenaline, Luis thought, adrenaline pumping through sheer lard: he will strengthen as I weaken.

Luis suddenly released Fat's other wrist and drove a fist into the drooping flab connecting neck and jaw. Fat moaned and his head snapped back, mouth gaping. Luis hit him again. Fat's jaw snapped together, a noise like dropped chinaware.

Luis rotated the unconscious man on his side and stumbled to his feet, arms crossed in front of his face. He could survive a chopped arm. He could not survive a chopped neck.

No swing of sharp steel was forthcoming, no severing blow.

Ugly did not have possession of the other machete. Judy did. Her body trembled, but her extended arm was steady. Ugly stood as rigid as a statue. The tip of the machete touched his now flaccid penis. His eyes bulged froglike and he did not appear to be breathing.

"We came to talk," Luis said. "We'll talk."

26

The six cabins shared one bathroom, situated at one end and just behind the row. It was the source of the sewage odor, Judy's investigation revealed, but at least there was running water. She asked the terrified girl if she could help her clean up. Her mouth was swelling where she'd been struck and she had ugly scratches on the insides of her thigh from Ugly's fingernails. Judy put her arm around the girl and escorted her outside, saying that she had tissues and first aid spray in her purse, and not to worry. The girl didn't comprehend a word, but Judy's delivery seemed to relax her. Luis felt no need to translate.

The girl was Rosa's age. She reminded him of both his babies. She could have been one of them. Esther or Rosa could have been *her*, beaten and raped by these animals.

Luis had a firmer grip on the machetes than he had on his temper. He was on the edge of hacking Fat and Ugly into dog food. Instead he hacked to pieces their pitiful possessions. A stack of comic books. Piles of dirty clothing. Gardening tools propped in a corner.

Fat was awake, seated where he and Luis had fallen. He alternately spat blood and ran his tongue along his gum line, taking inventory of his teeth. Ugly was equally docile, seated on the chair, waiting out Luis's tantrum.

Ugly finally protested when he sliced the handles of their gardening tools in two. "Man, please, I beg you, we're responsible for those, they're our living. They get busted, we got to buy new tools from management."

"They are usable. The handles are just shorter," Luis said. "You'll have to bend over. Good training. When the girl files charges, has you arrested and sent to prison, you'll learn the fine art of bending over. They'll do to you what you were going to do to the girl."

"Oh, man," whined a sneering Ugly. "You're pissed because you're an Indian and she's an Indian. A stiff dick never hurt nobody. She might've liked it, you hadn't come along and spoiled her chance. Your girlfriend, Indian-looking *gringa*, she knows how to handle a machete. She chop sugar cane or wheat or something back home? Lucky for you she grabbed my machete before I could, or we'd have a different story here."

Luis dropped the machetes and lunged at Ugly, who rose from his chair, balling his fists, yelling, "Ernesto!"

Luis sent a blow that originated in his toes into Ugly's gut. Ugly collapsed, making a noise like air being expelled from a balloon. He slumped into the chair and gagged. In the close stench of the shack, Luis was grateful that he did not vomit. Fat, meanwhile, was motionless, a mute spectator.

Luis stepped back, catching his breath and his senses. He found the machetes and silently cursed his own stupidity. Ugly was not stupid. He was goading Luis into a mistake that could have cost him the life Judy saved. Fortunately, Luis threw an effective first punch and Fat did not join in. The result could have been the opposite, Luis the victim of his wild temper.

Luis waited quietly until Ugly regained his ability to breathe normally and speak. He told Fat he should have jumped Luis and called him a cowardly, shiteating son of a whore. Then he asked Luis what he wanted from them.

"Your name is Juan and he is Ernesto?"

"My name is Juan. What did Juan and his fat, cowardly, shiteating friend, Ernesto, ever do to you, man?"

Ernesto grunted and spit out a tooth.

"Vance Dugdale."

"I told you before, man, he's just a gringo we do jobs for."

"You didn't tell me he worked here."

"He doesn't. They fired him. Wasn't any of your business is how I figured."

"It is my business. When and why was Dugdale fired?"

"A while ago. He wasn't selling condos and the manager thought he stole some stuff."

"Did he?"

"Where do you think those slot machines come from?" Juan said, smiling.

"Where does Vance Dugdale come from?"

"He's North American. Somewhere up there. I don't know. The manager didn't like hiring Dugdale. He don't like gringos, but some of these rich gringo condo buyers, they like dealing with gringos. They don't like dealing with Mexicans."

Luis's anger had diminished. Although he had control of himself, he was still short on patience. "Don't play dumb with me, boss. Where does Dugdale live, where does he hang out?"

Juan shook his head, but he wasn't looking at Luis. "He comes and goes. We see him. We don't see him. I don't know. He never said."

"I wonder how many years you get for rape?" Luis said. "You ought to hire a lawyer. Did Dugdale pay you well enough to afford a lawyer?"

"I didn't rape nobody, man. You saw. Me and Ernesto flipped a coin. I won. I got to have her first. Except you spoiled it."

Luis realized that the girl and her parents probably would not file a police complaint against Juan and Ernesto. They would fear the humiliation, the harassment, the intimidation. The odds of a conviction were as slim as a complaint. With her flat tire, this Indian girl had gone voluntarily to a cabin with two men, and that was that. "My friend and I will lie and testify you were raping her. We will convince the girl to cooperate."

"You're full of shit, man. No court's going to convict us of nothing even if the girl causes trouble. It's our word against yours."

Against my word as an Indian, Luis thought. He stretched his bluff. "My friend, the inspector who confiscated the Dead Dinosaurs money—"

"That's not legal, he pocketed our money. We worked our asses off earning that money. We was supposed to be paid out of that."

"I'll have my friend Inspector Salgado arrest you for rape. The girl and her family may or may not pursue the matter. They don't pursue the matter, all right, you will be released in, oh, three or four or six months from Inspector

Salgado's jail. His jail is not as filthy and disgusting as your cabin, but I would not care to live there."

"Man—"

"Should you survive three or four or six months, that is. We Maya drink too much, you know. Some of us do. This is a fact. We get drunk and tossed in jail. We wake up the next morning hung over and irritable. To pass the time of day, maybe we ask you what you're in for. You don't want to say, we ask somebody else, who tells us. Could be a coincidence, could be our own daughter you—"

"Man, I'd recite you Dugdale's life story if I could."

"Where does he live?"

Juan shrugged. "Up around Cancún, I think. Like I told you, man, he contacts us, we don't contact him."

"You worked for him. Doing what besides Dead Dinosaurs jobs?"

"Nothing."

"I asked you that question at Ho-Keh, remember? You didn't answer. What other jobs have you done for Dugdale?"

Juan did not reply.

"You stole the gambling equipment and TV out of the model unit."

"No. Not by ourselves."

"Then you helped him?"

"Dugdale had a key he gave us. We carried the stuff to the wall, at a spot where there's trees and brush, and lifted it over to him. That shit's heavy, you lift it up and over that wall and fence. He loaded it in his Jeep and paid us a few pesos. Man, all this fucking trouble, we worked too cheap."

"Dugdale didn't bribe Paco to close his eyes so you could haul your stolen property out the front gate?"

Juan shook his head. "Paco's psycho crazy. No one you'd want to meet in a dark alley. Dugdale paid Paco to let him in and out to see us. Paco wasn't in on the theft."

"When did you last see Dugdale?"

"When was it? Night before last, first casino night at your village."

"Speakeasy night," Luis said.

"Yeah. Dugdale called it a speakeasy. What's a speakeasy, anyway?"

"So you and Ernesto took the initiative to host Dead Dinosaurs tonight despite no Dugdale? You boys have ambition."

"We're too good to be planting shrubs, man."

"You hustled the cruise boat tourists by yourselves? You arranged for the bus? You bought the refreshments? You brought coins and chips? You gentlemen thought of everything."

"You don't think we could? We're too smart to be peons the rest of our lives."

Luis squatted and rested the flat of the machete blade on Juan's thigh. "I changed my mind. I won't have Inspector Salgado arrest you."

Luis jabbed the blade at Juan's crotch.

Juan managed a sickly smile.

"You're such a fine liar, Juan, the law would be unable to win a conviction. But of course I am no lawyer or policeman. I am no judge of evidence."

"Evidence?"

"I'll take this in with me," Luis said, jabbing again. "My lady friend and the girl will be happy to assist. We'll take it in to my inspector friend. Maybe he will decide it is too small to be a criminal weapon, a rape weapon. No charges will be filed."

"You're *loco,* man!" Juan said, pressing into his chair.

Luis smiled. "That is me, boss. An *indio loco.*"

"He was out today. He talked us into picking up the tourists and going out tonight to work. He said it would be the last time for Dead Dinosaurs and that he would give us a bigger cut of the money."

"Dugdale wasn't there," Luis said. "You could have taken a one-hundred-percent cut of the money."

"He was supposed to be, man. He didn't show."

"My feelings are hurt. Dugdale told nobody he was closing down at Ho-Keh. Why?"

"He said you were uppity Indians with bad attitudes. He said you were too negative. He mentioned you in particular. He said you pulled some shit on a tourist like you did on us about that voodoo curse. He said you were a negative influence, the rotten apple that spoiled the barrel."

Luis was flattered. "I didn't speak to the tourist about ancient curses. I spoke about snakes."

"Same difference, man. Vance said he had a hell of a time recruiting gringos for tonight. Word got out on the snakes."

"Why do you think Dugdale failed to come?"

"Who knows? Who cares? Fuck him. He treats us like garbage. He calls me Johnny. He calls Ernesto Ernie. He doesn't respect us."

"Where do I locate him?"

"I'm telling you the honest truth, man. I don't have a clue."

Luis stared at him.

"Look, man, I don't like you any better than you like me, but if I give you a tip on Dugdale, will you give me a break? I can't give you an address, but I can give you good advice."

Continuing to stare, Luis lifted a shoulder. "Give me the advice. If it is worth anything, I'll consider giving you a break."

"Dugdale has an ugly temper. Like yours. You haven't seen the temper through his smiling line of shit, but we have. Be careful when he loses it."

"What is he going to do to me if he loses his temper?"

"I can't say for sure, man. We never pushed him that far, but almost. This look comes over him like he's dead and don't give a damn whether you are."

"So?"

"I noticed once when he sat and crossed his legs. He's got this little baby pistol in this little baby holster he straps right above his ankle. You can figure he knows how to use it."

27

The Maya girl's name was Juliana. Judy told Juliana she should file charges. Juliana said she was frightened and didn't want any more trouble. She wanted to forget the whole thing. She had been on a waiting list for this job. Good jobs like this were hard to find and she feared losing it, and, please, could she just go home.

Luis said she was not the cause of the trouble. He ordered Ernesto to repair her bicycle tire, to do the good deed he originally promised. They would then lash the bicycle to the roof of the Beetle and drive her home.

Ernesto pointed at his bloody mouth and shook his head. Luis wagged a finger at him and said you don't patch a tire with your teeth, and you are an expert on two-wheeled vehicles, aren't you?

Ernesto mumbled as he worked, in pain and thoroughly humiliated by Indians and females. Juan seethed as Ernesto worked. Luis fixed him with a stare designed to ward off any thought of retaliation against Juliana.

Juliana lived half a kilometer south and half a kilometer west of the highway, at a rancho with her father, mother, and five siblings. She pleaded that she be allowed to ride home alone, so as not to disturb her family. She was the only one working steadily and her father wasn't well.

Luis and Judy reluctantly abided by her wishes, but they idled at the intersection until she had peddled safely to her cutoff and out of sight. It wasn't until they were in Judy's Akumal bed that Luis could thank her for neutralizing Juan and probably saving his life. Judy said no big deal, the bastard was so involved in what he and Ernesto were going to do to Juliana that he went for his machete late, like in Hollywood slow motion. I beat him to it easy. Piece of cake, okay? Common sense dictated where I aim the blade. I wasn't about to get into a Three Musketeers thing with him. Luis, what's the matter?

What they nearly did to Juliana, Luis replied, not adding that the fact that she, a woman, had saved his life might be contributing to his inability to perform. Judy hugged him and told him that what she meant by what's the matter was his anxiety, not anything physical. He was a man's man tonight because he *couldn't* perform, a compassionate human being. Luis fell asleep in her arms, somewhat confused and mightily relieved.

In the early morning, María Ek's funeral was conducted in her home. In darkness illuminated by candles, a Maya holy man from a nearby village said words over her. The Ek house was not large enough to accommodate everybody, so Luis waited outside with his family and no less than fifty other mourners. He did attend the burial at Ho-Keh's small, rocky cemetery. Francisco was stoic, arms wrapped tightly around his boys. In a few years, Luis knew, María's bones would be dug up to free a plot. María Ek would live anew in her home, in a box, at an altar.

Afterward, Luis went to the cenote. There was no evidence of Vance Dugdale's Dead Dinosaurs gambling speakeasy. No slot machines. No rickety palapa. No tables. No garbage, not even a cigarette butt. Francisco had been so thorough, it was as if he had sacrificed the blight to some ravenous god.

Luis had lunch with his babies. Black Coral would be closed today, but he still had detective business to take care of. Esther and Rosa were not pleased. They liked their father's North American lady, but they did not like the *lotería* case, did not like the murder, the fighting, the complicated problems. Luis kissed them and promised to be careful and to behave. They asked him in mock seriousness who would teach him, as he had no prior experience doing either.

As they drove to Cancún City, to Ricky's office, Judy said, "I'm looking forward to meeting him. Does he really look exactly like Desi Arnaz?"

"Except for Ricky's mustache, they could be twins," Luis said confidently.

"The dairy princess, what is the possibility of running into her there?"

"Better than it was at his apartment. They could still be lawyer and client."

"Wham, bam, thank you, ma'am."

Luis looked at her.

"American slang for loving 'em and leaving 'em."

"Yes," Luis said. "That is Ricky."

"For all we know, Rita and Ricky have a lead on Robert, a stronger lead than Thelma Chance gave me on the phone."

"They could have," Luis said without confidence. "Ricky is through with Rita in bed, but her interest in the lottery fortune will hold his interest."

"Could Ricky do anything for Juliana?"

"How do you mean?"

"He is a lawyer, okay? Civil damages, you know. In the States, those two slimeballs wouldn't have to go jail for a jury to award money for traumatizing a woman."

"In North America, yes," Luis said. "In Mexico, I don't think so. And those boys have no money anyway."

"Well, how about her suing the owners of Punta Paraiso? They must have super-deep pockets and they could be held liable for hiring those creeps."

"Their wealth is why they cannot lose a lawsuit."

"Then hush money. They pay her to keep her mouth shut."

"Hush money, that is a possibility," Luis said.

Ricky was at his desk. He seemed different to Luis, older but no wiser. Unhealthy, listless, near exhaustion, bags under his eyes. There was something else that evaded Luis, and it wasn't influenza.

He introduced Judith Maxwell-Chance to Ricardo Martínez Rodríguez.

Ricky could not summon the energy to rise for a gracious bow. "The second and unwedded Mrs. Chance. My condolences, dear lady."

"God, you are a double for Desi Arnaz. Condolences for what? Mikey Smith is dead, not Robert. He isn't, is he?"

"No, not to my knowledge, but he is a prime murder suspect and you are out of the loop regarding the lottery winnings."

"We'll see about that."

"Rita Trunkey Chance was going to hire you to draft a fair settlement of Chance's lottery fortune," Luis said.

Ricky shifted to Spanish. "Luis, the woman is insatiable. A hot-blooded blonde, I had no idea they existed. We Latins are known for our passion, rightfully so, but this *güera,* Luis, I am, essentially, her sex slave."

"I thought she was in your bedroom when I came to your apartment. Are you complaining, Ricky?"

"Oh no, not in the overall scope of the arrangement. She relishes sexual fantasies that are beyond even my worldly experience and imagination. The difficulty, Luis, is that Rita is so domineering of me and my time. I have to literally escape to come to this office and eke out a bare living."

"She is madly in love with you?"

"No, not in the sense that your companion loves you. Adoration is apparent in her face. No, Rita loves me as a—how shall I say?—as a toy. An object of sexual pleasure. She addresses me as her *hombre.* Is Judith an Ind—a Native North American, Luis?"

Judy nudged Luis. "Sorry to interrupt your boy talk, but I thought you said that Ricky wore a mustache."

The 'something else' that had evaded him. "Ricky, why did you shave? Answer me in English, will you. Judy doesn't speak Spanish. We are being impolite."

"A recommendation was made that I shave my—cookie duster."

"I'm picking up bits and pieces," Judy said, grinning. "The dairy princess made you shave?"

Ricky looked at Luis, eyes bloodshot and haunted. "Dairy princess is a frequent reference by Rita to her youth. Luis, what precisely is a dairy princess?"

"That is a long story," Luis said knowingly.

"I can tell you," Judy said.

Luis smiled at her and shook his head. "Later."

"She induced me to shave in order to become her Ricky Ricardo. My next fear is that she will dye her hair red."

"Are you having a good time, Ricky?" Luis said. "That is the important thing."

"Fantastic fun," Ricky said, managing a weak smile. "I am, however, comprehending why prudes urge moderation in various pleasures. My endurance is being tested."

"You do look kind of peaked," Judy said, straight-faced, but with playful eyes. "Ricky Ricardo in the old shows, he had a healthier glow than you do. And they were in black and white. Are you eating right?"

"Rita voiced an identical concern," Ricky said. "As we speak, she is shopping. For the duration of her stay she intends to cook for me, to 'put some meat on my bones' in her jargon. Cheeseburgers and chicken-fried steak are her specialties, foods that she alleges are rich in protein and nutrients. What is chicken-fried steak, Luis? Chicken and beef are separate meats. Is chicken-fried steak a high-tech North American hybrid? They have amazingly advanced agriculture up there, you know."

Luis shook his head. "I do not know chicken-fried steak."

"You'll like it," Judy said. "Greasy but yummy."

Ricky threw up his hands. "Irrelevant. I do not require fried meats. I require Spanish fly and ground rhinoceros horns. I am not a rude person, Luis, but it would be prudent if you and Mrs. Chance left. Mrs. Chance is due momentarily and I truly desire to avoid an explosive situation."

"I don't have a problem with her," Judy said. "If she has a problem with me, that's her problem."

Rita Trunkey Chance entered, cradling a grocery bag, cigarette dangling in her mouth. "*Hombre,* it's some kind of challenge hunting up real food in this town. The supermarkets don't cube round steak or they don't have round steak to cube or I wasn't expressing myself through the language barrier, one. Now, hamburger was easier to come by. What it's made of, your guess is as good as—"

Rita took notice of Luis and Judy, especially Judy.

Ricky had no sand in which to bury his head, so he covered his face with his hands.

Luis watched the women stare at one another. An introduction, he knew, would be redundant, perhaps foolhardy. He ransacked his brain for an appropriate conversational opening gambit.

The best he could do was, "Rita, what killed the dinosaurs?"

She laughed. "What kind of goofy question is that?"

"A question I ask visitors for no particular reason."

"Weird. You're asking the wrong gal. I did lousy in science. There's this joke, though. A dinosaur walks into a bar with a duck on its head. I forget the punch line."

She turned to Judy and asked a friendly question. "Have you seen my worthless husband lately?"

Judy smiled. "Nope. Have you seen *my* worthless husband lately?"

Luis thanked whichever god he didn't believe in for intervening. Ricky exhaled and crossed himself.

Rita rolled her eyes. "Don't I wish. Him and his Lotto annuity. But all I've got of Bobby is a faint, faint memory."

"I have Robert's credit card," Judy said. "And it's burning a hole in my purse. Let's go shopping."

Rita cackled. "That man always did have good taste in wives."

28

The two Mrs. Chances asked for shopping recommendations. Rita was partial to malls, Judy to quaint shops. Ricky and Luis assured them they could have both, at any of dozens of malls and markets, and at hundreds (thousands?) of shops, in the city and the hotel zone, quaintness and local color being dominant themes in Cancún merchandising. Instant Mexico, instant Yucatán, Luis said. Price and selection are the variables, Ricky added; you may save a little in the city, but be boggled by the luxurious options of the island.

Rita asked how much Twinkletoes had remaining on the card. Judy hadn't the foggiest, either the unpaid balance or the card's limit. Rita said Bobby had probably forgotten completely about the card, responsible guy that he was. She suggested they go for the classy arcades and surprise themselves when the card maxed out. Her motion carried.

"Vance Dugdale," Luis said to Ricky when they were alone.

"The instant rapport the ladies have, Luis," Ricky said, beaming. "It is a miracle."

"No. Not a miracle," Luis said. "Rita has you and Judy has me. Love isn't an issue, just money. Vance Dugdale."

"An extremely broad subject, Luis."

"Not a subject, Ricky. A request. A request that you tell me everything you know and I do not about the cultural theme park impresario."

Ricky sighed. "Your sarcasm is uncalled for, Luis. In fact, Vance and I, evidently, have terminated our business relationship. Vance is not an honorable man."

"Evidently?"

"I have not seen him in several days. On that occasion the man had the audacity to borrow money from me."

"Seeking further capitalization?"

Ricky shook his head wearily. "Ridiculing me with my own words, Luis, is an act of cruelty. This was a negligible personal loan situation. So Vance alleged, his Houston bank had botched a wire transfer of funds to a local account, creating a cash flow shortfall. He asked for a few pesos, walking-around money for a day."

"Ricky, you must have seen Dugdale lately. You're talking like him."

"Was he not at Ho-Keh yesterday evening?"

"No. Just his two trash half-castes. Dead Dinosaurs is dead, by the way."

"A shame, but predictable because of Vance's lack of integrity and slipshod management techniques."

"Ricky, *have* you seen Dugdale lately?"

"You missed him by moments on your last visit to this office."

"Dugdale was your mystery client? Why were you so flustered?"

"I cannot say in all truthfulness that I am proud of each and every aspect of my social and occupational life, Luis. I am like any man, flawed, and there are instances when my judgment is not perfect. I shall not, however, defend my frailties. Career pressures, our constantly eroding Mexican economy, agonizing over whether to accept or reject a golden, once in a lifetime opportunity, these elements, Luis, greatly impact a professional man's choices."

Ricky was sinking into philosophical gloom, Luis thought; a sign of extreme internal torment, a rare instance of his conscience wrestling on an even footing with his appetites and rationalizations. Ricky's conscience emerged and died like insects from a cocoon; a brief, frenetic life followed by a long period of dormancy.

"Talk to me, Ricky. You need to talk to me."

"Pointless, Luis. My dialogue would consist mainly of speculation and unsubstantiated allegations."

"Start, Ricky. I don't object to allegations. Maybe I can substantiate them for us."

"Dead Dinosaurs had incredible promise, Luis, unlimited potential. The science was accurate, the tourism demand infinite, the concept refreshingly original. Agreed?"

"I agree that Dead Dinosaurs was refreshingly lucrative for you and Dugdale. For Ho-Keh, the gambling was a deception. Dugdale had no intention of setting up dioramas and plastic Brazilian dinosaurs. He is a con artist who grabs tourist dollars with his jungle casino and moves on to the next village. If the army or the *federales* raid us, we pay dearly and Dugdale is long gone."

"While Vance is rascally and insensitive, gambling is not, I feel, inherently evil, Luis. Your Mr. Bob Chance, for instance. Had he not lost self-control, his gambling experience would have been, should have been, for him a paradise on earth. Vance's idea for using gambling as a stopgap until the cultural paraphernalia was delivered, this is not basically unsound. The flaw was Vance's character. He is driven by greed."

" 'Driven' reminds me, Ricky, a desperate car rental clerk is looking for you. He wishes to kill you before his boss kills him. You signed for Dugdale's Jeep?"

Ricky gulped and nodded.

"When you brought Dugdale to Black Coral you gave me the impression that Dugdale was generous and wealthy."

"Vance peeled money from a roll of bills to pay for the Jeep."

"But you signed."

"Vance's credit cards were in his luggage, which had been delayed in Houston. Evidently this was also a lie."

"Dugdale still has the Jeep?"

"I suppose. He did at the aforementioned visit here, my last encounter with him. He parked in the alley."

"How can I contact Mr. Dugdale?"

"Vance does the contacting. That is his style."

"So I understand. Have you any idea where he lives?"

"No. Why, Luis, please explain, if Dead Dinosaurs is shut down, why are you still so anxious to contact Vance?"

"Why were you so rattled when Judy and I came in, Ricky? Talk to me."

"Luis, you cannot conceive how difficult what I am about to say is to say."

"You sound as if you are going to confess something to me, Ricky."

"Confessing is a bit too strong, Luis. Informing is, I think, more accurate."

Luis shrugged. "As you like."

"Do you remember when you called on me here the evening you first visited Bob Chance at the InterPresidential?"

Luis nodded.

"You so generously referred Mr. Chance to me, an assignment to draw up a contract for him and the late Mr. Mikey Smeeth to sign, an instrument to resolve their lottery dispute."

Luis closed his eyes. He knew what was coming.

"I was on standby, so to speak, in the event that Mr. Chance desired to secure my services for the transaction. You were to notify me."

"How long after I left your office did you race to the hotel to solicit Chance? Did you run or take a taxi?"

Ricky fluttered a hand. "There is no point being abusive, Luis. Within the hour. Approximately."

"I should have guessed. Chance asked too many questions about you at the bullring the next day."

"I offered my services. However, I applied no high pressure. What is that North American phrase with which people abuse attorneys who merely solicit business to pay their bills and feed their children? Ambulance chasing, as I recall. It was not like that, I swear. Mr. Bob Chance and I had a friendly and productive dialogue. No fees were tendered, no documents signed. Unfortunately, the bizarre homicide of Mikey Smeeth rendered the situation irrelevant."

"I believe as Judith Maxwell-Chance does that Bob Chance did not murder Mikey Smith."

"No, Luis, Chance did not seem to me a man who could commit mayhem. He was gentle and confused and hapless. Should he possess the anger to kill, he certainly does not possess the physical efficiency. Yet, circumstantial evidence is not favorable to him."

"Keep talking, Ricky."

"Luis, I have bared my soul. Do you realize how hard it is for me, a college graduate and a professional man, to admit a blunder? Especially a blunder that may have hurt a loyal, wonderful friend, namely yourself? A blunder that could perhaps be construed as unethical?"

"A chunk of that blunder is sticking in your throat, Ricky."

"I may have related innocently in normal, casual conversation with Vance the extraordinary Bob Chance story."

"*May have*, Ricky?"

"All right, how often does one make the acquaintance of a fabulously wealthy gentleman, the recipient of three million gringo dollars? The topic was exciting."

"Did you deliberately bring Dugdale and Chance together?"

"No, I swear on the Virgin of Guadalupe I did not, Luis!"

"Did you normally, casually relate to Dugdale where Chance was staying?"

"Luis, you are too young to be so cynical."

"Yes? No?"

"Possibly. A room that costs hundreds of dollars per day is a noteworthy conversational subject in its own right, is it not?"

"Dugdale immediately drove his Jeep at high speed to the Cancún InterPresidential?"

Ricky sighed heavily. "There you go again. This is in the realm of speculation, but, yes, I am afraid that Vance may have capitalized on the slip of my lip."

"May have?"

"When I assemble circumstantial fragments of fact, yes, I might have to conclude that Vance and Mr. Chance reached a business arrangement."

"What kind of business arrangement?"

"Unholy. But I would not begin to speculate regarding the fine details."

"Bob Chance disappeared after Mikey Smith and I fought. Mikey Smith was found murdered in Chance's hotel room. Judy spoke on the telephone to Chance's mother, who said Chance telephoned her begging for money. We think he was calling from Yucatán State, in the vicinity of Chichén Itzá. Judy and I are going there for the equinox to investigate."

"Rich gringos begging for money, Luis. The world has gone mad."

"Did Dugdale promise to repay your loan on a specific date?"

"No. I assumed a day or two, when the Houston bank corrected their error."

"A day or two has passed."

"Oh, I am aware of that, Luis. I know how to read a calendar."

"Dugdale is hustling for money. Chance is hustling for money."

"Yes they are, Luis. What they are doing beyond that scenario, I would not speculate."

"Why would you speculate that far? Have you proof they're together?"

"I peered out my window just after Vance left, Luis. The passenger door of the Jeep was open. Bob Chance was clutching a can of beer and urinating in the alley."

29

The shoppers returned within the hour. Bobby Chance, the dummy, Rita Trunkey Chance explained, had forgotten to cancel Judy's plastic. The card had a high limit, but whoever said Mexico was *el cheapo* was talking through his sombrero. The balance zeroed out lickety-split.

"Speaking of which," she added, taking from the largest plastic shopping bag Luis had ever seen two of the most garish sombreros Luis had ever seen.

"The least we could do," she said, presenting them.

"You ladies are too kind, too extravagant," Ricky said.

"Yes," Luis concurred. The sombrero material was black and velvety. The brims were the diameter of umbrellas. The metallic stitching was so busy that Luis decided wearing them in a lightning storm could be suicidal. Luis thought of the Cisco Kid.

"How about us? How do we look?" Rita said, doing a model's twirl.

She wore an eye-piercing heliotrope sheath. Notable on her wrists and fingers were silver bracelets and rings set with semiprecious stones. Lapis lazuli, turquoise, rose quartz, and black coral. Luis was hurt and disappointed. He could have done better for her at Black Coral. Luis Balam accepted major credit cards.

"Bravo," Ricky stood, clapping.

"Look at Judy," Rita said, grinning. "This little gal's dolled up like a yuppie who could run the Boston Marathon."

Judy was indeed in North American jogging wear, a rainbow of skintight fabrics scientifically designed to breathe and to cost his income for one month. Luis was simultaneously aroused and reminded of Denny and Joyce.

Judy saw how he was looking at her and blushed.

Rita said, "Listen, guys, we got lucky on our timing and took a cash advance at an ATM before the next to last boutique. Their computer shot up a red flare on Bobby's plastic. This little snot clerk glared at us like we were two-bit whores and scissored the card into tiny strips, just like they do back home. Since we have some spare cash and we're well into cocktail hour, what say we take you two out for margaritas and a basket of tostados?"

"Bravo, bravo," Ricky said.

"My Ricardo *hombre,*" Rita said, kissing his cheek. "Always ready to please. You guys talk some business in our absence?"

"We did," Luis said.

"You look serious. I know the perfect spot."

Rita's perfect spot was the bar below Ricky's office. She said the place intrigued her. It struck her as the real Mexico. Ricardo would never take her in there, but on account of her and Judy buying, to hell with him.

If the bar had a name, Luis had never noticed. It was narrow and deep and dark and smoky. A jukebox guitar played at low volume. Judy and Luis had Leon Negras, Rita and Ricky margaritas. Judy said to Ricky, "How come nobody here seems to know you? This would be a superconvenient hangout and it's got atmosphere that won't quit."

Rita laughed. "Judy's thinking of Bobby. A watering hole this close to *his* job, he'd be a partner."

"Believe it or not, I have never frequented this bar," Ricky said stiffly. "This is a tourist trap, a cheap bar, not my type of establishment."

Rita sipped her margarita and shuddered. "One hundred octane. A cheap bar that makes a drink like this, it can't be all bad."

Luis knew that Ricky hated this cheap bar because it reminded him that he practiced law above a cheap bar.

"Yeah? What is your type of establishment?" Judy goaded.

"Hotel zone lounges and discos. They offer atmosphere."

They also offer single women and a partying frenzy, Luis thought further.

"Well, aren't they tourist traps?" Judy asked. "Besides Rita and I, everybody else here looks Mexican."

"Nary a gringo visible in the haze," Rita said, lighting up.

"A tourist trap for the budget-conscious," Ricky said. "They will arrive. Trust me."

"Well, c'mon, fellows," Rita said. "Out with it. You're dying to."

"Go ahead, Ricky," Luis said.

"Repeat my confession? Luis, you are twisting the knife."

"Not confessing, Ricky. Informing."

Ricky informed. He described the Ricky-Chance connection and the presumed Chance-Dugdale connection. Judy's jaw dropped. Rita exhaled smoke in Ricky's face and said, "Why, you little turdbird, you were holding out on me."

"Only to spare a vulnerable and sensitive and sensual lady the worry of unfounded speculations."

"Ricardo, I don't know whether you're naive or crooked or what. You hoodwinked us."

Luis saw Ricky's arm creep forward under the table.

"Your hoodwinky is not in my vocabulary, but, yes, naive and crooked. I have a tiny trace of those in me. Components of my charm, as it were."

"Don't do that in public, *hombre.*" She squeezed Ricky's cheek and turned to Judy. "Gotta love him, don't you? How can you stay ticked off at the Incredible Hunk?"

Judy was unhearing. "Dugdale murdered Mikey Smith, you know."

"He could have," Luis said.

"Well, remember when Inspector Salgado brought me out to Black Coral?"

"Always."

She ran the toe of her sandal on his calf. "I was in that weird car of his while he was in with you. Ricky and Dugdale came out and drove off in the Jeep. That was Dugdale, wasn't it?"

"Yes."

"The first thing that went through my mind was 'escaped child molester.' He looked that creepy. And he was smoking a cigarette."

Rita looked at Judy and butted hers. "I didn't take you as one of those cancer fanatics, but I never met a jogger who wasn't."

Judy smiled and otherwise ignored the crack. "The third person in Robert's room, Luis. The dirty ashtray. Mikey Smith didn't smoke. Robert didn't smoke. Dugdale smokes."

Luis stupidly said, "Mystery clue. Francisco Ek in our village, he told me Dugdale was out with a big man in his Jeep. I thought it was our fat friend who loves his motorcycle."

"They're partners," Judy said. "Dugdale killed Mikey Smith to gain access to Robert's Lotto winnings. With Smith out of the picture, he's sole owner of the ticket. Thinks he's sole owner, that is."

"Ignorance is bliss," Rita said. "Bobby has a couple of wives and doesn't know it."

"Nor does Dugdale know," Luis said. "Ricky?"

"Not unless Mr. Chance confessed to Dugdale. I certainly did not reveal the surprise. I was informed late of that aspect—you two lovely aspects—of the man's life. Your speculating is irrelevant, though. You overestimate Vance's capacity for violence. He has a fast, oily mouth, but he is hardly a murderer."

A young tourist couple came in and took a table. Their crimson faces glistened from sunblock applied too late. They wore T-shirts decorated with COZUMEL and a toucan.

"Keel-billed toucan," Judy said to Luis. "Extremely rare. Ever see one?"

Luis couldn't remember. "No. They're very very rare."

"This little gal and her birds," Rita said with affection.

"I admire anybody who goes out and learns something they don't have to. What I know about birds is how to flip one to somebody who cuts me off on the freeway."

"Don't be so sure Dugdale isn't violent, Ricky," Luis said. "His trash mestizos claim he has a bad temper and a small-caliber weapon strapped to his ankle."

Ricky's eyes widened.

Rita said, "With Bobby under the thumb of this guy, you gotta worry. This Dugdale, whether he killed Smith or he didn't kill Smith, it doesn't sound good for Bobby, him being more or less in this character's custody."

A mariachi trio materialized. As a jaguar smells blood, Luis thought, sidewalk mariachis follow the scent of suntan lotion.

"Luis, you are the best detective around," Ricky said. "Prove it. Liberate Mr. Chance and his remaining nineteen years of the lottery fortune."

The mariachis' sombreros were identical to Luis and Ricky's. In tight pants and matching jackets, they were speaking to the crimson Anglos. Luis said, "We'll start with Héctor."

"The chubby inspector? Good move. He strikes me as a bloodhound when he sets his mind to it. Ricardo and me, we'll go to his pad and fry up that meat before it spoils, unless it was spoiled before I bought it, which will be obvious right off the bat. Okay by you, *hombre?*"

Ricky licked his lips and stroked his long jaw. Luis read a gleam in his eyes. Ricky had regenerated without the benefit of rhinoceros horns or Rita's chopped meat.

"I will consult my appointment book, but if I recall correctly, my calendar is free this afternoon."

Judy paid the check. They stood just as the mariachi

trio began "La Bamba." Rita sat, tugging Ricky's arm. "Wait a minute, hon. This is an all-time favorite of mine."

Ricky slumped into his chair, eyes shut. Luis and Judy met the rotund pseudo-Texan of a car rental clerk as he came out of the alley.

"Was Attorney Martínez in?" Luis asked. "Does he have your Jeep?"

"Not in! No Jeep!" the clerk cried, throwing up his stubby arms. "What kind of lawyer is he, really? He has a disgraceful office he is never in to see clients I doubt he has."

"As I explained to you at your agency, Mr. Martínez is one of the finest lawyers in Cancún, if not all of Yucatán. He is probably in the field with important clients or away lecturing at a seminar."

"Splendid. I want my Jeep."

"So does Mr. Martínez, boss. Should I see him before you do, I'll relay your message."

En route to the Quintana Roo State Judicial Police and Inspector Héctor Salgado Reyes, Judy said, "You could have steered that poor man into the bar. You made it no secret you're pissed at Ricky."

"I was tempted."

"You saved his life and saved his afternoon," Judy said, laughing.

"You are my witness. He owes me. I would rather force him to repay a favor than to visit him in a hospital. You and Rita, Judy, you were—friendly. Ricky thinks it is a miracle. He may have a point."

"You expected clawing and spitting?"

Luis accelerated and slalomed through a busy intersection, oblivious to bleating horns and braking traffic.

"Jesus, Luis, you'll kill us yet."

"This is Cancún City. Too many cars. If you slow down, you're an easy target for a crash."

"Super logic. Everybody should drive a hundred miles an hour. Everybody would be too quick to get hit."

"Everybody in Mexico will drive a hundred miles an hour if they have the open road. No, I did not expect clawing and spitting, but I did not *not* expect clawing and spitting. You and Rita are both married to Bob Chance. Because he and Rita are not divorced, you and Chance are not married, although it is not your fault."

"Well, they say opposites attract. That applies to friendship too. We both think the other is weird. Nice but weird. The weirdest thing is that we both married Robert. We know we're too good for him."

"But you still care for him?"

"Haven't we covered this territory? Are you jealous?"

"No," Luis lied.

"I care for lost puppies too, okay? Rita does too. Don't you?"

"Yes," Luis lied.

"And we care for the money. We wouldn't be human if we didn't. Would we?"

"You wouldn't," Luis agreed.

Héctor was in, although in neither good health nor good mood.

"Are you sick?" Luis asked.

"My beloved Carmen inquired the same," Héctor said. "Except that she was smiling sadistically. I vaguely remember she was smiling, but I could not determine with certainty as I was retching at the time. A hangover derived from canned fruity booze is the foulest of the foul."

"Sorry," Luis said.

"The beverages are dishonest," Héctor went on. "Sugars and vitamins camouflaging the lethal chemistry."

"Anything new on Bob Chance?" Luis said.

"Only additional harassment. To employ that North American saying, the fan collided with the shit this morning. Tourism bureaucrats of every stripe and officials of his nation and ours make constant nagging inquiries. I inform them that reliable intelligence has placed Chance in Yucatán State. Not my jurisdiction, not my problem. They say, no, no, Smith was killed in Cancún, Quintana Roo State, therefore, Inspector, your intelligence is meaningless unless Chance is in custody. He could be anywhere and your jail is the preferred place for him, so why is he not there?"

"Why all the uproar over one dead American?" Judy asked. "Not that I'm making light of murder, but the killing wasn't political."

"Mikey Smith was a former North American–rules football star, was he not?"

"Junior college honorable mention all-American, according to Robert. Endlessly. Big deal."

"Big deal, indeed," Héctor said. "Those people up north, they martyr dead football heroes as we do professional wrestlers."

"Martyring Mikey Smith?" Judy said. "Come on, Inspector."

"Journalists instigate these headaches. Smith's hometown newspaper splashed the story in headline fashion. A faded football hero and a *lotería* tycoon, they are of enormous public interest. The tabloids are expected to write their versions. Mr. Bob Chance's mother is being interviewed relentlessly by the press and by law enforcement people. I understand she is a difficult lady. She tells them she may be coming to Cancún."

"Call out the national guard," Judy said.

Luis filled Héctor in on Ricky's anguished confession.

"Dugdale and Chance," Héctor said. "Rather fascinating."

"Dugdale is a smoker," Judy said. "The ashtray, right? He was the third man in Bobby's hotel room. He's the shooter."

"Perhaps, Señora Chance. Association of those two does expand possibilities."

"We have a reliable source who claims Dugdale carries a small-caliber pistol holstered on his leg."

"Fugitives come to Mexico, they feel they can operate with impunity," Héctor said, sighing.

"Fugitives? Dugdale? What do you have, Héctor?"

Documents were stacked on Héctor's desk in piles that seemed to Luis random. Héctor selected one half a meter high, propped it on his ample lap, licked fingertips, and began searching.

"Criminals such as Vance Dugdale are so arrogant that they falsely believe they can operate with impunity using their real names. What is Mexico? A sanctuary for cutthroats? The Casbah? The dark side of the moon?"

Thus far, Luis thought, Dugdale *had* been operating with impunity. He did not answer.

"Ah, here we are." Héctor pulled out a WANTED BY FBI poster.

"Hey, that's what hangs up in post offices," Judy said.

"Correct, señora."

"How long have you had this, Héctor?"

"Police departments trade information on fugitives and many facets of our profession," Héctor said defensively. "The sheer mass of the information is oppressive."

"Months?" Luis asked.

Héctor jabbed a finger at him. "Do not agitate a sick man, Luis. I warn you! Mere weeks, I estimate."

"That's him. Yucch," Judy said. "He's one guy mug shots really do justice to."

Luis looked at the photos. Lank stringy hair. Raptor's face. No, make that raptor's and scavenger's face. The poster was dated a year earlier and the tropical sun had not yet erupted Dugdale's splotchy freckles.

Luis studied the text. Vance Ralph Dugdale. Wanted by the FBI for Mail Fraud. Aliases: Ted Snowe, Maurice Johnson, Jack James, William Nelson. No stupidly similar names, he thought.

Occupations: car salesman, tour guide, investment broker, realtor. Remarks: talks fast, dresses stylishly. Stylishly was a matter of opinion, Luis mused, this Desert Fox and Los Angeles Pimp.

Criminal record: Dugdale has been convicted of Mail Fraud, Wire Fraud, Income Tax Evasion, and Assault. Caution: Dugdale, a master salesman, is being sought in connection with a fraudulent scheme in which 150 victims were swindled out of in excess of one hundred thousand dollars through their payment of deposits for a combined Civil War theme park and time-share condominium near Gettysburg, Pennsylvania. Dugdale has been convicted of assaulting a former wife. He is familiar with firearms and should be considered armed and dangerous.

"A cultural interval ownership entrepreneur," Luis thought out loud.

"He has also worked as a tour guide, Luis," Héctor said. "What else do you and he have in common?"

"Chichén Itzá," Judy said. "The equinox celebration."

"Chichén Itzá," Luis said.

"Wouldn't the celebration fit Dugdale's profile?" Judy said.

"It would," Luis said.

"How?" Héctor said. "Specifically?"

"Dugdale will try to sell Chichén Itzá."

Judy added, "Like the Brooklyn Bridge?"

"Plausibly," Héctor said. "Dugdale would sell anything."

"Judy and I, we are going sightseeing tomorrow, Héctor. Join us?"

"Not me. Your theory is not without validity, but I am not chasing wild geese outside my jurisdiction. No. My police colleagues in Yucatán State would not care to have me snooping in their back yard."

"Well, wherever he is, Inspector, Dugdale's dragging Robert around with him as excess baggage."

"No. Thank you anyway. Count me out, children. This is your party."

30

Luis spent the night at home. Not because he could not perform. No, that had been a temporary malfunction. But his babies were entitled to see him occasionally. Chichén Itzá would occupy him tomorrow and the next day, minimum. Esther and Rosa were running Black Coral on their own and deserved the presence of their father. Judy said she understood. Sort of. She certainly understood the guilt he was suffering. Not guilt, he told her; a sense of fatherly responsibility.

In the morning, Esther and Rosa asked Luis what was wrong.

"Nothing is wrong. What do you mean?"

"You were tossing and turning in your hammock throughout the night. We could hardly sleep."

Sleepless throughout the night was accurate, he thought. One half of the night due to lustful images of Judy, one half due to the announcement he now made to his babies.

"Chichén Itzá, Father?" Rosa said. "How can you know Dugdale and Chance are there?"

"We think they are."

"How can you pick two men out of thousands of tourists?"

"We have to try. Should we not find them there and soon, I promise to quit the case. It isn't right that you have to be at the shop all the time while I'm chasing people."

"Don't feel guilty, Father," Esther said.

"I'm not feeling guilty."

"When does your North American Indian lady go home?"

"She is not Indian. I don't know when she is going."

"You capture this man, her husband, does she go then?"

"I don't know. She can't stay forever, whether I locate him or not."

"Go. You should be with her while you can."

Luis hugged his daughters. "You can stay home today. Black Coral can be closed for a day."

"No," Esther said. "Then we would feel as guilty as you are. Go."

Luis picked up Judy at Akumal and said, "Do you think Juliana would like some hush money today?"

"You bet, but aren't we going to Chichén Itzá?"

"It's early," Luis said. "Juliana needs us to stick up for her."

"You're really gung ho on this."

"Gung what?"

"You know, zealous."

"We should do it. It's something we should do."

"I'm not arguing, Luis. Is everything okay with your daughters?"

She was probing his mind with hers. Luis imagined her

brain waves tickling his, tapping into the sense of fatherly responsibility transferring from his babies to another Maya girl. The curse of falling in love with an insightful woman! "Yes. Okay."

"You're wound tight, Luis. Relax, okay? As far as I'm concerned, you don't have any reason to be guilty. You're a nifty guy and a nifty dad. Lighten up."

Maybe Ricky had the right idea, he thought. Be attracted to women whose bust measurements equaled their IQs, and be attracted to them in quantity. "I am not guilty. I am lightened up."

"Zealots kill people, you know, whether they intend to or not. That condo manager doesn't deserve to die."

The Punta Paraiso manager arrived just ahead of them in a Ford Mustang with chrome dual exhausts and black louvers on the fastback window. He was out of the car, hand on hip, opposite elbow on door, talking to Paco. His hair and casual outfit were immaculate. He should be playing golf with celebrities, thought Luis, who gestured that they would also like to enter.

"Quite the sport, isn't he?" Judy said.

The manager nodded without enthusiasm and said something under his breath to hard-eyed Paco, who waved them through. Luis gave Paco the finger. Judy gave Luis's thigh a rough pinch and called him a brat.

At the model unit, the manager said, "Do you have my goods?"

"I recovered your television," Luis said.

"Yes, you did recover the TV, but it doesn't work. It smoked when I turned it on, blew fuses, and stunk up the model unit."

"Japanese workmanship is overrated," Luis said. "A couple of wires get crossed on the assembly line and the TV will fail."

"You ought to buy the extended warranty on expensive electronics," Judy advised. "You'll save yourself a lot of grief."

"That TV is of no consequence. Don't expect a fee unless you deliver the gambling equipment."

"Forget the gambling machines. They have been sacrificed."

"You're a funny little man," the manager said, unamused. "Save that brand of humor for your villagers. A smart-ass answer won't get you paid."

Judy touched Luis's arm. "Easy, easy."

"Your reward money isn't important, boss. I have another assignment, investigating attempted rape charges made by an employee of yours against two other employees of yours."

"That's ridiculous."

"So ridiculous that your ears are turning redder than your reddest golf shirt. I am chief private detective for Ricardo Martínez Rodríguez, the noted Cancún attorney who represents the victim."

"I never heard of him."

Luis and Judy looked at each other in disbelief, then Luis said, "Mr. Martínez is among the finest lawyers in Cancún, if not all of Yucatán. Listen, boss, Juan and Ernesto were within an instant of raping Juliana when they were interrupted."

"There are things worse than rape," the manager said philosophically. "There are degrees of rape that are not necessarily rape."

"What makes you think you're qualified to say what's worse than rape, you prissy piece of garbage?" Judy yelled.

Luis touched her arm. "Easy."

The manager replied without losing composure. "Juan and Ernesto, those slobs, they didn't report for work yesterday. I went to their cabin. They had cleaned out and gone."

"It happened, nearly happened, in their cabin."

"How do you know?"

"How do *you* know, boss? Please do not plead ignorance."

"Stories like that, they spread like fire, they get back to me. I pride myself in being a good, sensitive manager who looks after his people."

"A good, sensitive manager would comfort Juliana," Judy said. "A good, sensitive manager would stand up for her rights."

"There is a limit to how much a manager should interfere in the private lives of his staff. The stories were unsubstantiated."

"Attorney Martínez and I have substantiated the crime, boss."

"You have that Indian girl's version. The men she accuses are not available to defend themselves. That is not substantiation."

"As far as Attorney Martínez is concerned, Juliana has a substantiated case. The Cancún newspaper agrees."

"Newspaper?"

"Attorney Martínez has contacted sympathetic reporters. He has not given them permission to print the story yet. He is considering another approach, contacting your bosses, the Punta Paraiso owners, and asking for damages. He does prefer a combination approach."

"Which is?"

"Having the article printed and allowing it to be the instrument that contacts your bosses."

"What do you want?"

"It's not what we want," Luis said. "It's what she wants and what she *doesn't* want. She doesn't want retaliation. She doesn't want a fuss made. Speaking to her about the crime would embarrass her."

"I cannot help her if I cannot negotiate with her."

"She is a fine employee, isn't she?"

The manager's eyebrows lifted. "She is just a maid. She does her job."

"A super-good job, I'll bet," Judy said. "A candidate for the maid's hall of fame."

"Deserving of a raise," Luis said.

"A merit raise," Judy said.

"I pay my people well already."

"How much?" Judy asked.

The manager shook his head. "Confidential."

"A few pesos a day, the equivalent of two or three dollars," Luis said. "Maybe enough to buy food."

"The reporter can ask Juliana her wage and include it in the article," Judy said.

"It occurs to me that the young lady's probationary period has expired," the manager said, snapping his fingers and smiling through clenched teeth. "She is due for a management review and an increase."

"Fifty percent," Luis said. "And two weeks pay as a bonus."

"Coincidentally, the exact amount I had contemplated."

"Good. A final question. Where might those two boys be?"

"Look under a rock."

"A second final question. Where might Vance Dugdale be?"

"I don't know," the manager said. "But I hope you catch him. You deserve each other."

Judy and Luis drove northward in satisfied silence. They bypassed most of Cancún City, just grazing the spreading outskirts of ramshackle housing, cement factories, and bottling plants, and turned onto Highway 180. Nearly two hundred flat, monotonous kilometers to the west lay the Chichén Itzá ruins. Speed bumps in numerous villages en route slowed the traveler and significantly reduced the traffic death rate.

Two thirds of the way to Chichén Itzá, they came to a toll booth and a divided highway. "This looks all brand-new. How much did you have to pay? I saw big numbers of those bills," Judy said.

"Twenty-four pesos. Eight dollars."

"That's pretty stiff."

"And it is brand-new."

"Not that I'm knocking progress, but why a freeway in the middle of nowhere?"

"This is the beginning. They haven't completed much road yet, but someday you will be able to drive all over Yucatán from ruin to ruin at the speed of light and see everything in a day without seeing anything."

Fifteen minutes later, they took the exit to Valladolid and lunch. Seeing that Judy's head was on a swivel, Luis drove through the narrow streets at a leisurely pace.

"Wow, that plaza and those old buildings and churches. Colonial charm and then some. Really old and pretty. We've passed three churches already."

At a cafe on the main plaza, the *zócalo,* Luis said, "The Spaniards built and built cathedrals. They demolished Maya temples for building materials. A convenience for them and a lesson for the heathen savages. Every time we looked around, we had reminders that God and Spain were with us. Valladolid has a rich history."

"Rich and bloody?"

"Judy, did you know the Caste War began in Valladolid?"

She shook her head.

"In the 1840s the Yucatán bosses were going to secede from Mexico. They feared Mexican troops coming down. They would be outnumbered. They armed the Maya to fight for them."

"And their plan backfired?"

"Yes. We fought our bosses. There was much killing. It was the worst in Valladolid, where Maya were always treated like dirt. Once, a drunken priest saddled a Maya and rode him, slashing him with his spurs."

"That's terrible. The bosses won the Caste War, huh?"

Luis nodded. "We had to quit temporarily to plant our corn crop. Winning a war is no good if you starve to death afterward. When we finally went back, they had imported guns and supplies and mercenary soldiers."

"Tell me the truth, Luis, are you nostalgic?"

"Meaning?"

"Doesn't some part of you yearn to have been there, killing bosses? Not that I blame you."

"Truth?"

"If you don't mind."

Luis looked at his table knife and pictured his machete severing a Spanish neck as easily as a cornstalk. "To do what I had to do to win the war, yes, maybe."

"Let's change the subject, okay. Your veins are sticking out. Valladolid looks prosperous."

"No. No, it is not prosperous."

"Could have fooled me. Aren't those rental cars and tourists here, there, and everywhere?"

"Headed for Chichén Itzá, fueling their bodies and their cars. The spring equinox draws fifty times the usual number of visitors," Luis said. "Two days ago or two days from now, Valladolidinos would be staring at you because you were the only North American in town."

"Because the new freeway bypasses Valladolid?"

Luis asked their waiter for the check and said, "Yes."

"That's rotten. There's a jillion U.S. towns that's happened to. How far to Chichén Itzá?"

"Forty kilometers."

"The speed you drive, we've got ten minutes to plan our strategy for zeroing in on Dugdale and Robert. Your thoughts? Please don't be bashful."

In the car, out of town, Luis said, "Dugdale is at Chichén Itzá to make money, not to drink in the history. Dead Dinosaurs wouldn't work."

"No, it wouldn't. His gambling machines were sacrificed," Judy said. "The Brooklyn Bridge syndrome is the key. Whatever Dugdale's up to, it's big and a one-shot deal."

"Brooklyn Bridge," Luis said. "Opened 1883. Fifteen hundred and ninety-five feet long."

"You are scary, you know, you and your almanac.

Dugdale's dragging Robert along like an anchor. They should be conspicuous."

"Thousands of people visit. Dugdale and Chance may not be on the grounds either. There are villages and hotels nearby."

"We can narrow our focus and hope we get lucky. Dugdale was a tour guide. You're a tour guide. Think like a greedy, evil tour guide, Luis."

"At Tulum, I gather as many tourists into a group as I can. Charge a dollar or two per person and multiply."

"Don't get your feelings hurt, Luis, but something tells me Dugdale's thinking bigger than that."

"He is wanted in North America for swindling people out of money for a Civil War amusement park. He does have ambitious ideas."

"He could pull that off here. Convince buyers he's throwing together a Maya Disneyland."

Luis slowed, then stopped, then started, then stopped, then started.

"How far out are we?"

"Three kilometers. Four."

"Identical to a daily commute in Seattle. I'm getting homesick. What's the tie-up, tomorrow's big-deal doing?"

"Yes. I knew the crowds would be large. But—" Luis's voice trailed off.

"Oh boy," Judy said. "Wish us luck, Luis. If Dugdale and Robert are conspicuous, they're two conspicuous needles in a haystack."

31

Luis was certain that every car creeping ahead of them on the highway was filled with people who planned to stop at the Chichén Itzá ruins. He was also certain that these travelers were preceded by all the friends, relations, and acquaintances of their lifetimes. Where would tomorrow's day-trippers fit?

Compact, walled Tulum was claustrophobic whenever tour buses invaded in peak season, but never as congested as these ten square kilometers of airy grounds were now. Luis imagined that Cancún's entire annual production of T-shirts and Japan's output of cameras were on the tourists at Chichén Itzá. That people would travel thousands of miles and spend thousands of pesos and dollars to observe a trick played by a conspiracy of the sun and stonemasons dead for eleven centuries was beyond his comprehension.

Judy said, let's mingle, keep our eyes open, maybe we'll get lucky. Luis agreed with a sullen nod, thinking maybe they would get crushed. Trapped in the path of a stampede, a panic to buy up depleted stocks of souvenirs and film.

Judy had a smooth, serpentine knack for moving through the mobs, gliding, weaving, hardly banging an elbow or shoulder. She had Luis by the hand, pulling and repeating chill out, cool it. Point and narrate. You're a tour guide. This is awesome. What's Chichén Itzá all about?

Luis recognized that Judy was adapting to inconveniences with good cheer while he sulked. Chichén Itzá was originally a Maya city, he said. Some of the architecture is theirs. Some is Toltec, a rough-and-tumble people who stormed down from Mexico and conquered this city. They ruled for two hundred years and remodeled.

Luis pointed and narrated for the next two hours. The Caracol. A unique circular structure. An observatory. We had no optics, but we could predict the placement of Venus in the sky with an error of less than one minute per year.

There's Kukulcán, *El Castillo.* Enjoy it today. Tomorrow you won't be able to get near it.

There was this temple and that temple. Judy was intrigued by the several ball courts, rectangular patches bounded lengthwise by parallel stone walls.

"The carved stone circle high up on the wall," Luis explained at the largest. "The object was to put a solid rubber ball through it. The players wore cotton padding and, like soccer, couldn't use their hands. The winners were given clothing and jewelry by the spectators. The losers lost their heads."

"You're kidding."

"I'm reciting the popular story. It's tempting to believe, like sacrificing virgins."

"God, Robert would love to bet on a ball game like that. Football just ends with a whistle and another beer commercial. And speaking of sacrificing virgins, isn't Chichén Itzá supposed to be famous for that?"

"You decide," Luis said, taking the lead to the Sacred Cenote.

Judy looked down sixty feet of sheer limestone walls at the brackish green surface and said, "Yucch. Virgins tossed into this gunk dissolved."

"Not necessarily virgins. Men, women, boys, girls. They've dredged and brought up bones with artifacts, but can't determine their sex lives."

"Except that they came to an end. I'm dying of thirst."

Under an unusually hot sun, they stood in line for cold sodas. At a table, Judy said, "Regardless how our hunch on Robert turns out, I have to leave the day after tomorrow. At the latest."

She was looking at her drink as she spoke. Luis asked, "Money?"

"Uh huh. My jobs too. They'll write me off as lost in the jungle if I don't get back, and I can't deal with unemployment right now. Too many bills, this trip compounding them."

Luis almost offered his home. Him and his home, a package. Foolishly, he thought; I can feed and house her, but I cannot give her a life. And the ability to feed her was questionable. After paying for parking, admission, and sodas, no currency remained from the Bob Chance one-hundred-dollar retainer. Aside from a folded stash of emergency money in his billfold, he had only coins. Black Coral ownership and Tulum tour guiding were not making him wealthy either.

"Bob Chance can solve your money problems. All we have to do is find him and save him from Dugdale and himself."

"I'm worrying more by the minute, Luis. Dugdale lost interest in the Dead Dinosaurs Park when Robert came along. He has something cooked up and if Robert doesn't fit in with the scheme, he'll lose interest in him too."

"Bob Chance has nineteen years to go on his *lotería* fortune," Luis reminded her.

"Yeah, but this is only March. His next installment isn't until the first of the year. You can become pretty sick of Robert in ten months. Just ask Rita and me."

"Dugdale is greedy enough to have patience. Like you, I'm convinced he was in Chance's hotel room when Mikey Smith was killed. Who pulled the trigger? Who cares? Chance is the prime suspect. Chance and Dugdale are together. They are a double prime suspect."

"Well, I guess that's what's bugging me. Dugdale is not about to be arrested with Robert. No way. He feels the walls closing in on him, you know how he'll react, to hell with any future Lotto money."

Luis said nothing. He knew.

"That old saying, you know. Dead men testify at no murder trials," she added needlessly.

"We will find them before the police do and before Dugdale hurts Chance."

"I hope so. Of the jillions of people at Chichén Itzá today, not one remotely resembles those two clowns. I have to worry. All we're going on is secondhand hysteria from Thelma, mommie dearest, a drunken old dingbat."

Dingbat? A bird she watched? "When we finish our sodas, we'll walk around and ask questions."

"Ask who?"

"Maya employees. Groundskeepers, guards, ticket takers, souvenir peddlers, guides."

"Makes sense. But they look awfully busy. This place is like, you know, Christmas season at the mall," Judy said. "Still, if Dugdale and Robert have shown, they're likely to have seen them. But we? Wouldn't I just be in your way?"

"Would you rather sit here and fry?"

"I'd rather contribute. I'll mingle. I'll ask subtle questions, gringo to gringo. What person who has encountered Beavis and Butthead in the flesh could forget the experience?"

The names were unfamiliar, but no matter. They agreed to meet back at the same refreshment stand in an hour and a half. Luis queried Maya employees who were amenable to conversation and could spare a minute from their duties. He drew a blank and quickly realized why. The workers were not dealing with people, they were completing transactions. Their transactions spoke a foreign tongue and looked very much alike, perspiration coating far too much exposed pink or tan skin.

Luis was irritated by their callousness, their lack of observation. But he identified with them. When Tulum was mobbed while he was leading tours and when full buses disgorged their loads at Black Coral, he too regarded the North American mobs impersonally, as soft and fleshy cash-dispensing machines.

A hot and frustrated Luis Balam bought a soda with a portion of his reserve and sat heavily. His car needed gas, but coolant for him outweighed fuel for it.

Not a minute later, Judy and a grandmotherly Anglo joined them. The woman had a gray permanent and glasses. She wore loose slacks and a long-sleeved blouse. What skin Luis could see was like speckled lard. She was not at home in the tropics.

Judy and her new friend were carrying margaritas in paper cups, salt coating the rims. "How did it go, Luis?"

Luis pulled on his drink and said, "No mystery clues."

"Pardon me for asking, grumpy. Madeline, this is my detective friend, Luis Balam. Luis, while you were pounding the pavement, I went where sensible people go in this heat. Do you realize that the mercury's at ninety-five?"

"Where do sensible people go, Judy?"

"Unless you have an air-conditioned hotel room, which is impossible to come by for the next two days, you head to the hotel lounges."

Madeline closed her eyes, remembering. "Right under that ceiling fan, it was heaven."

"You hung around bars?"

"Don't get excited, Luis. Nobody tried to pick me up. It wasn't that dark."

Madeline cast Judy a grandmotherly frown and said, "You don't sell yourself short, honey."

"She's a doll, isn't she? Anyway, bottom line, Madeline has had contact with Dugdale and Robert."

"That isn't what they said their names were. The fat one, I don't recollect if he ever gave a name. The one with the fast mouth, he went by Jack James."

"Our old friend Jack James from the wanted poster," Judy said.

"It wasn't actually me who had contact with those birds, it was Rollie. He's in the room now, taking a siesta. Too much sun, too many *cervezas,* and him a bad boy about taking his blood pressure medicine. He's nearly melted."

"Rollie?"

"Rollie's my husband. Forty-second anniversary coming up in June. We usually take our vacation every summer at the lake. But Rollie retired last December. Forty-three years at Ford in Dearborn, not counting layoffs and strikes. Rollie says, we're living the life of leisure we can for once in our lives take a trip like they advertise in those commercials with the palm trees and the beaches. We're Midwestern car people, all our lives in Michigan. We're accustomed to mean and nasty winters, but those commercials looked awful good, although now I'm in Mexico, I can't say as I'm overly fond of sweating day and night."

Madeline chuckled and sipped her margarita. "Rollie did a bang-up sales job on me. I've never been south of Fort Wayne, where my sister lives. Not that we're made of money or anything. This Cancún package set us back a pretty penny. Rollie got a bug in his ear that we had to see this sun snake on the pyramid thing. We fell into a Hotel Mayaland room cancellation but it's costing a small fortune. We'll be going to the lake for two weeks instead of three come July, or maybe not at all after the fleecing Rollie took from your Jack James."

Judy patted Madeline's arm. "If anyone can recover your money, Luis can."

"I can? How was Rollie contacted?"

"Night before last in the same cocktail bar where I had the good fortune to come across Judy. I'd laid down after dinner and joined Rollie late for a drink. They were already close to wrapping things up, that's how quick this Jack James character works. Rollie, he had this look on his face I can't hardly describe except that I hadn't seen it since he hit eight out of ten on the football card they buy at bars around the plants from guys who, if you believe everything you hear, get these cards from the Mafia. Rollie's one dollar paid eighteen hundred. Matter of fact, when I sat down at the table, Rollie and the fat guy, Mr. James's mining engineer, were jabbering a mile a minute about pro football, trades and things, what coaches were fired. He acted like he'd been away from America for a long time."

"Mining engineer?" Luis said.

"Shh. The plot thickens," Judy said.

"Say, Luis, what's your reading on this comet thing?"

"The comet that killed the dinosaurs?"

"Yeah. They dated it at sixty-five million years ago. Isn't science incredible?"

"Yes, incredible," Luis said. "Mr. James and his mining engineer took you and Rollie to a village at night to see dinosaurs?"

Madeline squinted at Luis, then Judy. "Dinosaurs? What dinosaurs? *Live* dinosaurs?"

"Keep your shirt on, Luis," Judy said.

"Where he took Rollie, not me, Rollie and another fellow, this couple we met at the hotel, him and his engineer drove them out to this whatdoyoucallit, watering hole, in this candy-apple-red Jeep."

"Cenote," Luis said.

"Like this one where they sacrificed virgins in, except a whole lot smaller. Rollie said it was scummy and he darn near caught malaria just looking down into it."

"No dinosaur cultural theme parks?" Luis said.

"You speak English as good as some Americans I know, Luis," Madeline said. "But how you sometimes got your words arranged, you're not making a lick of sense. They went to the cenote to check out the iridium."

Judy said to Luis, "Iridium is the element found in unusually large amounts where a comet or meteorite hit."

"Mr. James spoke of iridium?" Luis asked.

"I'm learning more about iridium than I can stomach," Madeline said, sighing. "Iridium's in the platinum family and is rare as hen's teeth. It's heavy and hard. The alloys they use it for, nothing else will do. We didn't take James's word for its value, give Rollie credit for that. My sister in Fort Wayne, her second oldest boy works in Chicago at the Board of Trade. Rollie had me call her. Sis called her boy and called me back. They don't handle it where he's at. The stuff's so rare, there's only a few companies dealing in exotic metals that sell it. Comes in a powder form for the most part and they sell it by the gram. Multiply those grams into an ounce and guess what iridium goes for."

Luis shook his head.

"In the neighborhood of fifteen hundred bucks an ounce."

"Nice neighborhood, isn't it?" Judy said to Luis.

"That doesn't mean you're gonna go out there to those cenotes and trip over iridium nuggets."

"True," Luis said, grateful that Madeline had saved him from raising that point. "Did they find iridium at the cenote?"

"They brought *something* back." Madeline removed a balled-up facial tissue from her purse and handed it to Luis. "You tell me what. Judy says you're a jeweler along with being a private eye. Salting the mine, that's the oldest trick in the book."

Luis opened the tissue. Inside were pinhead-sized chunks of whitish metal. "I wouldn't recognize iridium, but I imagine Dugdale would. This looks like silver that has been cut up and hammered to appear coarse, like ore."

"Dugdale, that's him, our Mr. Jack James? Not a shadow of a doubt?"

"None, I'm afraid, Madeline," Judy said. "Vance Dugdale and Robert Chance, a pair to draw to."

"How much money did your husband pay him?"

"Not a fortune to some folks. We won't be on the breadline, but three thousand dollars is big money to us. Rollie drove the rental car on in to Mérida to a bank that would give him cash advances on our credit cards."

"Were there papers, documents?" Luis asked.

"Rollie isn't the total village idiot, though he'll feel like one when I break the news to him. The papers, they looked official. Those gilt-edged certificates. Of course, they were in Spanish, which is Greek to me. He had letters too from high officials in Mexico City on official-looking letterheads saying that James, oops, Dugdale and his company had rights to mine the iridium so long as they shared with the government and didn't harm the environment."

"May I examine the papers?" Luis asked.

"Don't have them with me. I guess I can sneak them out to you."

"Sneak them?" Luis said. "Your husband has to be told."

"Not now, not here. Rollie's blood pressure and his temper, oh, he has a doozie, he's liable to blow a cork. If I have to break the news, I'll wait till we're home, or maybe I won't. Maybe it's better he finds out on his own, gradual like, when he can't reach James and there are no dividend checks coming in.

"What I'm hoping, what the ideal thing is, I think, after lucking into you folks, is for you to grab Dugdale and make him give the money back. Have him tell Rollie they had trouble with the government or something and can't go ahead yet mining the iridium. Something so Rollie can save face."

"When did Dugdale sell Rollie?"

"Night before last. Rollie paid him yesterday. Haven't seen him since."

"That was the answer to my next question. Your husband's friend who visited the cenote with him, did he buy too?"

"His name's Leo. Him and June, they're steel people. He's retired out of Pittsburgh. No, I don't think he bought, but he sure nibbled."

"Can you do two things, Madeline?" Luis asked. "Sneak the papers out for us and find out if Leo and June are still in contact with Mr. Jack James."

"Hmmm. We could ask them to have dinner with us at the Hotel Mayaland. They've got good food. We'd been meaning to anyway. Hey, we'll have you join us. I'll pose you as somebody and you can pick their brains to your heart's content. Playing detective, it could grow on me."

Good food and too expensive for his joke of a budget, Luis thought. "We would be intruding. They might not talk freely in front of us."

Judy looked at Luis, then said to Madeline, "We couldn't. Really. Luis is right."

"My treat," Madeline said, reaching into her handbag.

"What time is dinner?" Luis asked.

"Who should we pose as?" Judy said.

32

In service since the 1930s, the Hotel Mayaland was noted for its colonial grace. A lobby of massive dark rafters, polished floor tiles, and pillared verandas enchanted visitors. The tranquillity and charm extended into the main restaurant, a two-story-high dining room of white walls and stained glass windows.

Colonial grace stifled Luis Balam, oppressed him. The Mayaland was as alien to him as Cancún's towering concrete, as irrelevant to his past as Cancún was to his future.

After introductions and drinks, the party of six ordered dinner. Rollie and Leo had heard good things about the pork; Rollie's favorite food was pork chops. Madeline and June were dying for a green salad, but had heard bad things about raw vegetables in Mexico, so they went for the Fillet of Pork Valladolid too. Luis wanted black beans and tortillas, but knew that was impossible. He and Judy made the pork unanimous.

Luis had, after some thought and consultation with Judy, told Madeline that they would rather pose as themselves. They would be honest and superficial simultaneously. He was a private detective hired to assist in the search for Judy's husband. Madeline just happened to bump into them on the grounds while Rollie was snoozing.

Luis and Judy would be a mystery clue. Rollie and Leo would be allowed to insert it-them into the coincidence of Robert Chance, missing husband, and a nameless mining engineer.

Madeline approved the plan. She said Luis must have known Rollie in a past life. Rollie hated being told he was wrong, especially when he had screwed up royally. He had to put two and two together himself. As for Leo, she didn't know him very well, but him and Rollie sure acted like two peas in a pod, in spite of Leo retiring white collar out of a cushy desk job, while Rollie had worked on the line.

Through drinks, the peas in the pods kept to themselves, conducting an intense and friendly debate on North American football clubs. Rollie and Leo expressed fierce loyalties to the Detroit Lions and the Pittsburgh Steelers respectively. They debated the merits of run-and-shoot versus a stout defense, and other arcana such as blitzing tendencies and two-minute drills.

June was an elfin woman, severely dieted and suntanned, with short hair bleached white. She was Madeline's age and fighting every day of it. "Your husband, is he a football fan?" she asked Judy.

Judy burst out laughing. "Is he!"

Leo's attention was captured. Lean and bronzed, a proper mate to June, he wore a hairpiece so obvious that Luis pictured a bird's nest partially dislodged by a high wind. "Yeah? What's his team?"

"The Seattle Seahawks."

Leo and Rollie burst out laughing. Rollie was chunky and florid, possessor of too many chins for good health.

"Sorry to be disrespectful, miss. You must be worried sick over your missing husband."

"Nope," Judy said. "I just want to get my hands on the s.o.b."

"Oh," Rollie said, winking heartily at Leo. "One of those deals. He's in the doghouse, eh?"

"Doghouse the size of a Cancún hotel."

Rollie and Leo looked at each other, then at Judy. Judy looked at Luis, who stretched out the anticipation several seconds before nodding assent. Judy then told her sad story of being not quite divorced from a man who had skipped out on her and everyone else after winning three million dollars in the Washington State Lotto. By prearrangement, the story ended there. No former dairy princess. No murdered lottery ticket partner. No swindler.

Rollie and/or Leo would request (out of curiosity) a description of the scoundrel, which would be accurately provided, the mystery clue deposited. Judy and Luis had agreed to spare the innocent parties needless complications.

"Holy Christ," Leo said to Rollie. "That's him, the guy in the papers."

"What guy in the papers?" Rollie asked Leo.

"I'll feel like a jerk if you haven't heard," Leo said to Judy.

"I've heard rumors," Judy said.

"What guy in the papers, Leo?"

"I first read it in a newspaper on the plane. It was front page, the murder. You pick up scuttlebutt in Cancún, but you don't get a peep out of the locals, no sir. Speak no evil."

"The murder?" Madeline whispered in Judy's ear.

Judy whispered, "Robert never killed anybody, Madeline. That's why we didn't say anything. The murder and the scam, they're two separate—"

"*That* murder," Rollie said, snapping fingers. "You mean the guy chasing his Lotto partner all over Mexico who finally caught up to him in Cancún? Then his partner killed him. Everybody's heard."

"Terrific," Judy said.

"The guy who vamoosed," Leo clarified. "He killed the other guy in a hotel room. Blew the side of his face off."

"No," Judy said. "Uh uh."

"A homicidal maniac," Madeline said, dazed. "You can't escape them. They're running around berserk everywhere."

"Your husband, this killer, what's he look like, you know, in case we cross paths? I haven't seen a picture or a mug shot or anything. We're really sorry, miss."

"Robert is not a killer," Judy said. "He's fat and shaggy. He's the world's biggest, gentlest, grossest puppy. He has a beer can grafted to his hand."

Leo and Rollie looked at each other. Then Rollie said to Luis, "You're a detective. What's the poop on iridium?"

"The rare metal associated with comets and meteorites?" Luis said evenly.

Rollie moaned. "Don't forget asteroids. Asteroids are jam-packed with iridium too. I'm an authority on iridium that's slammed in from outer space."

"We're on the same page," Leo said. "Wish we weren't, but we are. Mr. Balam, tell me, please, does the law in your country let us gringos dig iridium out of the ground and take it home with us?"

"I have a friend who is an expert on Mexican constitutional law," Luis said.

"Ricky?" Judy said.

"No. Héctor. I am certain he would confirm that Mexico covets her minerals, oil especially, but any precious mineral. The answer is probably no."

"Your husband, he got an engineering background?" Rollie asked Judy.

"Sort of. He was a planner at Boeing."

"Does he have a nervous disposition?"

"When he's afraid or has a guilty conscience."

Rollie said, "I think we got us an amazing coincidence."

"Apparently," Leo said, taking Judy's wrist. "Apparently your wayward husband, the killer, is posing as a geological engineer. He fits your description to a tee. It troubled me that he didn't give us a name."

"Faking it damn good too. Played the part and dressed the part," Rollie said. "Had me fooled. Mad, why don't you run up to the room and bring down that paperwork for these people to read."

Madeline dug into her purse. "Brought it downstairs to dinner with me. The papers and the traveler's checks. They say these hotel employees are as honest as the day is long, but only a fool takes chances."

She gave the documents to her husband, who afforded them a perfunctory and disgusted glance before passing them on to Luis.

A thick, professional bundle of fraudulent paper, Luis thought. Vance Dugdale had not shifted from the dead dinosaur business to the iridium business overnight. Letters and a contract signed by Rollie R. Hoopsma were on an IRIDIMEX letterhead with a Mexico City address. Iridimex as in Pemex, the nationalized petroleum industry, or

Cordomex, the henequen monopoly. Copied photographs and text on the 65-million-year-old phenomenon, perhaps from the magazine on display on the Punta Paraiso model unit coffee table. Copies of Yucatán State survey maps. Letters of credit in English and Spanish on plain stationery—crude forgeries, essentially gibberish, but impressive gibberish to the uninformed.

"I screwed the pooch, didn't I?" Rollie asked.

Luis could not translate the man's words, but he could translate his expression. He nodded.

"Hey, guy, anyone could be taken in," Leo said, clapping Rollie on the back. "I missed dropping five grand to them by the hair on my chinny-chin-chin."

"The slick-talking sidekick, who's he?" Rollie asked.

"He cheated people at my village. He may be the killer of the man in the hotel room. Leo, you didn't buy. Did you tell them no?"

"No, actually I didn't. I told them I was considering an investment, and that I'd be available at the Mayaland through tomorrow. Speaking of the devil."

Leo's voice rose and his jaw fell. Luis followed his gaze to the dining room entry and in the blink of an eye a round posterior that was unmistakably Bob Chance's disappeared.

Luis was the first out of his chair. He toppled it, tripped, and stumbled into the adjacent table. He pardoned himself for the spilled drinks in Yucatec Maya, his language of instinct, and ran after Chance.

Luis was no sprinter, but Chance, even in terror, was barely ambulatory. He thrashed and lurched rather than ran, as if swimming upstream, wasting too much energy to propel his large body at speed. Luis gained rapidly.

They were a sight, a fat man in khaki shorts and shirt,

wearing a pith helmet, pursued through the lobby and outside into the night by an Indian. Luis overtook Chance five meters from the red Jeep. He grabbed his collar and said, "Stop!"

Chance grunted, swatted at Luis, and dragged him along. Luis released Chance's collar, dove low, and wrapped his arms around his calves.

Chance landed on his hands and knees with a howl and a thud. Luis gripped him by an armpit and flipped him onto his back, like obstinate livestock. He straddled him and said, "Give up."

"Guess I have some explaining to do," Chance said in surrender, panting.

The rest of the dinner party caught up with them.

"Helluva open-field tackle," Rollie said.

"Terrific," Leo added. "One-on-one coverage at its finest."

"He does look like an engineer decked out that way," June admitted. "Or like a jungle scientist."

"Or in those old movies, the one who's eaten by cannibals," Madeline said.

"Hi, Robert," said Judith Maxwell-Chance.

"Oh God," said Bob Robert Chance.

"Small world, fatso," Judy said.

33

Leo and Rollie hoisted Bob Chance to unsteady feet. Each draped an arm over a shoulder and assisted their formidable load into the hotel and upstairs to Leo and June's room. June and Madeline soft-pedaled guests and staff attracted by the commotion.

"Our friend got sick," Madeline said. "He fell down and lost his cookies."

"*Turista,*" June said. "Montezuma's revenge. He got careless about drinking the water."

In the room, the men released Chance onto the bed. Chance and the mattress groaned. Leo and Rollie stood close, to prevent their prize from falling and to prevent his escape.

Madeline said, "Shouldn't we be notifying somebody? Murder and fraud, aren't those matters for the police?"

"Don't forget kidnapping," Chance said. "I gotta go on record. You're holding me against my will."

"Don't forget bigamy, Robert."

Chance flicked grit from scraped knees. "Bigamy, huh, what?"

"Lordy. Bigamy too?" Madeline said. "You folks have 911 down here?"

Luis shook his head. "No police, Madeline. Not yet. Murder and kidnapping and fraud and bigamy, they aren't always police matters in Mexico."

"I don't think I have diddly-squat to say," Chance said. "I don't have to put up with any Spanish Inquisition. Ow!"

June had removed a can of aerosol first aid medication from a suitcase and was spraying Chance's knees. "Oh, hush, you big pansy. The germs they have in this climate, you'll thank me for saving you from gangrene."

"You said you had explaining to do," Luis said. "Explain."

"Judy, were my ears ringing or did you really accuse me of bigamy?"

"I won't answer a weenie who won't look me in the eye. Answer Luis."

"In my situation, I'm smart to keep my trap shut." Chance looked at Luis. "I have rights."

Luis smiled. "Was that a question?"

Rollie danced a jig, shuffling and jabbing, like a prizefighter in his corner before introductions. "We can beat the truth out of him. He'll talk."

"Will you please act your age," Madeline said.

"Bob, would you like a cold beer?" Luis asked.

"Is the Pope Catholic?" Judy said.

"We have baby airline bottles of booze and baby Coronas in the baby fridge."

"An American beer for Mr. Chance," Luis said.

"Hey, thanks for remembering."

"I'll run downstairs," June said.

"I'm still zipping my lip. I probably ought to hire an attorney."

"May I recommend Ricardo Martínez Rodríguez? He is among the finest lawyers in Cancún, if not in all of Yucatán."

"Sorry, Luis. I should of fessed up at the bullfight that Martínez came to my hotel room and whipped a sales pitch on me. I'd be better off now, that's for sure."

"You and Vance Dugdale would never have met," Luis said in agreement.

"Who?"

Judy rolled her eyes. "For God's sake, Robert, stop playing dumb."

"What did I say, what did I say?" Chance said, whining. "I'm clamming up till I see an attorney and it's not gonna be Ricky. I need a heavyweight."

"You might be right, Madeline," Luis said. "This is a matter for the police."

"Bring in the inspector, Luis," Judy said. "He can take Robert for a ride in that creepy car of his."

"Salgado?" Chance said. "Him and me, we're tight. I paid him five hundred bucks. Money talks."

Five hundred? "No, Chance. The hundred-dollar bills are spent. Héctor is angry with you. No amount of money you pay him would buy you forgiveness. You killed Mikey Smith in your hotel room, which is in Héctor's jurisdiction."

"I didn't do it. I didn't, I didn't!"

"Tourism officials are applying pressure. Diplomats and journalists too. Everybody demands your arrest. Mikey Smith is a martyred football hero. They cannot wait until you are arrested, convicted, and sentenced to life imprisonment in a filthy Mexican jail. Héctor cannot wait. I have never seen my old friend in such a continuous tantrum."

"Sweet Jesus," Chance muttered.

June entered with a six-pack of longnecks. "Is Bud okay?"

"Yeah, super. Thanks," Chance said.

"Hey, where's ours?" Rollie said.

"You two birds can raid the fridge and drink the stewardess bottles."

"Why didn't I think of that?" Leo said. "Mr. Balam, can you do guard duty for a minute?"

Luis gestured for the North American retirees to go, moved in front of Chance, and intercepted the bottle June offered the prisoner. "Who killed Mikey Smith if you didn't?"

Chance licked his lips. He didn't reply.

"Who killed Mikey Smith?" Luis repeated.

"Luis, no disrespect, but I gotta play it close to the vest. You don't realize the problems I have. It's the mother of all third-and-long situations."

"Problems, Robert? You don't know the half of it. Word association. Quick. Dairy princess."

"Oh oh," Chance said.

"I didn't sign the divorce papers, Robert. Guess who else didn't sign divorce papers back in the good ol' days?"

"Oh sweet Jesus," Chance said.

"If you want my opinion, bigamy has gotta be the lowest of crimes, the absolute pits," Madeline said. "Bigamists, they crawl out from under a rock."

"Is Rita in Mexico?"

Judy smiled.

"Yeah, dumb question. Where?"

"She is in close contact with her attorney in Cancún City," Luis said. "Who killed Mikey Smith?"

Chance drained the bottle in one gulping swig and belched.

Luis said, "All right, Chance. I give up. You win, we lose."

"Hey, what about my three grand?" Rollie protested.

"I can't in clear conscience give you to Héctor," Luis told Chance. "In his state of mind, I couldn't guarantee your life. The local police, that's the answer. We'll drive you into Mérida."

"When do I get my attorney?"

"After you've confessed to murdering Mikey Smith. After you've told the police where Dugdale is."

"Who's Dugdale?"

Luis jerked Chance to his feet by his shirt pockets. Chance cried out in pain.

"Luis, take it easy, okay," Judy said.

Along with the pockets, Luis had inadvertently seized flesh beneath, boy tits. He released Chance and pushed him back on the bed. "Sorry, but I don't like being lied to."

"Honest, I'm not lying. I don't know this Digdale of yours," Chance whined, massaging his chest.

"Talk," Luis said.

"Okay, but off the top, before I say word one, promise me that nothing I say will be held against me."

"No," Luis said. "Start at the beginning and don't stop until the end."

"Well, I had to ask. Your lawyer buddy, after you came to see me, he came to my room. You'd sent him on over to offer his services if Mikey and I could ever negotiate on peaceable terms. Seemed like a nice guy. No commitments were made. Obviously that was a pipe dream."

"Obviously," Luis said.

"Hey, sorry about that, Luis. I'm not going to insult your intelligence by pretending I was surprised Mikey ambushed us. Mikey wasn't as stupid as people thought. I figured, you could take care of yourself, which is what I hired you to do. I was sort of surprised he got so violent with you."

"You cheated him out of a fortune."

"That's a gray area open for interpretation. The thing is, the situation came to a head and you went nose to nose with Mikey for me. I'll always be thankful to you for that."

"You ran out on me."

Chance shrugged. "Judy said it. I'm a weenie."

"Inspector Salgado put Mikey Smith on an airplane to Dallas. He caught the next available flight to Cancún. He was murdered in your room that same night. Why did you return to your room? How did you return to your room unseen?"

"I couldn't take off without packing a few things. I had a few bucks on me and that was it."

"You returned for your cat?"

"Yeah. My kitty. Good memory. I was close to being tapped out. When you're on the move, every penny counts."

"What?" Judy said in mock horror. "You didn't take your Super Bowl videos?"

"I was traveling light, you know. Just Super Bowl III, where Joe Namath and the Jets knocked off the Baltimore—"

"How were you able to return to your room unseen?"

Chance rubbed thumb on fingers. "I caused an outbreak of temporary blindness."

"Dumb question," Luis said.

"This fruity little manager, he confronted me in the hallway on my floor, said he'd been deputized?"

"How much?" Luis asked.

"Forty bucks. Every penny I had on me."

"You learn something new every day," Judy said. "Undeputizing costs twice as much as deputizing."

"Jack James showed up just as I was headed out. Must have been lurking there the whole time."

"That slicky-boy ought to go by Jesse James," Rollie said.

"You never knew him as Dugdale?" Luis asked.

"Nope. He was Jack James, client of Martínez and close personal friend and associate of yours."

"He knew of my fight with Smith?"

"Yep. Seemed to be tuned in on the entire situation. Offered his sympathies and an investment opportunity. He was buttering me up one side and down the other. I was a man of substance, blah blah blah."

"Iridium?"

"Didn't come right out and say it then. My head's still out of kilter over everything, but I could swear he started jabbering about dinosaurs and how you were some kind of consultant for him."

"Senior executive liaison and chief guide," Luis said.

"Okay, right about then there's a knock on my door. I go, who is it? and this voice goes, room service. This voice is imitating a girl's, but it sounds like a three-hundred-pound bullfrog. Guess who. He must have greased a palm or two to be back on the trail so quick. Well, I kind of panicked, went nuts. James, Dugdale, whoever he is, he goes, hey, estranged lottery partners are no problem, we'll establish a dialogue. Then he goes and unlocks the door and in comes Mikey, like a fullback on fourth and goal. Boom! You think Mikey's scary in a normal situation? He's red as a pomegranate. He's got this big dressing on the side of his head. I'm not exaggerating, he's foaming at the mouth."

"Foaming at the mouth, Robert? Come on."

"Well, spit's flying out while he's screaming and yelling, which is the same thing as far as I'm concerned. Jack's in between us, trying to sweet-talk Mikey, who throws Jack aside like a rag doll. Mikey's got me pinned to the bed and I'm telling him I'm almost tapped out. I'm begging Mikey. I'll sign any damn thing he says to. Mikey doesn't care at that point. You know how he is—was, Luis."

"You cheated him out of a fortune."

"Hey, no amount of money is worth a human life."

"Speaking of human lives, who killed Mikey Smith?"

"I'm getting there. Mikey's on top of me. All of a sudden I hear this pop. Mikey's head snaps sideways and Jack's rolling him off me. Jack's got a gun in his hand."

"Describe the gun."

"What do I know from guns? Automatic, I think. Cute little chrome jobbie, like a military pistol, except left in the dryer too long so it shrunk. He wears it in a holster on his leg down by his ankle."

"What did you do with the body?"

"Stuffed him in the closet. It was like shoehorning a size fourteen foot into a size nine shoe."

"Who replaced the gauze?"

"*Looked* legit," Chance said. "I'm not as stupid as I seem. I figured the situation out eventually."

"Why Chichén Itzá?"

"Because it's packed with tourists for this equinox situation. You'd have plenty of suck—, uh, clients to pick and choose from, and it'd be easier to get lost in big crowds if you had to. Safety in numbers, that's Jack's motto. The revised plan, the new game plan, was to use my kitty to hang out in the area and attract, er, investors.

"Jack'd been thinking ahead. He's cagey. That Iridimex crapola was already printed up. The iridium payments were seed money. He had fake ID lined up in Mérida. We'd go home. That was appealing. I could go home. Come next year, the scenario, as I see it, we'd pick up the next installment of the Lotto, then for eighteen years thereafter. What's his real first name?"

"Vance," Luis said.

"Robert, how many years do you think you and Dugdale would have been Siamese twins?"

"Yeah, it was starting to sink in. Next year I'd be a hundred and eight grand richer. Ten minutes later I'd be history, doing my civic duty as landfill. Jack—Vance, he's a restless guy."

"Where is he?" Luis asked.

"Laying low. We move once, twice a day. He sent me ahead to set this situation up. Sorry, Leo. He's waiting up the road. I return alone and by a certain time or he's gone."

Luis smiled. "He doesn't trust you."

"He trusts me to the extent he has power over me. He's my ticket out of Mexico. He hangs on to the cash and the ID. Me, I'm his golden goose. Him and me, Vance, we need each other in a sick way."

"What gauze?"

"Mikey Smith's dressing."

"Jack James was giving orders and I was following them. Tote that bale. I couldn't look at Mikey. Not at his face. Okay, concealing evidence is where you're coming from. Jack took care of the fine details. I was the grunt labor. Everything happened real fast."

"Dugdale took care of the evidence and took care of you from then until now," Luis said.

"My guardian angel," Chance said sourly. "We finish stuffing Mikey in the closet, Dugdale cranks the air-conditioning up and we're outta there. That guy's a sharpie, you know. He pulled the trigger, but I'm taking the rap. What I am, okay, is James's prisoner. Nobody saw him come or go. Nobody's got an APB out on him. And I'm supposed to be grateful to Jack."

"Are you grateful?" Luis said.

"Yeah, in a weird way. After all, he saved my life."

"Why did he bring you to Chichén Itzá?"

"Jack said that because of me he had to revise his game plan. His dinosaur deal—which he never did explain—was out the window. He made me feel like crap. I should of been guilty over Mikey getting murdered, but I'm feeling guilty over this guy screwed out of a business deal. Is that goofy or what?"

"Plans revised to iridium?" Luis asked.

"Yeah. Jack laid out the paperwork, briefing me line by line. The comet chock full of iridium and so forth. It looked legit."

"Legit?" Leo said. "You posing as a mining engineer and taking people out in the middle of nowhere to a salted iridium mine?"

Judy sighed and said, "Robert, you're a murder fugitive. How on earth do you expect to live in the United States even if Dugdale can slip you into the country? And how do you expect to collect next year's Lotto check without being arrested?"

Chance shook his head helplessly. "Hell, I don't know. Jack, Vance, he always seems to come up with an answer, always seems to land on his feet."

Luis detected Judy softening toward Chance. She was looking at him as if he were an animal that had been hit by a car. The realization was settling in that he would lose her. Not this minute, perhaps not to Chance, but he would lose her nonetheless. And he could not rule out Chance reentering her life. Judy might be overwhelmed by latent maternal instincts. The irresistible urge to nurse a pathetic, wounded ox.

"Will you cooperate with us to catch Dugdale?" he asked.

"Man, I don't know. I was between a rock and a hard place to begin with. I can't, you know, grasp where cooperation leaves me."

"Listen, Chance, you tell us Dugdale killed Smith. We need to catch him and deliver him to the police before you can prove it."

"Yeah, I guess so."

Rollie cleared his throat. "Don't forget my three grand before they lock him in the slammer and throw away the key."

"I guess."

"Commit yourself, Robert. Stop being a horse's ass."

"Okay, what's the game plan?"

Luis scanned Leo, Rollie, June, and Madeline. "You

people have to agree. My idea excludes the police for now. We capture Dugdale, then give him and Chance to my friend, who is with the Quintana Roo State Judicial Police."

"Whoa, what, wait, time out. Dugdale and *me?*"

"Héctor has to hear both sides."

"Robert, lighten up and grow up."

Rollie slapped his hands together. "You can sign me on, Luis. A sting operation beats the hell out of sitting around watching the humidity rise."

Leo shook a fist. "Make that two of us. What do we have to do?"

"Lordy," Madeline said to June. "We got us a couple of James Bonds on our hands."

"Chance, when do you have to report to Dugdale?" Luis asked.

Chance checked his watch. "Ten minutes till the deadline."

Luis took Chance's beer out of his hand. "Go. Tell Dugdale that Leo is buying. He has to convert plastic into cash."

"Okay, I think I can sell it. Where do we rendezvous?"

"Dugdale likes safety in numbers? Tell him Leo will meet him in this room tomorrow at noon. Leo?"

"Double-oh-seven, eat your heart out," Leo said dashingly.

"Can we trust a bigamist?" Madeline asked nobody in particular.

"Hey, you guys got me pinned deep in my own end. If Dugdale is tipped that I have two wives, two Lotto heirs, I'm worthless to him. I'm dead meat."

"Go, Chance," Luis said. "If you're late and Dugdale suspects, the game is lost."

After Chance left, June said, "Can we trust him?"

"No," Luis said.

Rollie swigged from a miniature bourbon bottle and shuddered. "Tomorrow at twelve. High noon. I like it."

34

Luis said that if Judy liked, they could return to Akumal for the night, as there wouldn't be a free room in the vicinity. Judy said it was already night and asked how far.

"In kilometers?" Luis asked.

"No, in time," she said.

"Three, four, five hours," Luis said.

"Three hours with you at the wheel," she said. "Doing a hundred miles per hour. I haven't seen a streetlight on a highway lately. It could be exciting."

"A hundred kilometers per hour," said Luis. "My car will go no faster."

"We smash into a cow crossing the road, what's the difference?" she said. "We survive and we have to turn right around. What's the answer? I refuse to sleep on the ground and be eaten by scorpions."

"They don't eat you, they sting you. You can have the back seat," Luis said. "I've slept in this car before. It is not the worst place I've slept."

"Okay. Where? Where do we park, I mean? There's no shoulders on these roads to pull over on and even if there were I'm not too excited about being raped and pillaged by bandits."

"We don't have too many bandits in Yucatán, but if we did, they would pillage me and rape you."

"Comforting."

"Just a minute."

Luis got out of the car with the paper sack of liquor miniatures Madeline and June had given them. Overruling good-natured protests by Leo and Rollie, their wives had allotted them three bottles each and the excess to Luis and Judy. More than three, Madeline explained, and the boys'll be dancing with lampshades on their heads.

Luis went up to the parking attendant at the entrance to the Hotel Mayaland. He returned to the car with a noticeably smaller sack.

"He is Maya and he loves Scotch whiskey," Luis said, shaking his head in disbelief.

"You bribed him?"

"I made his evening happier." Luis drove to the darkest edge of the lot. "He won't disturb us and he will make sure that nobody else disturbs us. Tired?"

"I could sleep. We aren't exactly in the lot, you know. With all these cars packed helter-skelter, we're nosed into the jungle."

"Exactly," Luis said.

She got into the back. After a few minutes of silence, Luis asked her how she was doing.

"Okay if you don't mind the fetal position."

After a few more minutes of silence, Judy said, "What I told you, you know, about having to head home the day after tomorrow?"

"Yes."

"It was half the truth. Those jobs aren't that great and if I lose this quarter at school, it's not the end of the world. I'm not carrying that many hours. I could call home or cable or something and borrow money if I had to."

"The other half of the truth?"

"Robert is alive and sort of well. The Judith Maxwell-Chance Scholarship Fund is a joke."

Luis did not answer.

"Okay, the other half, the big half, is that I don't want to care about you too much. It's too damned complicated. You're complicating my life, Luis Balam Jaguar."

"Sorry."

"Are you?"

"No."

Judy laughed and said, "You know, this seat is roomier than I thought."

"Yes, it is."

"And you knew that when you parked us in the weeds out of sight?"

Luis did not answer.

"Well, what are you waiting for, an engraved invitation?"

Luis went over the front seat and joined her.

35

Judy and Luis were up at first light. They had begun to change clothes in the car when Judy said, hold it, wait, it's a glorious morning, ideal for a run, to relieve our stiffness, before we get all sweaty in fresh clothing. Luis said that their footfalls would awaken the tourists, not to mention the crocodiles. Judy said that crocodiles were a crock, but she had a compromise.

Looking at birds, Luis thought. Birding, Judy said.

One hour, Luis said; no strenuous pursuit, no tree climbing. Then breakfast with the North American couples. Mooching breakfast off them? Judy said. Have we asked for a fee? Luis countered.

Judy accepted Luis's logic and terms, and marched him along roads and trails for two hours. Luis had to admit that he had never actually looked for wild parrots before, and that he did derive some pleasure when they were spotted. Yucatán woodpeckers and clay-colored pigeons too. He even feigned sympathy with her inability to tell a social flycatcher from a great kiskadee. As far as Luis was concerned, they were identical—black, white, yellow, and inedible.

They ate a leisurely breakfast with Madeline and Rollie

and June and Leo at the Mayaland. They discussed what Leo and Rollie insistently referred to as the "game plan." It was in theory simple. When Dugdale and Chance came to their door at or about high noon, June and Leo would lock themselves in the bathroom. Dugdale and Chance would be admitted, and it would be explained to them that Leo was in Mérida raising the cash and June, poor June, she was in the bathroom, stricken by a sudden case of *turista.* June, if required by Dugdale's suspicions, could retch on demand. Leo said she'd pull it off; this gal of his was a trouper.

Luis and Judy, meanwhile, would wait in the restaurant of the Hotel Hacienda Chichén Itzá, one hundred meters from and out of sight of the Mayaland. Upon the arrival of the criminals and a moment of amenities, Madeline would excuse herself to go downstairs for refreshments, then notify Luis and Judy, who would return to the Mayaland, burst into the room, and with the aid of Leo, Rollie, and possibly Chance, overpower Dugdale. Simple. Easy. Foolproof.

They shook hands on it. The men and the women, everybody with everybody. It was ceremonial and giddy, like a summit meeting. Rollie and Leo, Luis thought, two bored oldsters flushed with the prospect of adventure. He dearly hoped nobody innocent got hurt.

Judy and Luis went to the Beetle, debating whether to move it to the Hacienda Chichén Itzá. They decided no. Traffic was a mess, compounding yesterday's by a factor of two or three. Vehicles were parked on both sides of the road that led from the hotels to the highway, leaving one narrow traffic lane. The probability of Dugdale recognizing Luis's copy of Mexico's most common automobile was remote.

Blocking traffic on that narrow lane was an automobile.

Judy saw it too and asked, "Luis, could there be two cars like that in the entire world?"

"No."

They walked to the black Dodge Dart with blackened glass. Inspector Héctor Salgado Reyes stepped out.

"Héctor," Luis said. "You can't park there. You are blocking."

"Luis, you were once a policeman. Has it been so long that you have forgotten that an officer on duty can park wherever he chooses. Cars are not moving, anyway."

"Héctor, how did you find us?"

"Elementary. We merely used our eyes and searched for the scabbiest Beetle in Yucatán. Señora Chance, how are you today?"

"Super, Inspector. You're on duty, huh?"

"Yucatán State is out of your jurisdiction," Luis reminded him.

"I am a law officer pledged to maintain the public safety in the United Mexican States. A dangerous individual on the loose, he determines my jurisdiction. I am simultaneously on holiday, honoring my hero of heroes, Benito Juárez. It is a day of business and pleasure, Luis. It promises to be a full day."

"Héctor, do you have reason to think that Dugdale is at Chichén Itzá today?"

"I can no longer question your assumption. Our last conversation stimulated me to initiate a subsequent conversation with the Cancún InterPresidential night manager. He accepted twenty North American dollars from me under false pretenses. He was collecting money and playing the sides against the middle. He admitted that he and his flunkies not only monitored the movements of Bob Chance, but of a man strongly resembling Vance Dugdale, and furthermore, the coming of the unmistakable Mikey Smith. Since Smith soon passed away, his going was not monitored."

"The manager gave in to his conscience?" Luis asked.

"In my eyes he is now a saint for his cooperation. And, no, Señora Chance, he relieved his burden without benefit of torture."

"Didn't say a word, Inspector."

"Did you discuss the conditions in your jail and in Mexican prisons?" Luis asked.

Héctor smiled. "He is a delicate, fine-featured young man. I would be less than forthright had I not advised him of the inevitable horrors and depravities."

Just then, Rita Trunkey Chance climbed out of the back seat, saying, "It's too hot to sit in there and listen to this guano, guys. Inspector, have I told you lately that your car is a sauna and it smells like gunpowder?"

"I recall that you have, Señora Chance."

Ricky Martínez got out too, dabbing his forehead with a handkerchief. "Luis. Mrs. Chance. A lovely day to transact business and apprehend a criminal, is it not?"

Rita and Judy exchanged friendly hellos.

Héctor said, "This lawyer and his lovely companion are persuasive people, especially the latter party."

Luis looked at Judy, who wrinkled her beauteous nose. "There's definitely an ulterior motive in the air."

Rita lighted a cigarette and said, "Sure is, hon. After our powwow at that bar, I put on my thinking cap."

"After she ordered two encores of 'La Bamba,' " Ricky said, eyebrows raised to maximum altitude.

"Shush, *hombre.* It occurred to me that if we can break Bobby loose of Darth Vader, we can clear his name, take him home, and work out a loan for him based on future Lotto payouts."

"A remarkable financial mind to accompany a remarkable body," Ricky said gallantly.

"I figured if we didn't intervene pronto, Bobby'd pretty soon be dead broke or dead and broke," Rita continued. "I'm business manager at a lumberyard. I know credit. I've listened to all the b.s. pitches why a contractor can't pay the invoice when they pick up. I've chucked a few meadow muffins myself to sawmills when we were in a cash flow pinch and a big shipment rolled in. Ricardo and me brought the idea to the inspector, who's been a doll."

"Señora Chance regaled me on credit in North America, Luis," Héctor said. "A revelation. Impossible as it is to conceive, giant multinational banking organizations send you credit cards in the mail. You can buy a used car on your signature. Interest rates seldom exceed twenty percent."

"Essentially, Mr. Chance borrowing on future payoffs is akin to a farmer borrowing on next year's crops," Ricky said.

"A much surer thing," Rita added grimly. "You don't have droughts and critters to fret about. Now, don't get me wrong. This inspiration, if you can call it that, isn't totally mercenary. I'm figuring, as crafty as this Dugdale joker is, a light bulb went on in his head long before it did in mine."

Luis said, "Dugdale takes Chance to North America. They sign loan papers. The bank gives Chance money. Dugdale takes the money."

"Not the end of the story, is it?" Rita said.

Luis shook his head.

"Easy credit shortens Bobby's lifespan. How I got it pegged, they do the dirty deed and Dugdale has two options.

He kills Bobby or he turns Bobby over to the police. He'll exercise both options is what he'll do. He'll kill Bobby and make an anonymous call to the cops to direct them to the body of the infamous Cancún linebacker killer. Pocketing the cash beforehand, natch."

"Expeditiously fast options," Héctor said. "As soon as they are home. Before arrest warrants by North American police are cut and impede the credit approval process. Law enforcement cooperation between our nations is not always cordial or lightning-swift."

Rita pivoted a gold sandal on her discarded cigarette and said, "So, Luis, how's it looking at this end?"

Luis said, "Let's have coffee at the next hotel and talk. We are a large conspicuous group."

In the Hacienda Chichén Itzá restaurant, Luis and Judy relived their past eighteen hours, no detail too trivial. The sole omission was two hours last night spent in the back seat of the Beetle.

Héctor said, "Wild geese I can bag and return to my jurisdiction for appropriate justice. Luis, are you not glad I am available to process them instead of some Yucatán State police stranger who is indubitably corrupt?"

"Yes, Héctor."

"This game plan of yours and the old gringos, I approve. You and I, Luis, perhaps as we await our signal we should go to my car for appropriate weapons. You did say Dugdale is armed, yes?"

Luis visualized large-caliber guns and high explosives. Goose bumps dappled his arms. "Do you still have the crate of grenades you confiscated from that arms dealer you stopped coming up the highway from Belize?"

"No. Sadly not. I discarded them. I worried that the rough riding of my automobile would dislodge a pin."

Rita lit a cigarette. "This trip has been colorful, I'll say that. Grand Old Opry, it ain't."

"Too many people for gunplay, Héctor," Luis said, looking at the entrance and at a wall clock. "No time either. Our signal is here, ten minutes early and not happy."

Madeline, wide-eyed and shaking, began jabbering before her rear touched a chair. "The game plan's backfiring. It's going down the toilet. The telephone. We didn't think of the telephone."

Judy stroked her arm. "Madeline, calm down. What telephone?"

"The one in the room. We couldn't think of hardly anything to say and Chance is sitting there sweating like he's in a Turkish bath, so I say, how's about me going for refreshments while we wait on Leo, nachos and beer, and just as I'm standing up, Dugdale says why not use the phone to call room service and Rollie says it's not working, because I sure as hell can't think of anything to say. Then Dugdale picks it up and says, listen, a dial tone, it's working. And I say, gee, it wasn't a few minutes ago. And Rollie says, what do you expect for Mexico. And Chance is saying he has to go to the bathroom, and June, bless her heart, she won't be able to speak for a month, she's in there overhearing every word and faking puking her guts out so they get the message that the bathroom's occupied for who knows how long. And Dugdale, with those weaselly eyes of his, they're darting every which way, so I know he smells a rat, so I say, I ought to go on down for the beer and munchies and be back in two shakes of a lamb's tail. You know how pokey room service can be and I have to pick up picture postcards anyway. I'll be right back."

Madeline looked at her watch. "Which was eight and a half minutes ago. I'd be plumb out of breath if I wasn't scared half out of my mind. Rollie and our friends are up in that room about to have kittens."

Game plans, Luis thought, rising; simple, easy, foolproof. "Let's go. Before Dugdale goes."

They were too late. They came into the Mayaland lobby as Dugdale descended the staircase, Chance at his side, and Rollie so close in front of them that they were walking lockstep.

Dugdale wore rumpled beige chinos, a striped button-down shirt, and no bizarre accessories. "What's he being today?" Luis wondered out loud.

"Anonymous. He's blending in," Judy said. "Garage Sale Casual Wear."

Luis led the approach, Héctor alongside, Ricky bringing up the rear with the women. Dugdale saw Luis, halted four steps from the bottom, and said, "Lu. Rick too. *¡Ay caramba!* Where's Frank, *número* three-oh in your shitty troika?"

"Sacrificing gambling equipment."

"Not a good time for riddles, Lu. Not a good time for a social call either. Stand aside, boys and girls. We've got places to go, things to see."

Chance appeared dazed, Rollie petrified. Héctor moved beside Luis and said, "Not a good time for places to go, things to see. *You* stand aside, shitbag, and show me your hands."

"Your copper friend, Lu, right? The one at your trinket

stand the other day. Don't do a dumb, dumb no-no, Sheriff. Folks'll get hurt and folks we got, anxious not to miss the sun's gig on the temple. The lobby's a sardine tin. Don't go and be the cause of spilled blood."

"Don't," Rollie rasped.

"Listen to the man. My arm's at my side, okay, precisely behind Rol's posterior cleavage. Don't take a rocket scientist to guess what I'm palming? Instant proctology, surgery with a bang.

"I smelled a setup when Maddie bugged out. Ambush City. Bummer. Her and Rol, they were about to poop their britches. Way I see it, Rol's our insurance policy till we can walk off into the sunset. Everybody cuts their losses. No harm, no foul."

"You win," Héctor said, backing up. Then he said to Luis in Spanish, "We play by his rules until we're out of this building, out in the open."

Dugdale stopped at the landing. "No fair talking Mexican. Haul ass or the situation ratchets up from ugly to uglier."

Leo and June were squeezing through the crowd on the steps. Leo had a pugnacious set to his jaw and June was swallowing hard and clearing her throat.

"Oh no," Judy said.

"Oh no what?" Rita said.

"That older couple, that's Leo and June," Judy said, mouth cupped.

Leo overhanded a punch, then another. The first struck Dugdale's shoulder, the second his head. Dugdale flinched and grimaced, but didn't fall. He turned, bringing his gun arm up.

"For Christ's sake, Bobby, for once in your miserable life, do some-goddamn-thing!" Rita yelled.

Chance blinked, jolted into action, and groped across Dugdale's body, grabbing his arm at the horizontal. He jerked it wide, but Dugdale drove an elbow into Chance's gut. The lottery millionaire gasped, released Dugdale, and fell to his knees.

Leo had frozen in mid-stride, barrel of the baby, silvery, automatic pistol almost touching his nose. Rollie glanced a fist off Dugdale's ear. Dugdale spun and shot Rollie in the right shoulder.

Rollie lurched backward, more from surprise than recoil from the lightweight slug, and fell into an advancing Héctor and a screaming Madeline. They all toppled against Judy and Rita.

Luis slammed into Dugdale, seizing him by the wrists. Dugdale's momentum took them to the floor, but Luis was able to twist his gun wrist while digging in his fingernails, and the pistol tinkled onto tile.

"Help! Thief! My wallet! Help me! Hold him! Police! My wallet! Help!" Dugdale shrieked.

The gunshot had attracted the attention of every person in the lobby. Most were unaware of the prelude to the gunshot. They only knew that people were kneeling around a bleeding man and that a fellow tourist was on the ground wrestling with a native, an Indian who had stolen his wallet. If the pickpocketing Indian was not also responsible for the gunshot wound, it was one hell of a coincidence.

Luis was jumped by who knows how many Anglo men, wrenched from his victim, and held to the floor. Judy flew into the melee, and yanked loose one man's grip.

Héctor freed Luis, wrenching off Dugdale's remaining

rescuers by whatever purchase available—belt loops, the napes of necks, ears.

Luis scrambled to his feet and chased Dugdale out the door, down the steps, and into the congested parking lot.

Dugdale's head was swiveling, his Jeep misplaced. Judy appeared at Luis's side. She spotted it and pointed. They ran to it, their angle making up Dugdale's lead. He saw that he was cut off and dropped behind a car.

Luis went after him, assuming that Dugdale was going to maintain a crouch and duckwalk the automotive maze to the jungle or to a vehicle he could steal. But Dugdale popped up, waving a baby, silvery, automatic pistol.

"Surprise, Lu. One for each ankle," he said. "Do yourself a favor and move out of range and out of my life."

Luis backpedaled slowly. "What happened to the Civil War condo money, Dugdale? Did you spend it?"

"That I did, Lu. A man on the road generates high overhead. Ask Bob Chance."

Luis continued his steady retreat. He snapped off a radio antenna.

"Swordplay, Lu? Don't be a dipshit."

"Give up, Dugdale. Tell your side of the story while you can. The police won't let a murderer escape."

Dugdale looked at Judy, who was beside the Jeep. He advanced, waving the gun like a wand. "Murder? *Me?* Get real, Lu. Takes two to tango. Better idea. You and Chiquita there come with me. Replace the geezer. Hostages are interchangeable."

"Rape!" Judy screamed at the top of her lungs, jabbing a finger at Dugdale. "Rape!"

"Cunt," Dugdale said, swinging the gun at her.

Luis moved in front of Dugdale and flung the antenna.

It spun by him, a miss but a distraction. His shot went high and wide. The gunshot and the rape cry were bringing help on the run, men and women, American and Mexican.

Dugdale waved his pistol at them like a garden hose. "Nobody be a dipshit!"

Dugdale took a quick count of his antagonists. There were more dipshits than rounds in his clip. And that was between him and the Jeep alone. He ran fifty meters to the rear entrance of the archaeological park. Gatekeepers did not ask to see his ticket.

Judy and Luis pursued. Dugdale headed for Kukulcán. He skirted the pyramid and Luis wondered why. Dugdale was going into a crowd of thousands and thousands of people. No one else had a firearm, but the odds were daunting.

Then Luis realized Dugdale had slowed to a normal pace and his gun was in his pocket. He would blend into the masses and have a clear path to the tourist center and the main parking lot beyond. By the time security and police personnel could be organized, Dugdale would have stolen the vehicle of his choice.

Luis and Judy were ten meters to Dugdale's rear. Luis picked up a stone and threw it with all his strength, hitting him in the back. Reacting instinctively, Dugdale drew his gun and spun around, cursing.

"You won't shoot, Dugdale," Luis said, gasping for breath. "Too much attention. Too many people. Look at how many are watching you. How many rounds do you have left?"

"Good move, Lu. Kudos." Dugdale quickly pocketed the pistol and started climbing the north steps.

Again, Luis wondered why. When Dugdale was halfway up, he realized. Dugdale threw a leg over the west wall of the staircase. He was going to take a shortcut on one of the nine stone terraces upon which the staircases were built. Each terrace was seven feet high and half as wide. It would be a fast and safe jaunt around two corners and down the south steps, doubling back in the confusion and chaos to the Mayaland or the jungle in between.

The crowd howled. The sound was sudden and throaty, a collective protest to the outrage, the desecration. The serpent's head at the base was aglow and the sun had given it a zigzag body. Thirty meters long and canted forty-five degrees upward, Kukulcán lived. Dugdale was not only straddling a balustrade, he was straddling the event.

Dugdale could not see the event from his perspective, Luis thought. Or if the cultural park impresario could, he did not appreciate its significance.

Dugdale brought his trailing leg across, his unconscious mind interpreting the howl from below as a reaction to his being about to step on something tangible. Startled, he must have lifted his trailing foot before his lead foot was flat and stable.

Vance Dugdale lost his balance and came down headfirst and backward. Luis was among the first to reach him. Dugdale's eyes were open, his head cocked unnaturally. There was no reason to send for a doctor.

36

In excess of one million people annually fly in and out of Cancún International Airport. In the terminal they tend to congregate in clumps, herded by flight schedules, tour directors, and the demands of Immigration and Customs bureaucracies. The majority of the million people are in a hurry, to get to the sun or to get home. Impatience is generally futile.

In a small clump stood Luis Balam, Esther Balam, Rosa Balam, Judith Maxwell-Chance, Rita Trunkey Chance, Ricardo Martínez Rodríguez, Héctor Salgado Reyes, and the catalyst of the clump, the cause of its existence, Bob Robert Bobby Chance. Judy, Rita, and Chance were scheduled out on the same flight, but only Chance was in a hurry.

Esther and Rosa had accompanied their father to Akumal. They brought cut flowers to Judy, who was brought to tears. Seldom had Luis's babies enjoyed the opportunity to people-watch such a volume and variety of North Americans. Their eyes were wide and constantly in motion.

Judy and Luis stood close, touching without grabbing. Their eyes were on each other, not in motion. Not much was said; not much needed to be said.

Rita and Ricky were saying goodbye more spectacularly. The pretty older Anglo and the prettier, younger Latino were on the verge of violating public decency laws. Even the least patient travelers put a hitch in their step long enough to give the moaning, embracing couple a quick glance.

The remaining pair were neither people-watching nor trading fond farewells. Héctor was watching Chance and Chance was watching his watch. Chance's assertion that Vance Dugdale had killed Mikey Smith was logical and satisfactory. The weapon matched the wound. The late Mr. Dugdale's criminal history was eclectic, a range of offenses that indicated a potential for the ultimate violence.

The Mexican criminal justice system resolved the matter at a record pace. Open and shut. The killer could take his lying rebuttal to the grave. And the exonerated, an embarrassment in his own right, was preferably out of sight, out of mind.

In Rita's and Judy's pockets were signed and notarized agreements granting each of them one third of Bob Chance's Washington State Lotto proceeds for the next five years. At the end of five years, Chance was given a lump sum buy-out option. Should Chance choose not to exercise the option, he would be committed to a three-way split for the twenty-year life of his fantastic luck. For their part, the women agreed not to so much as utter the b-word—bigamy. They agreed to quietly divorce him, in chronological order.

In Héctor's, Luis's, and Ricky's pockets were riders promising payments for professional services. Unfortunately there was no cash money available to pay the fees immediately. Everybody would be forced to wait for next year's Lotto disbursement.

Ricky had initially balked at completing the papers without immediate compensation. Admittedly the documents were brief and rudimentary—his command of North American law was a fraction of his sketchy knowledge of Mexican law—but there were out-of-pocket expenses. Stationery, photocopying, the notary. Not to mention his time. As a professional.

Discreetly, he had inquired to Luis if there was anything he could do. Luis informed him that he and Héctor had also suffered out-of-pocket expenses. He informed him further that Chance had no assets unless you counted the Super Bowl tapes, which were in no great demand; no other North American visitor, to the best of his knowledge, visited Cancún to sit in a darkened room and watch North American football matches played years and decades ago. Ricky was, of course, free to ask Rita for money, but she had been generous with him in a number of ways already and there was a name for men who lived off the earnings of their women.

Ricky pouted. Luis hated Ricky's pouting. He told the attorney that they were even, that he had saved Ricky's life. Ricky pursed his pouting lips into a question mark, and Luis explained that while Ricky and Rita were being entertained by "La Bamba," he had lied to and effectively deflected the rental car manager who was perfectly happy to kill him for the overdue Jeep. Ricky said that Luis was blackmailing him. Luis said, yes, he was. Ricky did not again mention cash money.

Rollie, Madeline, Leo, and June had taken flights out earlier that morning. Rollie departed with a bullet in his shoulder and a tale to tell for the rest of his days. Danger in the tropics. Wild gun battles that would put stateside gang activity to shame. Madeline pleaded with Rollie to stay in the hospital the extra day or two the Cancún doctors had advised, but Rollie said, uh uh, gotta be joking, I'll convalesce up north. The germs they got down here, some of them they probably don't even have names for yet.

Judy was still watching Luis, but her eyes were darting to Chance.

"Something is bothering you?"

"Yeah, Robert is. And it's not what you're thinking, so don't turn green with jealousy, okay? I'm saving every penny, and I'll be back to see you the second I can."

Luis saw that Chance was animated, Héctor bored, the *lotería* tycoon apparently recounting to Héctor his valiant attack on Dugdale.

"His innocence is bothering you," Luis said.

"Peeking into my head, Balam, you voyeur. That's as bad as peeking up my dress."

"All right, I will peek up your dress instead," Luis said. "Book a later flight."

Her eyes glazed. "I wish."

"What bothers you?"

"How he's acting, peppy and happy as the world's fattest clam, like, you know, a kid who got away with something. He's pumping out his lifetime supply of testosterone."

"Got away with murder, you mean? It was you who couldn't believe Bob Chance was capable of killing a man."

"Neither could you. But it's beginning to sink in, Luis. Not that I didn't have a hint in my past life, but Robert can be molded like clay."

"A conspirator, a murderer's assistant," Luis said.

"Is it possible?"

"Yes."

"Problem is, we're relying on intuition. Maybe Robert's smugness is twisting us. We're inventing things, making him out to be something he really isn't."

"Physical evidence bothers me. Possible physical evidence."

"Such as?"

"The fresh gauze replacing the dressing that Dugdale shot through to kill Mikey Smith. Where did it come from?"

"And the third party in the hotel room. With the nicotine habit. We know Dugdale's our boy, but when did he have time to sit down for a smoke?"

Luis stroked Judy's back. "Come on. I haven't said goodbye to Chance yet."

Chance's arm was across Héctor's chest in demonstration and he was saying, "Suppose Jack—Vance, suppose Vance'd been running, packing the ball, and you clothesline him how I did, a forearm shiver is what they used to call it. His momentum stops right now. That was the problem. He was just standing there and I didn't have any leverage. Clothesline him how I did—boom!—it's fifteen yards. Automatic. Every ref in the stadium drops his yellow hankie. I'm not kidding, the NFL's gone pussy. In the old days you take the hump out of a guy's Adam's apple, hey, no big deal."

"In the old days of leather helmets and no jockstraps, huh," Judy said.

Chance opened his mouth for a snide comeback, but looked at Luis looking at him, gulped as if he had snared an insect, and averted his eyes by squinting at a wall clock. "Our flight's due in from Dallas any minute. It turns around and we go home. What's the odds it'll be on time? You know, *mañana.*"

Héctor shoved Chance's arm away from his chest and stared at Ricky and Rita.

"If the airplane left North America on time it will arrive at Cancún on time, will it not?" Luis said.

Chance shrugged.

"I am unclear," Luis said to Chance. "Vance Dugdale, clever as they come, admits a madman to your room."

"I told you. Jack—Vance—he could sell refrigerators to the Eskimos. Frost-free and the optional icemaker, no lie. Mikey was pounding and pawing the door like an animal, yelling that he was going to do to Vance what he was going to do to me. Vance quiets him down like he shot him with a tranquilizer dart."

"How, Robert?"

"Said he was from the IRS. You know, the Internal Revenue Service. The IRS scares the hell out of anybody with half a brain. Mikey has—had—half a brain so he shuts up and listens. Vance makes him promise not to get physical and lets him in. He gives Mikey this line about how he tracked me down and how I'm in arrears on my taxes and in a humongous jam. I'll be in less of a jam if I split with Mikey. I'll owe half as much in back taxes. I'm catching on and playing along. Mikey's semi-mellow. Vance says he'll mail Mikey some forms to sign, then he'll get his half."

"The tax man impersonation was not in your earlier version," Luis said.

"I cut a few corners, okay. I was under a ton of stress when you were giving me the third degree. The ending's the same. Mikey went berserk, jumped me, and Vance saved my life by shooting Mikey."

"Why would Mikey go berserk if Dugdale had mellowed him with promises of his money?"

Chance hesitated, thinking. Thinking and perspiring. Finally he said, "Mikey wants what he wants right now. He'd chased me halfway across Mexico and wanted to be paid. Right now. Mikey has—had—a nitroglycerine temper, you know."

Luis fluttered a hand. "Chance, you shift from past tense to present tense on Mikey Smith. You can't accept his death. Your conscience can't accept his death."

Chance frowned and shook his head. "Nope, no way. I got nothing to feel guilty about. I just blacked out on some of the fine details."

"Details such as the gauze," Luis said.

"You're trying to confuse me with that detective jazz. I already answered."

"You or Dugdale did not go out to buy fresh gauze. Dugdale ripped the tape, shot Smith, and restuck the tape."

Héctor was paying attention. He said, "Temperamental as the late Mr. Smith was, the late Mr. Dugdale certainly possessed excellent eye-hand coordination if he was able to withdraw his gun from his ankle holster, rip aside Mr. Smith's dressing, and fire a round."

"Unless he had some help from his friend," Judy said.

"Seated at the table perhaps," Héctor said. "Mr. Dugdale enjoying a cigarette during their conference. That is one for you, Señora Chance. Mr. Smith smells a malodorous rodent. His mood darkens. Mr. Chance loses his composure, his courage.

"He bellows at Dugdale for assistance. Mr. Dugdale has subtly withdrawn his effeminate albeit effective pistol. Perhaps Mr. Smith hears it being cocked on Mr. Dugdale's lap. Mr. Chance, while overwhelmingly outmatched, clutches Mr. Smith's hands, restraining him for the one or two seconds required to complete the task, knowing that if he doesn't, Smith will overpower Dugdale and kill them both."

Héctor looked at Judy. "Henceforth, they form a man-to-man cohesion—what is it termed?"

"Male bonding," Judy said.

"Exactly," Héctor said.

"In the last conversation I had with Dugdale before his death, he said it takes two to tango," Luis said.

"An old gringo adage," Héctor said.

Chance gestured toward the doors leading to the flight line. "Those people streaming in, that's our plane. It's like, you know, the two-minute warning. Ball game's damn near history. I'd better be checking in."

"Airplanes depart for North America constantly," Héctor said. "You should remain and we can have a nice conversation."

"No way, José," Chance said. "I'm officially off the hook, remember?"

"Yes, you are. But perhaps you shouldn't be. Self-defense or a conspiracy. We should talk."

"It's been a blast," Chance said, saluting. "I'm done talking."

"Judy!" Rita had broken her clinch with Ricky and was pointing at the arrivals. "Do I see who I think I see? Déjà vu from once upon a time?"

Judy followed an invisible line from Rita's fingertip to a short, scowling, leathery woman. "Oh my God, you do."

"Hasn't changed one iota in seventeen, eighteen years. Usually when you say that it's a compliment, but she was born ugly."

"Oh Jesus," Chance muttered. "Oh sweet Jesus."

"Her?" Luis asked Judy.

Judy replied by waving at the woman. "Mom! Hi, Mom! Over here!"

"Oh God, I have a plane to catch," Chance said, pushing between Héctor and Luis.

Luis flattened a palm on his spongy chest. Héctor took his arm and said, "I am not arresting you, but I would be a wretched human being if I did not facilitate a reunion of mother and son. I am a passionate advocate of motherhood."

Judy kissed Héctor on the cheek, took Luis's hand, and headed for the boarding gate, but not before waving and yelling, "Yoo-hoo. Thelma. Bye."